Miss Landon and Aubranael

Tales of Aylfenhame, Book 1

Charlotte E. English

D1444598

CHAPTER ONE

Mornin', folks, an' how do ye do? My name's Balligumph—Mister Balligumph, if ye don't mind—an' I'm the guardian o' this here toll-bridge ye've fetched up at. Ain't she a beauty? Not altogether big enough to merit a toll, ye may be thinkin'—but don't be worryin' yer heads about it. The toll's not steep. All I'll be askin' fer is a scrappit o' information—a secret, if ye're minded to call it that. Here, whisper it in my ear—don't be shy, now! I may be a sight bigger'n you, but ye won't find a gentler troll across the whole o' Lincolnshire, that I guarantee. Or one better dressed.

There, that'll do. Thas one mighty interestin' nugget o' truth fer me, an' free passage into the pretty town o' Tilby for you. Been here before? 'Tis an ordinary enough town, most times, though once in a while somethin' special happens.

The last time was exactly a year ago today! Began around the first o' May—Beltane, as ye'll know. Many a strange thing can happen on Beltane. Perhaps ye'd like to hear the tale? 'Tis a fine mornin', an' I'll not keep ye more'n an hour or so. Well... not very much more, anyhow.

Ye would! Well, then, step out o' that carriage and take a seat on this here handsome patch o' grass, an' I'll begin. It's to the Parsonage we're goin' first: that buildin' just away yonder, do y'see? There's a new family there now, but a year ago it was the home of old Reverend Landon an' his daughter, Miss Sophy.

It's Miss Sophy tha' this story is about. The sweetest, sunniest young woman in all o' Tilby, she was, an' a nimbler set o' fingers with a sewing needle I never did see...

Miss Sophia Landon—Sophy, to those who knew her well—wrapped a piece of court plaister around her bleeding finger, and sighed. She had dripped blood on Thundigle's new shirt. Turning the tiny

1

garment around in her hands, she tried to persuade herself that the speck of rapidly browning blood wasn't visible.

'Not very visible, at least,' she muttered under her breath. It was the second shirt she had made that morning, and her fingers had almost escaped unscathed. Almost.

Laying the new shirts side-by-side, she surveyed them both. The contrast between the two amused her, and her smile broadened. The first shirt was for her father. It was large, to accommodate the generous girth he had acquired through years of good dining. It was made from the best linen they could afford; this still placed it several cuts below the fine garments worn by some of their neighbours, but still, it was respectable and she was proud of it. Her father, a clergyman with only a modest living, loved his table far more than his clothes, and he hadn't had a shirt this fine in years. Sophy had worked every stitch as carefully as she could, determined that it should be perfect. And it was.

The second shirt was only as wide as her palm. It was dwarfed beside the Reverend George Landon's. She had made it from the scraps of linen left over from the first project, so it was every bit as good as her father's—except for the speck of blood. She had sewn it with every bit as much love, because this shirt was for a friend.

Picking up the tiny shirt, she left the parlour and made her way to the dusty room upstairs that had belonged to her mother. The chamber remained in much the same state it had been in when she had died: it was comfortably furnished and prettily decorated, albeit in the style of ten or fifteen years before In spite of its furnishings, it possessed an air of emptiness, for her mother's possessions had long since been lovingly adopted by Sophy herself. Neither she nor her father had found the heart to make use of the room, however.

One corner of this faded chamber was different. A set of miniature furniture stood fastidiously arranged: a little oak table with two matching chairs, a tiny closet and a rocking chair. Sophy herself had sewn the tiny rag rug that covered the floor, and the cushions that covered the rocking chair's hard seat and back.

Sophy sat down on the floor nearby, heedless of the folds of her dress, and laid the shirt carefully across the little table. She placed a tiny bowl of honey beside it, and a second full of clear water.

'Thundigle!' she called. 'I have a gift for you.'

A puff of light erupted in the air before her, and the Landon household brownie appeared. He was a diminutive creature with dark brown skin, wild curly brown hair and eyes the colour of autumn leaves.

'Miss Landon,' Thundigle said with a graceful bow. 'You are generous, as always.'

Sophy smiled. 'You haven't seen what it is, yet.'

Thundigle smiled back, his expression still faintly shy despite his several years' residence in her family. 'Dear Miss Sophy, what need have I to see it when I can smell it? It is lavender flower again, isn't it? The most fragrant honey...' He turned to the table, his black eyes alight with anticipation, but when his gaze fell on the shirt he stopped. 'But what is this beautiful thing?' Picking it up in his gnarled hands, he turned it about, holding it as though it were very fragile. Sophy discreetly eyed his twelve-inch tall frame, and smiled in satisfaction. The shirt was correctly proportioned and should fit him, and the fine fabric would, she hoped, last a good while.

Thundigle looked up at her with quivering lip, a gleam of moisture shining in his dark eyes. 'Miss Landon, this is far too much.' His hands were shaking as he held the shirt. 'Such fabric as this—I can feel the fineness of the weave—each individual thread...' He tailed off, overcome with emotion.

Sophy suppressed an urge to giggle: Thundigle didn't like to be laughed at. He was a remarkably well-dressed brownie; most of his kind wore rough garments and were offended by offerings of clothes, but Sophy had won her brownie helper's heart years ago when she had discerned his eye for sartorial elegance. She had made him a number of outfits, cobbled together out of scraps from her father's worn-out clothes: long trousers of beige cloth, shirts with full sleeves and snowy cravats, a waistcoat of dark wool and even a deep red cutaway coat.

In spite of this regular bounty, Thundigle was overwhelmed whenever she presented him with a new piece for his wardrobe. It was quite endearing.

'Better yet,' she told him, 'your hat is almost ready. I am collecting it today.'

Thundigle stared at her, eyes shining, his new shirt temporarily forgotten. 'Hat,' he breathed, as if the word contained some kind of special magic. 'Hat! Is it—is it like—?'

She nodded, knowing what he meant to ask. He had forever

admired the tall, glossy hats worn by the gentry of the county, but such a project lay beyond Sophy's abilities. Instead she had bartered her skills as a seamstress with a hatmaker's family in order to acquire one for him.

Thundigle drifted towards her and leaned against her leg, as though exhausted by the demands of receiving gifts. He was muttering something. Leaning down, she caught the words: 'Thankyouthankyouthankyouthankyou...'

This was too much for her self-control. She laughed, ruffling his curly dark-brown hair to show she meant no harm by it. 'You need not thank me. I can't think what we would do without your help, for there is far too much work about for Mary to manage alone.' She sighed, her smile fading. 'I do wish I could be of more use, but you know what a liability I am! Why, I have burned Papa's tarts yet again this morning. I can never manage the oven right: it is either too hot, or not hot enough. But Mary hadn't time to make them, and now how disappointed Papa will be without a fresh supply!'

Thundigle eyed her seriously. 'Since the topic has come up, Miss Sophy, would it be impertinent of me to request that you leave the dusting of the drawing-room to me? I noticed... that is, I could not help observing that another accident has occurred.'

Sophy blushed. 'Papa's pipe! Oh dear, yes. I cannot think how it came to end up on the floor; only I was so busy I didn't notice it upon the mantel, and by the time I did, it was too late. It can be mended, of course, but the ash upon the carpet? Is it so very bad?'

'I believe I can remove the stain,' said Thundigle gravely. 'With a little effort.'

Sophy smiled down at him, her cheeks still pink with mortification. 'You are too good. If only I were not such a hopeless housekeeper! One would think that at my age—mistress of my father's house these ten years and more—' she broke off. 'Well, but it cannot be helped, for I cannot change. I shall do as you ask, only do so hate leaving everything to you and Mary.'

'Not quite everything. There isn't a better clothed household in the county, I wouldn't think; possibly in the whole kingdom. Why, I haven't suffered so much as a loose button in years!'

'Well, if that is to be my sole contribution to our collective comfort, it will have to do.'

'It is my pleasure to assist with the rest, Miss Sophy.'

'You are a treasure. I know Mary thinks so as well.'

Thundigle beamed. He had changed his attire somehow without her noticing: the old, threadbare shirt lay discarded on the floor, and he had left off his coat in order to show her the fit of his shirt. The crisp white linen shone against his nut-brown skin, and in spite of the incongruity of the attire, it suited him.

'You look marvellous,' Sophy told him. 'Now, I don't know if you have time to help Mary a little, but I know she would appreciate it very much. Father has requested another goose for dinner, and I have just managed to contrive the purchase of a small one. There is the plucking to be done yet, and soon, if it's to be ready in time.'

Thundigle swept her another bow. 'At once, Miss Sophy,' he said, still beaming, and vanished.

Sophy stood up slowly, her legs tingling from sitting too long on the floor. She didn't know how he contrived to work in the house without dirtying his clothes, but so he always did. But that was the peculiar thing about brownies: they seemed to enjoy the work, considering it even as a kind of privilege. Most families in Tilby had at least one brownie in residence; some, like the Adairs and the Winbolts, had scores of them.

Quickly brushing down her gown, Sophy descended the stairs just in time to hear the commotion of someone arriving. The front door flew open and closed with a bang, and quick female steps sounded in the passage. 'Sophy!'

The charming young face of Miss Anne Daverill appeared below. The girl clutched at her light straw bonnet as she stared up at Sophy. 'There you are! The morning is almost gone; do tell me you are disposed to walk, for I am going this instant and I simply must have a companion.'

Sophy laughed. Anne was a whirlwind of activity, always flying about in pursuit of some errand or other. As usual her bonnet was slightly askew, her ribbons flapping untied and her red hair escaping from beneath.

'I shall be happy to walk with you, only I must go to Mr. Peck's; shall you mind that?' Reaching the bottom of the stairs, Sophy quickly set her friend's bonnet and ribbons in order.

'Of course I shan't mind,' Anne replied, submitting to these ministrations without complaint. 'Is your father to have a new hat at last? Miss Gladwin will be pleased, for she has been shaking her head over that shabby old thing these two years at least.'

Thinking of the worn hat her father always wore, Sophy smiled ruefully and shook her head. 'I tried to persuade him on that score, but without success. He is fond of his faithful old hat, and refuses to part with it. He instructed me to get a few more birds for dinner, if I was so intent on spending money.'

'Which I hope you will not, for one can hardly help noticing that—Oh, Mr. Landon! Good morning, sir.'

Sophy grinned as her friend made a hasty curtsey, her face flushing. She needn't have worried: Reverend Landon was turning somewhat deaf, though he would never admit it.

'Sophy, my dear, you are not going out?' His eye travelled over Anne's bonnet and spencer and settled on the light pelisse that Sophy had just collected.

'Yes, father, for a walk. We will not be long.' She hastily tied the ribbons of her bonnet and made for the door.

'Are you sure that is wise, Sophy, Anne? For there is a strong wind today, you know; perhaps you have not noticed, but I can see the branches waving from my study window. And I am not at all sure it will not rain...?'

Sophy gave him a peck on the cheek. 'It is a beautiful, glorious day and we shall be quite safe. Come along, Anne!'

She stepped briskly out of the house, satisfied to hear Anne's quick step following along behind.

'Rain! Why, there is not a cloud in the sky,' Anne said as she caught up with Sophy.

'Try not to blame poor Papa,' Sophy replied. 'Ever since Mama, you know, he has had a horror of chills.'

'Oh, yes; I quite forgot. Still, on such a wonderful day as this! It is strange, Sophy, you will not mind my saying so.'

Sophy could only own that this was a perfectly fair observation. Her father's ideas were a little strange at times, and his overzealous care for her health could be maddening. But she never truly minded, for it was all borne out of love and care, and how could she mind that?

Anne talked on as they walked, chattering comfortably about the doings of her own family, and those of their mutual neighbours. At nineteen, she was almost ten years younger than Sophy, and her conversation tended to reflect that; for she talked a great deal more about the doings of unmarried young gentlemen than Sophy cared to hear. It was of no interest to her how much money Mr. Snelling had, or whether Mr. Adair was likely to choose a wife soon; neither was likely to affect her prospects, nor those of her friends. But she let Anne talk uninterrupted until they arrived at Mr. Peck's shop.

'I shall not come in with you,' Anne said promptly, 'for Miss Sargent has just got a new bonnet in and I am wild to try it.'

The milliner's shop being just opposite, this suggestion could only please Sophy, and she readily agreed. It was the work of a mere few minutes to complete her business with Mr. Peck, the more speedily accomplished for not having an audience, and she soon stepped out into the street once more with two hatboxes in hand: one unusually large, and one remarkably small.

She noticed at once that Anne had not gone into Miss Sargent's shop at all, for she had noticed Mr. Ash in the street and had, with well-meaning enthusiasm, pressed him into conversation. Mr. Ash was a tall, rather serious young man, well known for the dedication he applied to learning his father's business. It was widely agreed across Tilby that Mr. Ash spent far too much of his time attending to his work, and Miss Gladwin and Miss Lacey were particularly forthright in their belief that he would wear himself away to nothing. With many a charming smile and much good-humoured laughter, Anne was doing her best to avert this terrible prospect.

Mr. Ash bore her conversation with patience, but Sophy could see that he was anxious to resume his errand, whatever it had been. Stepping quickly across the street, she walked straight up to the couple and immediately said:

'Forgive my interruption, Mr. Ash, but you have accosted my companion and I am much desirous of having her back. Shall it inconvenience you very much if I reclaim her at once?'

Mr. Ash shot her a look of mild relief, mumbled something vaguely affirmative and rapidly made his escape. Sophy noticed that he cast a quick, shy look at Anne on his way past.

'I am not sure whether to be vexed with you or not, Sophy,' said Anne once Mr. Ash was out of hearing. 'He almost smiled! Would have, I am sure, had I had another moment's conversation with him.'

'And is it your mission to induce smiles in every young man?'

'No; only the stubborn ones, like Mr. Ash. Most of them need no encouragement.'

Sophy smiled herself, but made no reply to this sally. Instead she said: 'Now, Anne, I am going to the bridge. I do not ask you to come with me if you would rather not.'

Anne eyed the enormous hat box in her friend's hands and made a face. 'You are not visiting with the bridge-keeper again, are you? I know he is a great friend of yours, but... a troll? I do not know quite where trolls fit into society, but a bridge-keeper cannot rank very high.'

'All of that is quite immaterial! Balli is a dear creature, gentleman or not, and I am going to give him this gift right away.' She turned and set off, leaving Anne to catch up if she would.

'But—but—Sophy,' Anne panted as she struggled to keep up with the taller woman's pace, 'it is not his profession so much as his unusual approach to it! Always wanting news and information and secrets. I do believe that many would infinitely prefer to give him money, like all the other tolls.'

'Why should that be? Everyone is always wild for news, and gossip is traded with considerably more enthusiasm than mere money. Mr. Balligumph is merely more honest about it than the rest of us!'

Anne's only response to this was an inarticulate noise of incredulity; but she kept up with Sophy all the way through the village and out to the bridge. The weather was indeed fine, and as the sun beat down upon them both, Sophy began to regret her choice of a long pelisse, instead of a short spencer jacket like Anne's. It was only that her gown, an old favourite in yellow muslin, was looking so shabby now, and she had just enough pride to want to cover it up. Her spencer was fraying at the cuffs, and until she had found a way to mend it neatly, her pelisse would have to do.

As the old stone bridge came into view, Sophy was glad to see that it was empty; no carriages waited to cross the worn stone structure, and there were no other walkers in sight. Stepping lightly into the middle of the bridge, she paused and called, 'Mr. Balligumph?'

Almost before she had finished speaking, she heard a familiar low chuckle. 'Well, Miss Sophy,' said a rumbling voice from somewhere beneath the bridge. 'I was beginnin' to think you was avoidin' me.'

An enormous, vividly blue face emerged to peer at her from beneath the bridge. She smiled as the rest of the self-appointed bridge guardian stepped out into the sun. He was much taller than she was; much bigger in every respect, for his eyes were as big as the palms of her hands, and the two tusks that showed around his congenial smile were as long as her forearms. She had no idea how he contrived to fit himself under the Tilby Bridge, which was by no means large enough to accommodate him.

'Good morning!' Sophy called. 'I have not been avoiding you; the very notion is absurd, as you well know. Here I am in the flesh, and with another visitor for you!'

Balligumph turned his enormous golden eyes on Anne, and smiled toothily. 'Always a pleasure, Miss Daverill.'

Anne mumbled something that sounded like 'pleasure', and inched a little closer to Sophy.

'Aww, now, I'll not be after hurtin' ye! I only smitherise them as have ticked me off, an' no friend o' Miss Sophy's has ever been known to do that.'

'Smitherise?' Anne said faintly.

'Pulverise,' Balli elaborated, his smile widening. 'Bash to smithereens, that is. An' I may as well add, anybody who's clunch enough to tick off my Sophy is likely to get smitherised likewise, an' I'll be happy as can be t'extend tha' offer to her friends as well.'

Anne stared at him.

'That is most kind of you, Mr. Balligumph,' Sophy said. 'Fortunately there will be no need to smitherise anybody today.' The look of strangled horror on Anne's face and the beaming congeniality on Balli's made her desperately want to laugh, and she had to cough a time or two to cover it up.

Balli eyed her. 'Well now, I can't help noticin' that ye ain't exactly empty-handed, Miss Sophy. Is tha' fer me?'

Sophy held out the enormous hat box with a sunny smile. 'It isn't very likely to do for anyone else, is it?'

'Tha's what I was thinkin',' the troll said smugly, his eyes lighting up at the gift. He took the box from her, taking great care not to crush her small hands with his gigantic ones. He ripped off the lid, threw it casually over his shoulder, and shook out a hat.

It was a tall hat, a little like Thundigle's but quite distinct. Where the brownie's aped the tall, polished, slightly conical hats that the gentry wore, Balligumph's was shorter, wider and blockier. Moreover, it was earth-brown instead of black. It also had a wider brim, the better to shade his eyes from the sun.

Sophy had chosen the style with care. I'm no gent, me, Balli had often said. Just a workin' troll. A hat like Thundigle's would never have suited or pleased him, but this one matched perfectly with the slightly shabby, city-attorney-crossed-with-a-farmer attire that he chose to affect.

Balli began to chuckle, his huge chest heaving with laughter as he plonked the hat onto his head. 'Ain't you a rare one! I can think o' nothin' more perfect.' He posed for admiration, his messy pale hair sticking out crazily from beneath the brim, his smile larger than ever.

Sophy applauded, relieved to see that the hat fitted him. 'You're a vision,' she told him, grinning.

Balli bowed low. 'Only watch them ladies try t' resist me now! Won't be possible, mark my words.'

Stealing a glance at Anne, Sophy noticed that she looked utterly appalled. 'He is quite safe,' she whispered while Balli busied himself with inspecting his new hat. 'Have you ever heard of Balli harming anyone?'

'No…' Anne admitted. 'But he is so big.'

'Well, he can hardly help that,' said Sophy reasonably. 'You are a great deal larger than a sparrow; does that mean that you intend to inflict harm upon any that you see? Of course not.'

Anne did not seem convinced; but just then Balli looked up again. 'Top notch, this,' he informed Sophy. 'Mr. Peck's work?'

Sophy nodded.

'Ain't cheap, then,' he said bluntly. 'Ye'll forgive me fer askin', for there never was a sunnier nature this side o' Aylfenhame. How's a threadbare miss such as yerself come up wi' a shiny piece such as this?'

Sophy shook her head. 'That is an impertinent question which I shall not answer!'

Balli twinkled at her. 'Impertinent I may be, but that's me: the manners of a goat, an' at least twice the hair. But it would be impolite not t'answer me, now, would it not? An' you bein' a proper gentry-miss wouldn't care to be rude.' He winked roguishly and Sophy couldn't help smiling back.

'I bartered for it,' she said with dignity. 'The use of my sewing fingers in exchange for some of Mr. Peck's time.' And it had taken her many hours of work to earn Balli's hat, for Mr. Peck—while not unkind—was canny, with an eye to the profit. But she would not tell Balli that.

Balligumph nodded thoughtfully. 'It's that nice o' ye, I'm minded to make a gift in return,' he said.

'That is not necessary at all, I assure you,' Sophy demurred.

'No argument out o' ye,' Balli said, waving a fat-fingered hand. 'I'll do as I please, and no shrimpin' scrappit such as the likes o' *ye* is goin' t' stop me, understand?'

Sophy suppressed a grin, and curtseyed. 'Quite understood.'

'Good.' He eyed her seriously, from the top of her blonde-curled head to the tips of her booted feet, and said abruptly: 'How's that old man o' yours?'

Sophy blinked. 'Papa is well enough, thank you.'

'Yes? His health is good?'

'I—well enough,' Sophy said again, with less certainty. In fact, a lack of exercise in his daily routine combined with an overabundance of rich food had caused a steady deterioration in the Reverend Landon's health, but she had no wish to own as much.

She feared that Balli knew that already, however, for he nodded knowingly and tapped one sausage-like finger against his cheek in thought. 'An' what o' ye? Any nice young men comin' callin'?'

Sophy flushed, and managed a laugh. 'No, of course not. Why should there be?' She had no need to elaborate: at her age, without either money, or connections, or even particularly striking looks to recommend her, her prospects were not bright. When one took into account her lack of musical ability or other accomplishments along with her hopelessness as a housekeeper, well… she had never really expected to wed.

To her mingled relief and pain, Balli chose not to challenge her on this point. Instead he looked at Anne. 'Well? Is she tellin' the truth?'

Anne looked uncertainly at Sophy and hesitated. 'I… know of no gentlemen, sir,' she said.

Balli nodded. All of his hearty good cheer had vanished; he began to look ready to… well, to *smitherise* someone. 'Come back in two days,' he said abruptly. 'Just Miss Sophy, if ye don't mind, Miss Daverill. First o' May. Don't be too late, now.'

Bemused and rather mortified, Sophy quickly agreed. Unsure of how to recover from the awkwardness of Balli's enquiries, she bid him goodbye and hurried away, Anne following close behind.

Now, will ye look at that? As fine a woman as any could wish fer, Miss Sophy—a prize fer any chap as has sense. But there ain't a scrap o' sense to be found in these parts, for all the young men to pass her over just 'cause she ain't rich, an' her features is perhaps not so well arranged as the imagination might fancy! Crowd o' great loobies, the lot of 'em. I had to do somethin'. *All the town knew tha' the silly old Reverend was eatin' himself to an early grave, an eatin' her inheritance with it; and what would become o' my Sophy then? I 'atched a plan, that's what I did. Listen some more, an' I'll tell ye all about it...*

CHAPTER TWO

Sophy left her father's house sharply at one o'clock on the first of May. The two days had passed slowly since Mr. Balligumph's offer, and she remained none the wiser as to what he had in mind. The sun was strong, the skies blue and the wind fair as she made her way back to the bridge; mindful of the weather and the lack of company, she had chosen to wear her spencer jacket and felt considerably more comfortable for it.

The fine weather lifted her spirits as she walked, and the breeze cleared her head. She had spent the morning housekeeping, a process which always left her feeling disheartened: for all her efforts and care, she often felt that she created as many problems as she solved, and left more work for Mary and Thundigle to do. But there had been such an excess of work to be done that she had been left with no choice but to do her best. Now, towards the end of a trying morning, a visit to Balligumph was very welcome indeed; he always had a smile and a jest for her, and cheered her considerably.

Thundigle had retired an hour ago, back to wherever it was that he lived when he wasn't at the parsonage. She was a little surprised, therefore, to find him waiting for her when she reached the bridge.

'Miss Sophy,' he said, offering a polite bow. 'I hope the labours of the day have not left you too fatigued.'

'Not at all, I thank you,' she said, frowning in puzzlement. 'What brings you to the bridge today?'

He opened his black eyes wide in surprise. 'Why, Mr. Balligumph particularly requested my presence.'

His manner suggested that the matter ought to be clear to her, which only puzzled her more. But then Balli himself clambered into view and sat weightily down, and she directed a smile at him instead. 'Mr. Balligumph, I hope I am not too late. There was a great deal of work to be done this morning, as Thundigle will tell you.'

'Not at all, Miss Sophy,' he rumbled. 'Yer timin' could scarcely be better, in fact, as it's taken me much o' the mornin' t'secure this pretty.' He held up something that twinkled in the sun, and offered it to Sophy.

She took it a little doubtfully. It was a glass sphere, just big enough to fit into her curled hand. At first she could see nothing remarkable about it—nothing at all to explain why Balli had gone to such lengths to find and present it to her. But as she held it, a spark of light grew in its depths until it began to shine in more colours than Sophy could count.

'Balli… what is this?'

He winked. 'A bundle o' feisty entertainment, Miss. Now, I want you to go a little way yonder—' he pointed out into the fields—'an' let it go. An' then ye must follow my little chap wherever he goes— don't let him out o' your sight! Thundigle will be goin' along t'mind ye.'

Sophy's gaze strayed back to the little ball of shifting light in her hand, and she stared at it, half mesmerised. 'Let it go?' she repeated. 'But I do not *wish* to let it go.'

'It will be worth yer while to do so, that I promise.'

Sophy blinked and shook her head, breaking the strange trance. 'It sounds as though this may take some time, and I have not much to spare this afternoon. I shall come back on the morrow.' She directed a smile at Balligumph and started to thank him, but the genial troll was shaking his great head.

'Ye must do it today or not at all!'

Sophy wanted to object; his words made no sense, and her own arrangements seemed considerably more logical. But she would have to trust him. He had never led her astray before, nor would he now. She nodded, and clutched the sphere more tightly, afraid to drop it too soon. 'Thank you,' she said with a smile. 'I am not sure what I am thanking you for, but I am much obliged to you for your kindness.'

The troll winked and cocked his head in the direction of the fields. 'Ye'll soon find out, Missy. Off wi' ye now.'

Sophy curtseyed by way of reply, and crossed the bridge. 'Off after her now, Mr. Thundigle,' she heard Balli say. 'An' mind ye keep up!'

Thundigle's quick, light steps came pattering after her. 'Not too fast, Miss Sophy!' he called.

Sophy tried to slow down, but a strange kind of eagerness had seized her as she crossed the bridge and she began to hurry along. Before she could think about dropping the sphere, it jerked itself out of her hands; but it did not fall instantly to the floor, as she might logically expect. Instead it rose up into the air and floated away, streaming light and colour as it went.

'A will-o-the-wyke!' Sophy realised, her heart beating faster at the thought. All the folk of Tilby knew never to follow a will-o-the-wyke, if one chanced to encounter such a thing, for they were notoriously mischievous and known to lead unwary folk astray. But Balli obviously trusted this one... she stepped quickly after it.

'Slow down just a little, Miss Sophy!' Thundigle called, and she tried, but her feet had rejected her command and now followed some other purpose. The wind picked up, catching at her clothes and her hair, and the sky clouded over, hiding the golden spring sun. The wisp shone still brighter in response, its colours growing more brilliant in the deepening gloom. When a white mist came rolling in, the wisp shone against the background of thickening fog like a tiny multi-coloured sun. Her heart beating fast with excitement and alarm, Sophy could look at nothing else.

She heard a stifled curse as Thundigle caught up with her, panting and wheezing, and collided with her legs. He clutched at her skirts as the mist began to clear, revealing a green landscape.

At first, she noticed nothing amiss. A field of flourishing grain stretched ahead of her; the sun shone overhead in wide blue skies; her nostrils detected the fresh and floral spring fragrances that she loved.

But as she stood, dazed and blinking, the differences began to intrude themselves upon her notice. The tall, waving crop in the field around her was of no variety that she recognised, and tinged besides with a hint of blue. She inhaled a lungful of air, rich and heady with a pungency of fragrance that made her head spin. A gust of wind brought with it the sound of distant bells; no church bells, these, but a melodic chiming that had never reached her ears before. Even the air tasted rich, like honey on her tongue.

'Mr. Thundigle,' she said slowly, 'this is not Tilby.'

Thundigle was grumbling crossly under his breath, but now he spoke up. 'How like a troll! A fine trick, to send an unsuspecting human across with only a brownie to guide her steps—and without even a word of warning to the lady beforehand! Without asking her leave! Why, it is so—so very—'

'It is of no particular matter,' Sophy interjected.

'—so very RUDE!' Thundigle finished.

'The manners of a goat, and twice the hair,' Sophy agreed, with a wry smile. 'He said it himself!'

Thundigle continued to bristle. 'Of all the hare-brained, empty-headed, sap-skulled notions to spring on a helpless young lady...' Thundigle began to stamp in circles, shaking his head and working himself up into a fine rage.

Sophy put out her hands, alarmed. 'Stop! There is no harm done; I am sure Mr. Balligumph had a good reason for acting as he has done, though it may not be clear to either of us just yet. And I, dear Thundigle, am hardly helpless.'

Thundigle subsided, though the sceptical look he bestowed upon her at her closing statement was not entirely flattering. Sophy let this pass.

'What we need to do,' she said reasonably, 'is remain calm.' Her words belied the flutter she was in, for to find herself inexplicably *elsewhere*, without warning and with no obvious means of return, alarmed her more than a little. She took a few deep breaths to soothe her rapidly beating heart—noticing anew the peculiar fragrance of the air, and the way her head swam under the influence of it—and looked around. 'I wish Balli had given some idea of what he meant for us to do,' she added.

Thundigle occupied himself with straightening his cravat, and said nothing.

'We are in Aylfenhame, are we not?' Sophy hazarded. Aylfenhame was the name given to the lands that mirrored the mortal worlds—home of Thundigle's people, and Balligumph's, and many another creature from the stories of Sophy's childhood. Some of its denizens migrated across to the human world, making their homes anew around human hearths (and bridges). Most chose to remain.

'The Faerie realm,' Thundigle said with a sigh. 'Yes, 'tis to Aylfenhame we are come. And don't you run away being all delighted,' he added, eyeing Sophy with grave disapproval. 'Tis perilous, and we must take care.'

Sophy turned in a circle, shading her eyes from the sun. All around her she saw neatly-tended fields, well-kept hedgerows and, in the distance, a collection of rooftops. 'Perilous? It looks perfectly harmless to me.'

'That's the crossing,' the brownie replied, nodding wisely. 'The Humanfolk are remarkably good at self-deception; 'tis a known fact in Faerie. What you are seeing is—mostly—what you expect to see. Fields, farms and so on, yes? That will change.'

Sophy did not like the sound of this, but she swallowed her disquiet. Balligumph had no logical reason to wish her harm; quite the contrary. So he must intend for something good to happen to her in this place. 'He has sent you along as my guide, has he not? Then please: by all means, lead on!'

Thundigle grumbled a little, but he set off in the direction of the rooftops Sophy had seen. Putting aside her fears, Sophy followed.

She soon realised that Thundigle's prediction had been perfectly accurate. As they walked, colours shifted in her vision; shapes turned fluid and reformed; the light changed, scents grew stronger and more alien and strange sounds began to reach her ears. Gradually, bit by bit, the pretty fields faded away, the hedgerows disappeared, and Sophy found that she was walking through a meadow of golden grass, peppered with luxuriant, sweet-smelling blooms and buzzing with colourful insects. As they drew nearer to the rooftops, Sophy saw that they were not neat tile, as she had thought, but instead composed of grey wood topped with erratic thatch, the likes of which she had never seen before. A sloping hill stretched away to her left, sparsely dotted with gnarled silver-barked trees with abundant foliage. As the branches swayed in the breeze, she realised that here was the source of the chiming she had heard. Someone had decked the branches which coloured ribbons and dozens of silver-and-gold bells.

'Beltane,' Thundigle said when she pointed them out. He offered no further explanation, and his mood being evidently still poor, Sophy asked no further questions.

A few minutes of brisk walking—brisk to Thundigle, at least—brought them to the edge of the village Sophy had seen from a distance. They passed through a stone gate just wide enough for perhaps three humans to walk abreast. Over the gate hung a neatly-painted sign announcing the name 'Grenlowe'.

'Grenlowe?' Sophy wondered aloud. 'That's the name of this town?'

'Yes. I can only imagine that Mr. Balligumph meant for me to bring you here, though I know not why.'

Sophy looked around with great interest. She saw at once why Balli had sent Thundigle with her, instead of accompanying her himself: Grenlowe was far from spacious. Its buildings were small, its streets narrow, its doorways and gates sized with more diminutive folk in mind. This was no home for folk of Balli's size.

The town was enchanting, and she soon forgot her fears and even her confusion in enjoyment. Nothing was ever planned in Grenlowe, that she could judge; most of the houses she passed appeared to have started out as a single room, and others had been haphazardly piled around and on top as they were needed. They were thatched in erratic patterns, like a head of tumbled curls; most were built from stone or grey wood, with small, paned windows bright with colour.

'Why are all the windows frosted over?' she whispered to Thundigle.

'The people of Grenlowe value their privacy,' he answered.

Sophy frowned, noting that most of the frosted-glass windows also had shutters and curtains. Privacy was *deeply* valued, she concluded, and immediately felt uncomfortable for staring. But the curtains were brightly coloured, and the shutters cheerfully painted; the overall effect was more welcoming than otherwise.

When they reached a village square—passing numerous houses, small shops and inns along the way—they encountered a market in full swing. Sophy was delighted; everywhere she looked her eager eye discovered ribbons, fabrics, foods and myriad goods, each more riotously coloured than the last. But Thundigle stopped her.

'Careful, Miss Sophy,' he said in an undertone. 'I advise against looking too closely.'

'But whyever not?'

'Things aren't always as they seem in Aylfenhame, remember? For certain you should not eat anything here, for if it does you no other harm, it may oblige you to stay. It changes you.'

Sophy had not time to answer. As they entered the market, only then had it struck her how few other folk she had seen in the streets of Grenlowe. They were all *here*, bargaining and buying, jostling and pushing each other, and Sophy along with them. She saw goblins and brownies like Thundigle, stocky gnomes in colourful overalls, nymphs and sprites and many other creatures she did not recognise. Some wore rags; others wore finery more splendid than anything Sophy had seen before.

She noticed many folk who looked human, too, except for a slight point to their ears, shades of blue, green and purple in their hair, and eyes coloured like earth and trees and meadows of flowers. Their skin ranged in hue from palest white through to deep, dark brown. These were the Ayliri, she realised: the ruling class of Aylfenhame by right of beauty, and birth, and power.

All seemed equally eager to acquire the proffered wares, rich and raggity alike. As Sophy fought to keep her feet in the crush and to remain near Thundigle, someone thrust an enchanting little cake under her nose. It was the colour of summer sunshine, and it sparkled with flecks of gold as the vendor turned it for her perusal. She smelled honey and nectar and at least a dozen other heavenly things.

'Sun cakes!' bawled a scratchety voice immediately next to her ear. 'Sun cakes, fresh! Going fast! Hurry!'

Mindful of Thundigle's warning, Sophy tried to turn away, but the beauty of the little cake held her. She inhaled another lungful of the delicious aroma, wondering if she had money enough in her purse for the treat.

'Sun cakes!' bawled the vendor again, and the cake was withdrawn. 'Fine spirits and good moods for a week; that's a guarantee!'

Dismayed, Sophy looked around for the seller, already reaching into her reticule for her purse.

'Miss Sophy!' Thundigle hissed. 'Remember what I said!'

'I know, I do truly remember; only it is so very—' her attention was caught by an array of ribbons fluttering from the awnings of a stall opposite. They were decked with flowers and bells and tiny butterflies with fluttering gossamer wings, and Sophy was enchanted anew. 'Oh, but look! I must have that lavender ribbon—you must allow me that much, Thundigle, for I assure you I have no intention of eating it.'

'We need to get away from this market,' the brownie muttered. With that he took hold of Sophy's skirt in one small but insistent hand and began to haul her away. He was surprisingly strong for one so small; off-balance as she was, Sophy found herself propelled some distance from the mesmerising ribbons before she could muster any objection.

'This is too bad of you,' she protested, really feeling disappointed. 'I cannot believe a single ribbon could do me any harm.'

Thundigle marched on, implacable. 'It begins with a ribbon...' he said grimly.

'And ends, perhaps, with an entire gown, and a pair of boots to match! I can see no probable outcome any worse than that, so do please be reasonable.' She finally managed to halt Thundigle's march, wresting her gown free of his tight grip.

Barely had she caught her breath, however, before someone large and heavy barrelled into her, sending her spinning away. She collided with a disagreeably solid wall, narrowly avoiding knocking her head against the unyielding stone.

'Well, really!' she gasped, clutching at her bonnet and reticule. 'People in Aylfenhame have fully the *most* disagreeable manners I have ever—'

She broke off, her eye fixed upon the fleeing figure who had almost knocked her over. He was unmistakeably Ayliri, tall and lithe, dressed in pale trousers, a dark blue tunic and a wide-brimmed hat. All she could see was his fleeing back; his dark brown hair was long and loose, flying in the wind.

He was chasing after an enormous purple cat.

The creature was magnificent; easily three times the size of a typical house cat. Its fur was quite, quite purple—the hue of lilacs in bloom—and highlighted with a sheen of silver. Sophy stared until the cat and the man had disappeared around a corner.

Intrigued and outraged by turns, and with confused notions in mind of admiring the cat and berating its pursuer, Sophy started down the street after them. She soon left the market crush behind and found her way clear; breaking into a run, she hastened to catch up.

The corner gave way to another, and another. Turning a third time, Sophy encountered a dead end. Her quarry stood at the end of it, man and cat facing each other in some kind of stand-off. They were both crouched low, ready to spring; were they going to attack each other?

'Stop!' she called, hurrying down the narrow street towards them.

The cat flashed golden eyes at her in the briefest of glances. The man chose that moment to pounce; but, even distracted, the cat evaded him with ease and tore away back down the lane towards Sophy.

She had no time to move out of the way before it was upon her. But instead of colliding with her, the cat leaped up into the air and began to run along the side of the building, with as much ease as though it ran on level ground. It missed her by a whisker; as it passed, Sophy had just time to observe that it was carrying something in its mouth.

She watched, astonished, as it ran the full length of the street sideways to the road, and finally vanished from sight.

Her attention was caught by the sound of laughter coming from behind her. Turning, she saw the stranger doubled over with mirth.

'Very well; you have earned your dinner!' he called, straightening. His gaze fell on Sophy, and he stopped laughing.

Sophy regarded him in silence, keeping a wary distance. His skin was dark brown; he was much browner than any person she had ever seen before. She could discern little else, for the wide brim of his hat and his unruly hair covered much of his face. Only a single bright brown eye was visible, twinkling with merriment and fixed upon her.

'Well, madam, you have made a mess of my contest, and given the victory against me. To what do I owe the honour of your interruption?'

His accent was unlike anything she had heard before, either, and very pleasant, full of lilting musicality. He did not sound cross, but

Sophy—as the injured party—bridled. 'A pretty comment, sir, when it is you who has interrupted me! You almost knocked me down a few moments ago.'

'Ah! I had thought it was a wall I had connected with, but thinking on it, I did find it a little softer than one might expect of a stone structure.' His one visible eye twinkled at her more merrily than ever, and his tone was full of laughter.

Sophy lifted her chin and stared him down. To be mistaken for a wall! She was taller than most women, this was true, and she was not especially blessed with physical endowments; but still! A wall!

'An apology is considered customary, under the circumstances!' she said.

'And have you really followed me for such a purpose as that?' he marvelled. 'Hey! Well, an apology costs nothing. You may have several, madam, if that will please you.' He proceeded to sweep her a low bow, and said, 'Apologies once, twice and thrice, and I am delighted to see that I have done you no lasting injury.'

Sophy could hear his smile, even if she couldn't see it. His peculiar manner began to strike her as charming, and she smiled in return. 'No injury indeed, though perhaps I had better ascertain the health of the wall. *You* may not have collided with it, but *I* did, and rather hard at that.' Hard enough to bruise, she judged, for she could feel a dull ache in her shoulder and back.

He laughed at that, and held out a hand. 'Walls are exceptionally good at taking care of themselves, I do find. May I know your name?'

Sophy advanced with a little caution. What manner of introduction was this? No proper one, certainly, for she ought to be introduced by a respectable third party. Moreover, she found he did actually mean to shake her hand, for he continued to hold it out to her.

'Miss Landon, of Tilby,' she said, curtseying. Evidently the customs of Grenlowe differed from those of her home town, but still she could not bring herself to actually shake his hand.

'Miss Landon of Tilby,' he repeated, withdrawing his hand. To her amusement he mimicked her gesture, and curtseyed very prettily to her. 'I am Aubranael!'

'Very well, Mr. Aubranael,' she began, but he cut her off.

'Not "Mister". Just Aubranael.'

Sophy frowned. Proper etiquette required that a lady address a gentleman by his title and his family name; did he really expect her to call him by his first name?

But, she remembered, this was Aylfenhame. Perhaps people here did not *have* family names. Or titles.

'Aubranael,' she repeated, trying it out. The name was so odd that the lack of title did not seem so peculiar after all; but she felt compelled to make up for the deficit in politeness by making another curtsey, which drew a laugh from him.

'You do not reside in Grenlowe, I think,' he said. 'Or even in Aylfenhame, I would judge. This Tilby of yours is situated in...?'

'England.'

'Ah! Distant shores! And how came you to be travelling here, Miss Landon of Tilby?'

'It was not a plan of my own making,' she replied, and explained the circumstances behind her arrival. To her surprise he appeared to have heard of Balligumph, and on the mention of the troll's name his manner towards her (already thoroughly friendly) warmed even further. This civil exchange culminated in an invitation to take tea with him: 'For,' he said gravely, 'your kind is famed for love of that particular beverage.'

His offer posed a dilemma, and she paused to consider. It was one thing to converse briefly with a gentleman one had happened to bump into (or vice versa); it was quite another to accept an invitation to tea, and without any other companion! Sophy found that she dearly wished to accept, for there was something about him that charmed her enormously; but she could not bring herself to be so bold.

She was saved by a slight cough from behind her. Turning, she found Thundigle glaring up at her.

'Oh! True, indeed, I had forgot. I must not eat or drink anything here, my friend assures me,' she said, turning back to Aubranael. 'Which is a shame, for I am rather thirsty.'

'No matter: you may watch me drink tea, and I will endeavour to make it every bit as entertaining an experience as drinking it yourself.'

With Thundigle to go with her, Sophy could see no further objections to this plan, and she smiled her approbation of it.

But then something strange happened.

The great purple cat came leaping back, sailing past Sophy's head without warning and making her jump with fright. The cat leapt straight at Aubranael's face, but instead of attacking him—as Sophy's startled mind expected—the creature collided with his great hat, and sent it tumbling to the floor. At the same time a cloud slipped over the sun and a great gust of wind came howling down the street, blowing back Aubranael's long hair. For the first time since their meeting, Sophy was afforded a clear view of his face, and she could not help but stare.

He might once have been handsome, but some accident had wrested from him forever the power of being considered even tolerably pleasing. His face was a mess of twisted, scarred flesh; only his eyes, velvet brown and suddenly sad, had escaped unscathed.

His expression changed as hers did. All his sunny merriment drained away, and he looked stricken.

'Apologies,' he said quietly, bowing his head to hide his face, once more, behind his hair. 'I should not have asked; now I have made you uncomfortable.' He spoke without a trace of bitterness or resentment, or even self-pity, and he made no attempt to chastise the cat. His apology seemed sincere, and Sophy cursed herself for her reaction. What could it possibly matter, when he was such congenial company?

'In England,' she said, summoning back her smile, 'it is considered impolite to withdraw an invitation once given, especially to a lady. Here I had taken you for a gentleman!'

Aubranael studied her for a moment, perhaps weighing the sincerity of her words. At last, his smile returned; faint, but growing stronger.

'And you, Miss Landon of Tilby, are every inch a lady, I am sure,' he said. He offered her his arm, and without hesitation, she took it.

'Will your companion be joining us?' he enquired, looking down at Thundigle.

The brownie drew himself up to his full, diminutive height and looked down his nose at Aubranael's knees. 'Miss Landon requires a chaperon, sir, as you would know if you were *indeed* a gentleman.'

Aubranael's face lit up in a delighted grin. 'Does she? Excellent! By all means, do come along and protect the lady from unwanted attentions. Who knows but what I may do, if left unspied-upon?'

Thundigle eyed him, very ready to take offence.

'Do please come along,' Sophy begged him. 'I am in need of your company rather more than your chaperonage, I assure you.'

Mollified, the brownie nodded stiffly and bowed. 'It would be my pleasure,' he pronounced.

The whole party set off under Aubranael's direction. He chatted easily as they walked, and joked often; Sophy found herself perfectly at ease with him. She thought, though, that some part of his mood had not recovered from the unveiling of his face. His merriment was, perhaps, a little forced. She felt she had much to make up for, and worked harder to be agreeable because of it.

The tea-room he selected was called The Golden Queen, and it was thoroughly enchanting to Sophy. The aromas of strange teas and untasted beverages tormented Sophy's nose, and she was sorely tempted to ignore Thundigle's advice. She persisted, however, her good sense winning over her curiosity; and besides, Aubranael was such an agreeable companion that she had no cause to repine.

She was touched to note that Aubranael was served with only a glass of water, no doubt on her account. He may not know the customs of England, she thought, but he had the spirit of a gentleman as far as courtesy and consideration went.

At last, the sun began to sink and the shadows lengthened. Late afternoon arrived, and Sophy began to talk of returning home.

'Though I do not know quite how,' she admitted. The matter ought to give her more concern, but she felt serene and at ease in a way she had rarely experienced before.

'But it is Beltane, and therefore the simplest thing to achieve,' Aubranael assured her. 'I do not know if I wish to tell you any more, however.'

Sophy blinked in surprise. 'Whyever not?'

'Perhaps... because I do not wish you to leave.'

Sophy smiled, but shook her head. 'We have only just become acquainted. I cannot believe you are so *very* pleased with my company as all that.'

'From this I judge that you are by no means so enchanted with me. But you are a little bit pleased; that is more than I tend to hope.' He stood up before Sophy had chance to reply, and offered her his arm once more. 'I will show you a little more of Grenlowe, if you've no objection, and then I will send you home.'

Sophy accepted readily enough, feeling slightly uncomfortable. Truthfully, she *was* delighted with him and did not at all enjoy the prospect of her imminent departure; she may never see him again. He had been far more agreeable than the other young men she knew, who saw only her lack of fortune, her lack of connections or her faults of face and figure, and offered her politeness as a mere matter of form.

But it would not be at all proper to say so, and besides, she could not find the words. So she walked along in distracted silence as Aubranael toured her back through the market square—now much more peaceful than before—and showed her street after street of eccentric, jumbled up houses, shops and gardens.

Sophy was struck by the weird beauty of everything she saw. The buildings might be irregular and outlandish in design, but they were painted and decorated and hung with all manner of adornments in a display of good cheer which warmed her heart. Gardens overflowed with peculiar blooms in hundreds of colours; fruit trees stretched over the paths, laden with many-coloured produce Sophy had never seen before; she saw metals, wood and sparkling stones that would fetch a great price in England, lovingly set into doorways and window-sills, walls, roofs and garden paths. The riot of colour would probably offend the people she knew in Tilby, especially those of higher status: pale hues, regular structures and relative simplicity of design were considered much more the thing. But to Sophy, the golden afternoon sun softly illuminating this feast of colour warmed her heart and lifted her spirits.

She was disappointed when Aubranael stopped at the Grenlowe gate. Beyond it she could see the verdant meadow she had passed through on her arrival, and the bell-bedecked trees, and beyond all this the promise of a great forest to explore.

'If it is your wish to return, you need merely touch the gate,' Aubranael told her.

Sophy stretched out her hand, then paused. Did she truly wish to leave this vibrant, exciting place? Much was said of the dangers of Aylfenhame, or Faerie; she had heard many such stories ever since her infancy. But she had seen nothing of danger. She had seen only colour and life and beauty, and met with kindness and considerable charm.

She hesitated.

But if she stayed, where would she go? What would she do? She had no home here, and could hardly expect anybody to provide her with one. And what of her father? Had she forgotten him? Her cheeks flushed warm with mortification at the idea, and she berated herself for her selfishness. Who would look after him if she did not?

'I thank you, sir, for your kindness,' she said to Aubranael. 'I have been most happily detained, and I cannot think when I have enjoyed an afternoon more. But I must return home.'

She thought she saw a flicker of regret in Aubranael's dark eyes, but he beamed at her and swept an extravagant bow—taking notes, she thought, from Thundigle. 'Very well, fair lady! Well met and I wish you health and prosperity and joy and, indeed, anything else good you can think of.'

His grin was irresistible; though his words suggested a belief that they would not meet again, she could not help smiling back.

'I wish you the same, tenfold,' she said. Then, quickly before she could change her mind, she gathered up Thundigle and pressed her palm flat against the cool stone of the gate. In a trice, the meadow and the gate faded as her vision blurred. She blinked rapidly to restore her sight, and found herself looking instead at the familiar fields of Tilby.

She stood near Balligumph's bridge, but she did not wish to summon him, for her thoughts were too busy and her heart too heavy for conversation. But as she crossed the bridge, she trailed her fingers over the cold stone and whispered, 'Thank you, you sly old troll.'

She thought she heard an answering chuckle from somewhere under the bridge, but Balligumph did not appear. Sophy turned her steps towards home and her father, leaving the wonders of Aylfenhame behind.

Now, dunnot look at me that way! I did naught amiss. Ye're as bad as that meddlin' brownie. Made her unhappy with her own world, that's what he said. I made her long fer summat out o' her reach. But did I? What if Miss Sophy is made fer different things?

Well, it weren't so simple as either of us expected, that's the truth. An' if ye'll allow me, I'll go right ahead an' explain why.

CHAPTER THREE

A number of days wandered lazily by in Aylfenhame, and Aubranael wandered with them: through the streets of Grenlowe, over its surrounding meadows, and far beyond. His only companion was the cat, Felebre.

'I think something is wrong with me, Fel,' confided Aubranael on the fifth such wandering day. 'All the world seems dull and drear. I can take no pleasure in anything. Exploring? Pfeh. Let the hills sleep in peace. Food? Hmph. It tastes of nothing. I no longer care what lies beyond the next rise; it will not be *Tilby*, and therefore it is of no interest to me.'

Felebre was a feline of taciturn nature. She rarely made any reply to Aubranael's musings, and she made none now.

Aubranael sighed. He was leaning on the gated entryway to Ahrimir Wood, some way from the town of Grenlowe; now he leaned his ruined face on it, too, so he would no longer be troubled with the effort of holding up his head. 'This is the problem with you,' he said to the cat, who had somehow balanced her considerable bulk along the top of the fence. 'There is no finer companion in all of Aylfenhame, I am sure, but I do wish you might be a little more communicative.'

Felebre twitched the tip of her long, shining tail and closed her shining golden eyes.

'Yes; perhaps sleep is the best idea,' he agreed. But he could not sleep, any more than he could eat. His thoughts were too busy, too confused, too troubled.

31

It was not the first time Aubranael had longed for a talkative companion. He had done so without pause ever since his childhood, and the incident that had destroyed his face. He had lost his best and only friend and his beautiful Ayliri visage at the same time; down all the many years since that day, he had been an outcast.

For some, his repulsive appearance was deterrent enough. The Faerie of Aylfenhame loved beauty, and deplored ugliness. The latter category certainly included Aubranael.

But if he had ever expected a different attitude from others among Faerie—the awkward and ungainly hobs, for instance, or the decidedly malformed goblins—his hopes had long since died, for they loved beauty, too. Some tried to curry favour with the beautiful by mimicking their behaviour, and rejecting those whom they rejected; others considered Aubranael unlucky to be close to, as if his particular, unique form of ugliness might in some fashion infect them.

Whatever the reason, Aubranael had grown used to being alone.

Until the strange lady from Tilby had arrived. Fortune had, for once, favoured him: his hair had hidden his features, and he had been granted a few precious minutes to talk in the way that real, whole, unblemished people do.

Even when she had discovered his true face, she had been kind. He blushed to remember the look of surprised horror in her eyes when the winds and Felebre had conspired to reveal him; but he quickly suppressed the memory. She had been kind. Even when relief and fear and hope had rendered him flamboyant, garrulous and absurd, she had still been kind. She had treated him as though even his appalling aspect might hide a mind worth knowing. If she had been pretending, well… she had done so with skill.

Perhaps she had not been pretending. Perhaps, in faraway England, people were not so fixated upon beauty as the folk of Aylfenhame. Perhaps they ignored faces altogether! Could it not be true?

No; absurd. The horror in Miss Landon's eyes told him that much.

He was glad, then, that he had resisted the wild impulse to fly after her, and try his fortune in England instead.

But he continued to think of her. It was her smile, he thought, that attracted him so; for it was sunny and warm, full of a simple delight in life and—perhaps he flattered himself—his company. There was something in that merry, half-dimpled smile that reminded him of Lihyaen... a very little. But he hurriedly dismissed *that* reflection from his mind. He had made many a pact with himself, all down the lonely years, that he would not dwell upon the past.

A few more days slipped by, and Aubranael began to regret the curious chance that had thrown him in the way of the Tilby lady. Until that day, he had lived in blissful ignorance of how much he missed real companionship. And now? He felt that he would never know peace again.

It was Felebre, surprisingly, who resolved his difficulties. By way of a tilted head, lashing tail and prowling in circles, she gave him to understand that she wished for him to follow her. He did so without argument; indeed, without even particularly noticing that he was doing so, and for some time he merely followed in a daze as she led him across meadows, over bridges and through dense woodlands.

Only once was he distracted from his internal reflections. He and Felebre were in the midst of a deep, dark forest when a wholly unexpected sound split the air: a shriek of high-pitched laughter, which rang and rang until, finally, it ended in a snort. The sound was repeated moments later, and Aubranael began to look around for the source.

Felebre had led him into the Outwoods, he realised; it was one of the largest forests in Aylfenhame, so dark and dense as to be almost impenetrable in places, and many avoided it altogether. Aubranael had no fear of it, however, for he and Felebre had spent many long days exploring it. He had heard many tales of its dangers, but little had ever threatened him here.

A gust of wind parted the thick canopy overhead, and a shaft of sunlight shone briefly upon Aubranael. And he saw ahead of him one end of a large dining table sitting incongruously among the trees, its sides lined with high-backed chairs. Each chair was occupied: he caught glimpses of hobs and goblins and brownies and other fae all talking loudly together. The table-top was covered in tea-things.

Intrigued, Aubranael changed course and set off in the direction of the peculiar picnic in the woods. But the faster he chased the table, the further away it seemed to be; and at last it faded away altogether, leaving him puzzled and panting in a silent, empty clearing in the Outwoods.

A gentle bite on his ankle recalled him to himself. He scowled down at Felebre, who stood gazing up at him with an air of irritation.

'Well, I am sorry. But you must admit it was the strangest thing!'

Felebre made no such concession.

'I have never seen or heard of that before, have you?' Aubranael tried.

Felebre stared at him with unblinking eyes.

'I suppose not,' he sighed. 'Very well; on we go.'

And on they went through the endless Outwoods. The table soon faded from Aubranael's thoughts, and he returned to the contemplation of his own troubles, scarcely noticing the route they were taking or any feature of the landscape around him.

When at length they finally stopped, Aubranael blinked as if waking from a long sleep. Felebre sat watching him with her tail wrapped neatly around her paws.

'What's this, Fel?' A glance around revealed nothing of obvious interest, except for the fact that he had never been to this place before. They stood at the bottom of a wide valley, in a little hollow clear of trees. Everything else around them was thickly forested; trees marched in clustered rows up, up and away over the steep sloping sides of the valley, crowded so thickly together that they blocked much of the sunlight. Or moonlight, in fact, for Aubranael realised with some surprise that it was now deep twilight.

He could see nothing that might explain Felebre's choice of this exact spot, and he said so.

Felebre blinked her enormous eyes, as golden as the rising sun, and said nothing.

Aubranael was about to say something more; something a little bit irate, perhaps, since they had undertaken a great deal of walking to no obvious effect, and he was cold and tired; but a voice much more powerful than his own interrupted him.

'Who is at my door!'

It wasn't so much a question as a statement, redolent with the suggestion that whoever it was would shortly be suffering no end of punishments for their unauthorised proximity. Aubranael jumped, his straining eyes searching for the source and finding nothing.

'I... am called Aubranael,' he said, trying to sound confident. He defeated all efforts to the purpose when he added, 'And I do not know why I am at your door.'

There was silence for a long moment. Aubranael spent the time nervously awaiting smiting, cursing, pulverising or any other variety of retribution, and searching without success for any sign of the disputed door. No retribution came, however; there was only the creak of a door opening, and then a space appeared ahead of him.

The door had no business being there at all, he thought with obscure irritation, for it appeared to be opening in the middle of a tree. Beyond it, a gleaming light showed him no tree trunk but a perfectly ordinary room, and a large one at that.

A figure appeared in the doorway. From the timbre of her voice he judged it to be a she, but nothing about the figure encouraged any such conclusion. So swathed in layers of cloth was this probable *she* that he could not even discern what manner of creature she was.

'Felebre,' said the figure. 'Brought me another one, have you? Hmph.' She nudged the cat with her toe, none too gently. Fel bore this interference with untouched serenity.

'Come in, then,' she said. 'And quickly; the night grows cold.'

Aubranael followed the lady inside, judging that a regular acquaintance of Fel's must be a safe person to visit. He hoped that the shiver in his limbs was not leading his wits astray. Inside the peculiar chamber he found a crackling fire; a great quantity of light provided by a number of floating glass lamps; and a heady aroma like the pure essence of summer, rich with nectar and sunshine and a warm evening breeze. He inhaled deeply, and smiled.

'Thank you, thank you,' said his host, as though he had spoken his appreciative thoughts aloud. 'I do like to keep it pleasant.'

He turned to discover that she had thrown off the robes that had shrouded her figure before. He could think of no conceivable reason why she should conceal herself, for the sight that met his eye was one of blazing, shocking beauty. She was almost as of a height with him, and in possession of the most perfect figure he had ever beheld. Her face was perfectly shaped, her skin smooth as silk and unmarred by the smallest blemish. Her soft lips were red, her eyes a glorious blue, and these were fixed upon him with an expression of amusement. A wealth of tumbling golden locks completed her perfect visage, and he swallowed, suddenly feeling very uncomfortable indeed.

'You approve of my art, then,' said the beauty, gesturing at her face. ''Tis a pity it is not real; but then, few are troubled by such minor matters as reality and fakery, are they?' She flashed a brilliant smile.

He blinked at her stupidly as his mind struggled to focus on her words instead of her face. 'I beg your pardon? Not real?'

She shook her head, smiling, as her eyes changed from summer-sky blue to a dazzling emerald green. 'Such a simple trick, beauty, and yet it holds remarkable powers, does it not?'

'Glamour,' Aubranael croaked. 'You are a witch.'

'One of the very best,' she said modestly. 'And you are here because you are in need of my help, yes? Or so Felebre tells me.'

Aubranael glanced at the cat, who had followed them inside and now lay stretched in front of the fire. 'I don't understand. We have been friends for years; why would she now decide that I am in need of help?'

'Something has changed recently, perhaps,' suggested the witch.

'So it has,' he agreed, thinking of a smiling face framed in fair curls. 'But who are you?'

'I am called Hidenory,' she answered. 'Sometimes.'

'Why do you conceal yourself behind this facade? What is your real form?' Aubranael asked the questions with beating heart, anticipating a story somewhat like his own, but she dashed his hopes with a mysterious smile.

'It is far too soon to be asking such personal questions,' she chided. 'But then, I must ask some of you, must I not? Isn't life unfair sometimes?'

Aubranael had no idea what to say.

Hidenory sighed a little, sat down in a large rocking chair and began to gently rock herself back and forth. 'Very well, let us get on with it. What is it that you wish for?'

A vision flashed through Aubranael's mind in an instant: himself with a *face*, a proper one, like everyone else's. What would he look like? Would he be handsome? Perhaps he would have regular features! An arched nose, a strong chin. Perhaps he would even be beautiful.

The thought prompted a curious thickening in his throat and a dampening of his eyes; unable to speak his wish aloud, he gestured at his face, hoping she would understand.

She did, but with understanding came a look of regret and Aubranael's heart sank lower than ever. 'I cannot,' she said. 'Glamour is my art, glamour and illusion. I cannot change reality, only hide it behind something else. And only temporarily, at that.'

Aubranael nodded, looking at the floor. He could muster no reply. Though he had enjoyed only a few seconds of hope, he felt utterly crushed in the aftermath.

'Come, now,' Hidenory said. 'You have endured this misfortune for some years, I collect; there must be a reason why Felebre has brought you to me today. What is it that you truly want? What is it that you would hope to gain, with a mended face?'

He swallowed, thinking of Miss Landon. Slowly and in a low voice, he told Hidenory the story of his meeting with the merry English lady and why it had mattered so much. The witch heard him speak without interruption, and when he had finished he was heartened to see that a smile had returned to her face.

'You wish to follow this creature! There is nothing simpler, I assure you. The journey may be a little unpleasant, but worth the enduring, I am sure? Do you wish to go at once?'

Aubranael stared at her, his head spinning. Go at once? Right away? His heart sped up and a smile tugged at his lips—and quickly died away. Go at once? As he was?

A succession of images flashed through his brain: of Miss Landon's face once she had seen his; of himself adrift in England, subjected to revulsion and humiliation anew as strangers caught sight of his features; of Miss Landon's inevitable rejection of him, once she grew tired of being kind.

He looked at Hidenory's beautiful face and saw his own transformed into handsomeness. People would like him—love him, even! Miss Landon would not be repulsed; she would not have to be kind. She would *want* his company.

'Can you... glamour me?' He asked. 'Give me a face like yours. A beautiful face.'

Hidenory gave him a long, measuring stare. He waited, heart pounding. 'I can,' she said, 'but only for a time. Glamour is a flimsy, ethereal thing. It wears away, and the truth inevitably shines through.'

Aubranael nodded, undaunted. If he could have just a little time to convince her of his worth...

'Tell me something,' Hidenory said. 'Do you intend to tell this Miss Landon your true identity?'

He thought about this for a moment, then shook his head. If she knew right away, her perception of him would be coloured by her memories of his true face, and much of the effect would be destroyed. He would present himself to her all bright and new, as a congenial stranger; they had got along so splendidly before, why should they not do so again? But still better, this time, with his perfect new face.

Hidenory's eyes narrowed and she stared at him as though she was reading his mind. Perhaps she was. 'One month,' she said. 'That is what I can offer you. But there is a condition.'

Aubranael waited, breathless, hoping it would not be beyond his power to accept.

'I will participate in your deception, but only to a degree. At the end of your month, you must tell her the truth. Do you agree?'

Aubranael's imagination helpfully offered him vision after vision of the probable outcome of that, none of them good. But he agreed. Of course he agreed! He would agree to anything, now.

But one further matter remained unresolved. 'Wh…how much will it cost?' he asked.

'I have yet to decide.' She eyed him speculatively. 'I will consider the matter. For now, shall we say that you will owe me a good turn?'

'Yes!' he said. 'Anything!'

Hidenory smiled wickedly. 'Anything? Well, now. You should be careful of unlimited promises to witches. If I were not such a fair and generous soul… but, no matter. Let us begin.'

Aubranael was startled to notice a great silver cauldron where none had been before. It was full of water, and an image slowly bled across the surface.

A gentleman of England stood there. He was tall and handsome, with thick dark hair and a strong chin. He was dressed in clothes of a type Aubranael had never seen: long pale trousers, a coat with tails, and a tall hat. He stood leaning elegantly on a polished wooden cane, surveying his surroundings (whatever they were) with the self-satisfied smile of a man who has everything he could possibly wish for.

Aubranael had never smiled that way.

'Is this what you had in your thoughts?' Hidenory enquired.

Aubranael could only nod dumbly. He couldn't articulate the longing he felt on beholding this piece of perfection; there were not words enough.

'Very good. That's easy enough,' said the witch, and her prosaic tone broke his reverie. He stood watching her, scarcely breathing, as he awaited the transformation.

'What are you staring at me for?' Hidenory said. 'Behold your own face.' She gestured at the cauldron.

He looked down to find that the stylish gentleman had gone. The water was now as clear as a mirror, and in it he could see his own reflection.

The sight stole his breath and brought tears to his eyes. Gone was the ruined face he had for so long despised. In its place he saw chiselled features; an aristocratic nose; the strong chin he had admired on Hidenory's image; clear brown eyes and a smiling mouth. His hair had not changed in colour, but it had been considerably shortened. Looking down at himself, he saw that he was wearing the strange costume of the English gentleman.

He stood a little straighter, rolling back his shoulders. A wide smile made its way onto his fine new mouth, and refused to be repressed.

Hidenory was laughing at him. 'It will suit you admirably, that I can see,' she said. 'Do not grow too used to it, mind. You have but a single month.'

Even this sobering reflection did little to dampen Aubranael's spirits. A month seemed a veritable age! What could he not accomplish in so generous a span of time!

He made his kind benefactress a low, grateful bow, and his fine shiny hat promptly fell off onto the floor and rolled away.

'Hm,' said Hidenory as he scrambled after it. 'You will need a little more help, methinks.'

Aubranael caught the hat and rammed it back onto his head. 'Never mind, dear lady,' he said, beaming at her. 'I shall soon grow used to it, I am sure.'

'I am not nearly so sure,' she answered dryly. 'Certainly not in one month. Besides, it is not enough merely to look the part of a gentleman; more will be required of you.'

He looked down at his beautiful new garments—sneaking another glance at his beautiful new face along the way—and said: 'What more could I possibly need?'

'A name. A house. Carriages, horses, considerably more clothes, ready money, and… friends.'

Aubranael blinked at her. 'A formidable list.'

'Quite, and beyond my power to provide.'

He began to feel dismayed, but she held up a cautionary hand and smiled. 'I know just the person to assist you. If you would be so good as to step through the door, it will all be arranged in a trice.'

What door? He thought, but as the words formed in his mind he noticed an oddly-shaped door fading into view in the wall directly behind Hidenory. It was round and jaunty in style, and painted in at least twelve different colours.

'Grunewald is a glamourist, like myself, and very well able to assist you,' Hidenory continued. 'You will, of course, convey my *very best* regards.'

Aubranael paused on his way to the door, searching for a suitable way to thank her.

Hidenory grinned at him. 'No need; I know all that you wish to say.' She studied his face for a moment, and a wicked gleam entered her eye. 'Grant me one small trifle by way of gratitude: a kiss. Seldom have I been so pleased with my own artistry!'

His cheeks warmed with both pleasure and embarrassment. Would this be the outcome of his new appearance? Ladies would be desirous of kissing him? How magnificent! And yet, how difficult, for he had never kissed a woman before—nor, indeed, any other creature. As Hidenory pressed her pretty lips to his, he hoped she would not notice his lack of experience.

This meeting of lips was not, as it turned out, all there was to the business of kissing. A great deal more happened, involving other parts of his mouth and body, and it went on for some time. When at last Hidenory released him and stepped away, she did not seem at all displeased.

Neither, he found, was he.

'Excellent,' she said, eyeing him. 'Excellent,' she said again, the word emerging a trifle breathlessly. 'Are you sure it is Tilby you wish to visit? You do not wish to extend your visit to me?'

Aubranael shook his head, and then nodded, confused as to which part of the question he was answering. 'Yes—that is—I wish to go.'

Hidenory sighed gustily, but her eyes twinkled as she said: 'Ah well. I may always create another one, of course. Off with you!' She pointed imperiously at the door, and Aubranael stepped through it.

'You take care, now!' she called after him. 'And mind you listen to Grunewald!'

CHAPTER FOUR

Now, before we get too carried away with the story, allow me t'catch ye up on a few small matters.

I ought t'make clear that I knew nowt o' this at the time, an' sorry I am that it was so, for matters might ha' been much less complicated-like later on, if I had. Still, to be all-knowin' is beyond the power of any bein', much as I may wish it otherwise.

Grunewald, though. Grunewald I did, and do, know. He's a bit of a legend in these parts. He's a witchifier, like Hidenory—thick as thieves, them two—but for reasons known only to hisself, he's made his home in England. 'Gentleman Grunewald', they call him, for he likes to pass hisself off as a gentry-cove. Mighty talented he is at it, too. Nobody knows what he really looks like, but nobody much cares.

At the time o' tellin', Gentleman Grunewald was loiterin' about in Nottinghamshire. He 'ad a house right on the edge o' Sherwood Forest, an' thas where our good friend Aubranael was goin'.'

On the other side of Hidenory's door, Aubranael found a large mansion house. The door opened onto the hallway, quite as if he had come through the front entrance. The building was old, and the décor eccentric: a frieze ran around the walls near the ceiling, depicting nymphs and satyrs frolicking with a variety of woodland creatures, and the rest of the walls were panelled with wood and painted dark green. His heels clacked loudly on the stone floor as he crossed it.

'Hello?' he called. The sound echoed off the cold stone walls, and no answer came.

Aubranael stood, feeling thoroughly uncomfortable. Here he was in someone else's house, with no particular invitation, and not a soul in sight to greet (or, indeed, repel) him.

He waited for some time, unwilling to call again. Then, just as he was filling his lungs for another shout, he heard footsteps approaching.

A grand staircase stood immediately before him, its gilded banisters carved with a plethora of foliage and its steps made from pale stone. It was upon this fine contraption that a figure finally appeared: a tall, spare figure, dressed similarly to Aubranael, and with a fine head of tousled (in fact, rather mad) red hair.

'Morning!' said the figure brightly, and trotted energetically down the stairs. 'My deepest apologies! I was still dressing, late though it is. It is these dratted neck-cloths. I can never get them quite as I wish.'

What is a neck-cloth? Aubranael wondered dazedly. He supposed the person must mean the complicated white fabric construction which adorned his neck, the folds of which looked impossibly complex to Aubranael's eye. It struck him of a sudden that he, too, might have to manage this aspect of his wardrobe henceforth.

'Are you Grunewald?' Aubranael enquired.

The man's eyes—a bright, leafy spring green in hue—sharpened, and his expression turned wary. 'I am known as Frederick Green,' he said with a polite smile.

Aubranael nodded, satisfied that he had found the right person. His host's face had shown no trace of confusion or puzzlement whatsoever. 'My name is Aubranael,' he said, and bowed—this time without losing his hat. 'Hidenory has sent me to you.'

'Ah!' said Grunewald, or Green, and his eyes brightened. 'A project! This is tremendous. I was growing awfully bored.' To Aubranael's surprise, he took a tiny painted box from some concealed spot within his clothes, opened it up, and took a pinch of something from inside. Then he put his fingers to his nose and inhaled.

Aubranael blinked at him.

'Snuff,' said Grunewald. 'It is quite pleasant; you'll try it sometime. But where was I?' He hid the box again, watching Aubranael's face through lazily narrowed eyes—an expression which, Aubranael felt sure, concealed a tremendous alertness and sharpness of mind. 'Why did Hidenory send you?'

Feeling desperately awkward, Aubranael tried to explain his circumstances in the briefest and most impersonal manner he could manage. He felt that he carried it off fairly creditably, and to his relief Grunewald did not appear to take against him for knowing that his handsome face hid a decidedly less attractive reality.

'Ah, yes—poor fellow—quite understand,' said Grunewald. 'Isn't Hidenory marvellous? Very skilled, she is—very skilled. Now then, you must have a powerful reason for adopting this amusing facade— am I right? I wish you to tell me all about it.'

Aubranael began the story. As he spoke, Grunewald guided him to a small parlour which was as madly decorated as the hallway, and waved Aubranael to a chair. A tray of tea things was already set out, somehow, and it had not been there long, for the cup that Grunewald presently handed to him contained steaming hot tea. Aubranael sipped gratefully at it as he told his tale; the day had been long and eventful, he appeared to have skipped the night altogether, and he was quite tired.

Grunewald nodded along enthusiastically, devouring several small cakes and tarts as he listened. He handed over a small plate piled high with more treats, still warm from the oven. 'Eat them all,' he advised. 'I should think you'll need to, after all that.'

Aubranael, being ravenous as well as tired, was happy to follow these instructions. The cakes tasted marvellous, and he polished off three in quick succession as Grunewald ruminated on his story.

'So!' said his host said at last, 'there is a lady in the case! I might have guessed. There usually is.' He beamed at Aubranael. 'Well! Then you will be needing—let's see—clothes, carriages, a good house—all the necessaries for impressing a lady. Nothing could be simpler. Where did you say she is living? Tilby?'

'Yes,' Aubranael said around a mouthful of cake. He swallowed quickly, and as Grunewald continued to look at him blankly he added: 'It is in a place called Lincolnshire.'

'Ah! Lincolnshire. A fine county, not too far off.' He paused, thinking, as Aubranael ate two more tarts. 'Yes! Absolutely. No question about it. I shall go with you.'

'Oh, no!' Aubranael demurred. 'Such a deal of trouble for you—I couldn't possibly—'

'Not at all,' Grunewald interrupted. 'It will be an adventure! I am, as I think I already said, quite bored.'

Aubranael began to smile, charmed by his new friend's enthusiasm and irrepressible good cheer. He was secretly relieved to know that he would have a companion through the coming weeks, and Grunewald's calm acceptance of his true face heartened him as well. They were two of a kind, Grunewald and Hidenory; neither had made any bones about his lack of beauty. Perhaps because they dealt so freely in glamour themselves, they felt that mere reality was unimportant.

But then, both had chosen handsome faces for themselves... perhaps it wasn't quite that simple.

Grunewald sprang up from his seat in a fine show of energy and clapped his hands together. 'Good! Capital! Best get on. We have a great deal to do.'

'I—thank you—' Aubranael began, realising that he had failed to respond to his host's offer of accompaniment.

'Not at all,' Grunewald said, waving a dismissive hand. 'I ask only that it be entertaining, this projected adventure. No doubt Tilby will be a lively place, with plenty to do.' He smiled hopefully at Aubranael, who spread his hands.

'I know nothing about it,' he admitted.

'Well, we shall see. Now, your name. It is perfectly excellent, but it will not do in these parts. You will need something more English, and preferably unremarkable.'

'Like Frederick Green,' Aubranael noted.

Grunewald beamed. 'Precisely. Let me think a moment.' He did so rather visibly, staring into space and scrunching his brow. 'I have it! Aubrey! Ha, ha! It is perfect.'

Aubranael frowned. 'It is perhaps too similar?'

'It is to be complete concealment of your identity, is it? Even from the lady? Very well. It shall stand as your first name; no one ever uses those.' He thought some more. 'Aubrey Stanton. How do you like that?'

Aubrey Stanton. Mr. Aubrey Stanton. Mr. Stanton. Aubranael turned it over in his mind, and found that he liked the sound of it. It was, as Grunewald had said, very English, and quite unremarkable. 'It is excellent,' he said with a shy smile.

'Capital!' said Grunewald. 'Well then, Mr. Stanton. Let us see to the matter of your wardrobe.'

If Aubranael had expected to be taken to a tailor's shop for his new garments, he was mistaken. Instead, Grunewald conducted him up the grand staircase in the hall, up another flight directly after, and then up two more increasingly narrow and winding staircases before he finally stopped before a bright red door and knocked upon it. He went inside without waiting for a response, and Aubranael followed.

Beyond the door was a large room, and inside the room were several goblins. They were all furiously busy with piles and piles of fabric, thread and assorted tools. Aubranael could not determine precisely what they were making, but the fact that they all wore exquisitely tailored coats like Grunewald's seemed to offer a clue. The coats sat oddly on their spindly frames, looking completely incongruous with their knobbly elbows and knees and their greenish-brown skin.

As Grunewald entered, they stopped what they were doing and turned to stare at him—and then at Aubranael as he followed his host inside.

'Hey! We are busy!' said one, waving a half-finished coat in illustration of his point.

'Lovely work,' said another, eyeing Aubranael's coat. 'Yours, sir?'

Grunewald shook his head. 'Hidenory's.'

'Ahhh! May I touch it?'

'No.'

The goblin's shoulders drooped, and Aubranael felt rather sorry for the creature. Grunewald forged briskly ahead, however, allowing him no opportunity to intervene. 'My guest is in need of your assistance! Two or three coats, please, at the least. The usual range. Quickly, quickly! We have much to do.'

The goblin tailors chorused an assent and instantly swarmed over Aubranael. Knotted ropes borne by nimble goblin hands circled his waist, chest, shoulders, arms and neck—even his legs and head. Rough goblin voices shouted out measurements, and a scriber chalked everything up on a blackboard.

Then there was a flurry of activity as fabrics were sought for, offered for approval, chosen and discarded. Grunewald asked Aubranael's opinion on a variety of hues and shades, but all he could do was nod dumbly at them all. What did he know of the differences between dark blue and dark red with his (borrowed) colouring? What did he know of wool or cotton or superfine or whatever else? Grunewald soon stopped asking, and settled the decisions himself.

Choices made, the goblins leapt into activity, swarming over the long tables set up throughout the room and throwing fabrics around with terrific energy. Grunewald quickly shepherded Aubranael out of the room and shut the door on the goblin tailors. 'Better leave them to it,' he said wisely.

Aubranael blinked. 'Why are they here?'

'No idea at all,' Grunewald replied cheerfully. 'They turned up at the house—oh, a long time ago. I gave them this room and they've been here ever since.'

'Making coats?'

'Yes. They love it above anything.'

'Do you pay them?'

'Pay them? My dear fellow, do you have any idea how much they cost me in food, not to mention cloth and so on? No idea at all what they do with most of the things they make—sell them, for all I know. Making a few for me and mine is the least they can do in return.'

Aubranael had the feeling that Grunewald was not being entirely honest with him; that he was holding back some important piece of information that would have clarified the situation considerably. He had to be satisfied with this, however, as Grunewald had already opened the next door in the long passageway—a blue one—and gone inside. Aubranael hastily followed.

He was greeted by a scene remarkably similar to the first, only these goblins were all wearing voluminous, snowy-white shirts over their patched knee-britches. Aubranael had to submit to another episode of frenzied measuring as Grunewald ordered shirts for him—'Ten at least, please, and quick about it!'—and then they were moving on once more through a yellow door, and then a green one, a brown one, a purple one and an orange, behind each of which lay another team of tailors. This mad procession continued until Grunewald had ordered trousers, waistcoats, boots and shoes, hats, neck-cloths and nightshirts. At last he turned to Aubranael and said, with unimpaired cheer, 'Those will be ready by morning, I should think! Shall we see about the carriage next?'

Aubranael, who felt completely drained, would have preferred a few minutes' pause in this whirlwind of activity, but he could not think of a way of saying so without displaying an intolerable degree

of ingratitude. So he said nothing, and followed in silence.

Grunewald chattered chummily about commonplace things as he led his guest back through his enormous and complicated house and out into a coach-yard, but Aubranael's thoughts were too busy to pay much attention. Ready by morning, he'd said? Which morning? For the windows in the goblin tailors' sequence of rooms had all appeared to display a different time of day, from dawn to the depths of night.

And why did Grunewald have such an astonishing quantity of goblins living in his peculiar house, all delighted to do his bidding? Had they been calling him "sir" or "sire"? Aubranael eyed his new friend, wondering whether the true form hidden behind his handsome facade might prove to be somewhat shorter, knobblier and greener.

Grunewald caught him at this covert surveillance, and smiled. 'Don't overthink it,' he recommended, and winked. 'Now, then: we shan't need anything new, I shouldn't think. Just a few alterations!' He set about delivering instructions to yet another crew of goblins, these armed with the tools of blacksmiths, upholsterers and engineers. As they leapt to do as he asked, Aubranael merely sighed and rubbed at his tired eyes.

Aubranael's tireless host kept up this ruthless routine for most of the day, pausing only for meals (to Aubranael's immense relief). The food was always excellent; he pictured to himself a kitchen full of pies, syllabubs and flummeries, cakes, breads and all manner of good things, probably prepared by a small horde of goblin chefs.

Night had fallen, and remained for some hours, by the time Grunewald's limitless energy finally began to flag. 'Sleep a little!' he said, clapping Aubranael on the shoulder. 'We're almost ready to depart. Capital day's work. Only need to collect your wardrobe in the morning, and off we'll go. See you bright and early!' He pointed Aubranael in the direction of a closed door—a plain white one, this time—and disappeared behind the one opposite before Aubranael had chance to reply.

'Good night,' he said belatedly. Venturing into his assigned room, Aubranael paused only long enough to take note of the enormous bed—large, soft and deliciously comfortable-looking. He would have fallen straight into it, but a pair of goblins approached.

'Let us help you with that, sir,' said one. They each took hold of his coat and began to drag it off him; it was a tight-fitting garment and it took considerable effort from both of them to prise it away from his shoulders. He wondered vaguely how he would ever get it on again.

The rest of his attire came away rather more easily, and his goblin attendants speedily replaced them with a nightshirt and cap. Aubranael was as unused to the process of being dressed and undressed as he was to the garments themselves, but he was far too tired to object. The moment the night-cap had been twitched into place on his head, he turned back the covers of his glorious new bed, collapsed into it, and instantly fell asleep.

He was woken sometime later by an offensively loud clanging noise. Opening his bleary eyes, he dimly perceived a goblin standing near his head, banging a gong.

'Wake! Wake! Master says to get up!'

'I'm awake,' Aubranael grumbled. He had not slept enough, and the goblin's appalling racket threatened to give him a headache. But these things mattered not a whit when he remembered where he was. Today was departure day! How long would it take to reach Tilby? Perhaps he would see Miss Landon again this very day!

He leapt out of bed, and submitted with impatience to his goblin attendants as they encouraged him to bathe, and then reassembled his strange but handsome attire. The coat required almost as much effort to restore as the rest of the dressing process combined.

At last—bathed, shaved, groomed and dressed, his hair wet and his heart light—Aubranael followed a goblin guide down to the dining chamber, to find a noble breakfast already laid out. Grunewald was there, sipping a cup of chocolate as he perused a stack of newspapers. 'Eat plentifully, but quickly!' he advised. 'The coach is all ready to go, and so must we be, soon.'

Aubranael followed these instructions with gusto. A flutter of nervous wings in his belly rather damaged his appetite, but he forced the food down—he had never enjoyed being hungry. This task completed, he went with Grunewald back to the main hallway.

A pile of clothes was stacked near the front door. An *enormous* pile of clothes. It spread across so much of the floor as to partially block the doorway, and towered almost to the ceiling.

'They may perhaps have been a little too enthusiastic,' Grunewald said thoughtfully. 'No matter! We will take it all.'

As if these words had been a signal, a line of goblins streamed into the room and began to take parts of the pile away through the huge front door and into the large coach that stood waiting outside. The tower quickly collapsed, dumping quantities of shirts, boots and waistcoats onto the heads of the goblin porters. Undeterred, they clambered free and resumed their task, not stopping until all of the garments had been taken away.

Surveying the coach, Aubranael frowned. Large it may be, but he had no notion at all as to how the porters had managed to fit all the clothes inside. By his reckoning, they would need at least four coaches of similar size, but no others stood waiting.

'Don't overthink it,' Grunewald said gravely, a twinkle in his eye. 'Come now. Hat—' he plonked Aubranael's tall hat unceremoniously onto his head—'Greatcoat'—he threw a voluminous, shockingly heavy mess of fabric into Aubranael's hands and quickly shrugged into his own ankle-length coat—'and we are away! Come along!'

He strode out of the door and stepped into the coach, Aubranael following close behind. 'I hope you are feeling rested,' Grunewald said as they settled themselves inside, 'for we have much to do!'

'Do?' Aubranael said blankly as the coach—manned, to all appearances, by humans rather than goblins—began to move. 'What can we possibly do in here?'

'I will teach,' Grunewald beamed, 'and you will learn.'

'What am I learning?'

'Etiquette, my dear fellow! The rules of gentlemanly behaviour, and all that. If you think the Faerie of Aylfenhame are irrational, wait until you see how the folk of England behave.'

CHAPTER FIVE

The first I saw o' these fine fellows was a day or so after, when they passed over my bridge. I took 'em at face value—what else was I likely to do? Told me all about their good selves, they did—sold me a fine pack o' lies! I let 'em pass. Should've pushed them into the river instead.

Their arrival set the whole town to talkin', as ye may imagine—flashin' money about an' makin' a fine show o' wealth as they were. We shall see how my Sophy handled the news by an' by.

Sophy felt in low spirits after her return from Aylfenhame. The colours of Tilby in Spring, however vivid, could not compare to the scintillating hues of Grenlowe's meadows which had delighted her eye and her heart in equal measure; the food served by poor faithful Mary and Thundigle, though excellent in its way, smelled and tasted of nothing in comparison to the mere fragrance of the fare of Aylfenhame, which she had not been permitted to eat. To return to her small life in Tilby—to her father's selective anxieties and habitual neglect, Anne's raptures over trifles and her own bleak future—sunk her spirits so low she found it almost impossible to maintain her usual semblance of cheer.

'Are you quite sure you are well, my dear?' her father enquired on the third day after her return. She had been detained in Aylfenhame rather longer than she had intended; she had returned to find him in a little fever of alarm, and he had never been satisfied with her vague explanations as to where she had gone.

'Of course, father,' she said, mustering a smile for him.

He peered at her face, his own drawn with concern. His gaze lingered on her cheek; but if he was fancying her thinner, he must be mistaken. A mere three days of picking at her meals could not possibly effect any material alteration so soon.

Anne noticed her listlessness, too, though Sophy was careful to tell no one where she had been. Tales abounded of maidens lured into Aylfenhame by mischievous fae-folk, only to waste away upon their return. Sophy could understand their feelings quite well, supposing such stories to have any truth to them at all; but she was made of sterner stuff than these wilting young ladies, and had no intention of starving herself into an early grave in such absurd fashion. She would have no one suspect her of it, either.

Besides, though Balligumph had not explained the reasoning behind his actions—only chuckling, and looking mysterious, when she asked him—she could not believe he'd had any such nefarious object in mind. Thundigle was not so sure; or perhaps his concern for her overrode his reason, for he glared darkly whenever Balligumph's name was mentioned, and stared frequently up at Sophy's face with almost as much concern as her father.

All this care was gratifying, or so she told herself, and she really tried to feel it. But it was wearisome to be treated as an invalid when her health had suffered no ill effects whatsoever.

And so, when news came—news of a sort to divert all attention and speculation away from Miss Landon—Sophy was considerably relieved. The news regarded an *arrival.* Tilby was a small town, its society usually unvarying; as such, any visitor at all could command a great deal of attention. How much the better when it proved to be a double arrival! Two visitors at once, actually taking a house, and meaning to stay for some weeks at least! When it was discovered that the two visitors were gentlemen, and wealthy, and to all appearances unmarried, Tilby went into raptures—and no one more enthusiastically than Anne.

'Sophy! I have never seen such handsome gentlemen!' she announced, sailing into the parsonage one morning with her bonnet askew and her reticule in a tangle about her wrist. 'I saw them both at church yesterday—how strange, by-the-by, that you did not attend! Were you not well? Are you recovered now? Your father could hardly remember the words of his sermon for worry over you, I am sure of it. Well, but their names are Mr. Stanton and Mr. Green, and they are marvellously fashionable, and *quite* rich besides! They have taken Hyde Place, which no one thought anybody would ever do. They came out of Nottinghamshire, so Miss Gladwin says; though I cannot find out quite where, or why they should want to come *here* of all places.'

She paused for breath. Sophy, suffering pangs of guilt over Anne's description of Mr. Landon's sufferings, had hardly attended to the rest of this speech. Searching for a passable response, she managed: 'I daresay they are very agreeable.'

'Oh, to be sure! At least, Mr. Green must be, for I never saw anyone smile so much. I am wild to find out more, so please, do come with me into town!'

'I am not sure how a walk into town will further this praiseworthy ambition,' Sophy said, amused in spite of herself. 'I hardly think young men are to be found peering into shop windows on such a fine day as this. They will be out riding.'

'Perhaps they may, or perhaps not! We will never find out, unless we go, so do please say you will come.'

Sophy agreed to it—not because she entertained any expectation (or any particular desire) of encountering the newcomers, but because she had an errand to perform in the town, and to be seen walking may settle some of her friends' disquiet about her.

'I will come with you, if we may go to Miss Sargent's,' Sophy offered. 'I am in sorry need of new ribbons.'

'Oh! Yes, for your summer bonnet I suppose. Very well, we shall go there directly.' In half a minute she was out the door and hurrying away; Sophy had to hurry to catch up.

After the glorious ribbons Sophy had seen in the Grenlowe market, she could muster little real enthusiasm for the wares of Tilby's milliner, but the process must be gone through; and Anne, at least, would take some pleasure in the business. She walked along beside Anne, listening with only half her attention to her friend's chatter, the rest of her thoughts wandering in Aylfenhame. They reached Tilby's principle street before she was aware; and then, to her surprise, she saw two unfamiliar young men walking towards them.

'Ah!' cried Anne in delight. 'There! I told you we should see them.'

Sophy had felt so completely secure in her belief that they would not meet the two newcomers that she felt a degree of chagrin, as well as surprise, on beholding them. Her errand must now wait while Anne performed whatever ritual of rapture she deemed necessary. Sophy, of course, would stand by, safely unregarded.

'Indeed,' answered Sophy. 'You have shown yourself very clever. But what shall we do with them, now that we have found them? Are you acquainted with them? For I am not, and otherwise we shall not be able to speak with them at all.'

She studied the approaching gentlemen as she spoke, concluding that—as unlikely as it may seem—Anne had not exaggerated. They *were* uncommonly handsome. Mr. Green was slightly the shorter of the two, with fine red hair and a coat as green as his name. Mr. Stanton was even more handsome than his friend, with dark hair worn in a fashionable style and a fine figure. Both were clothed in the first stare of fashion, with every possible accoutrement that could suggest wealth. Both bore themselves like men of consequence, and smiled upon the world with the complacency of gentlemen who knew themselves to be entitled to anything they could wish for.

Sophy observed their approach with misgiving.

'I am not acquainted with them,' Anne said in tones of despair. 'Still, it is a great deal only to see them. How fine they are!'

Sophy shushed her, for they were rapidly drawing within earshot of the two young men. She expected them to pass by, and so they did; but they slowed as they did so, and Mr. Stanton's gaze turned upon her in a manner she did not at all like. He not only looked at her; he *stared.*

Young men did not stare at Sophy out of admiration. Indeed, they never had; not even in her first youth and bloom. At the age of eight-and-twenty she was fully resigned to this, and was not especially cast down to see no obvious signs of admiration in Mr. Stanton's fine dark eyes. What she did not expect to see was a kind of intensity, as though her presence mattered to him in some strange way.

She supposed that some aspect of her appearance offended him. Well, with her uninteresting face and shabby attire it was hardly surprising; but as she could do nothing about either disadvantage, it was remarkably rude of him to stare at her so.

To her horror he actually slowed down further—hesitated—seemed about to address her! What could he possibly find to say? She took a deep breath, bracing herself for the insult, when his friend intervened.

'Stanton! Do hurry up, or we shall be awfully late.' Mr. Green cast one swift, intent glance at Sophy—giving her time to observe his very startlingly green eyes—and touched his hat. In a trice both young men were gone, vanishing around a turn in the street.

'Well!' breathed Anne. 'Gracious, Sophy, how Mr. Stanton did stare! He must be pleased with you.'

Sophy thought her tone was slightly piqued; Anne was certainly more used to attracting attention than Sophy.

'I hardly think so,' she replied, concealing her mortification behind a smile. 'Nothing in his looks or his manner suggested that he was the slightest bit *pleased.*'

Anne appeared to regret her momentary lack of graciousness, for she linked her arm through Sophy's and squeezed it. 'I shouldn't wonder if he was pleased! But for my part, I think Mr. Green the handsomest and most agreeable gentleman anyone could wish to meet.'

This statement announced her intention of falling in love with Mr. Green, with all due haste. Sophy did not object, choosing to satisfy her feelings with a private resolution of avoiding them both— especially Mr. Stanton.

* * *

In most respects, Aubranael and Grunewald's descent upon Tilby could only be described as a complete success. Being so well-supplied in all the most important blessings (principally wealth and beauty, and with more than a little charm besides), the two gentlemen found themselves in high demand almost from the very first moment of their arrival. Their various merits were instantly perceived by the local community, and instantly categorised as deserving of the highest position within Tilby society—alongside such luminaries as the Adairs and the Winbolts, even! It did not matter that the house in which they took up their abode was only hired, and not even a particularly good house at that. Tilby was even so good as to overlook the peculiarity of two gentlemen taking a house with no ladies present to do the honours. They were welcome everywhere that they went, and frequently received invitations to bestow the blessing of their company upon every one of the worthier households in the town.

It did not take Aubranael very long to understand that the combination of wealth and beauty was a very potent one indeed.

The novelty of being not only welcome, but actually in demand, was a significant one to Aubranael. Their first few days in Tilby were quickly beguiled away, under the charm of popularity; he found himself with a steady stream of visitors to contend with, as it seemed that almost every gentleman in the town wished to introduce himself and his family to the notice of the two young men. First and foremost amongst these were the older gentlemen, with—Grunewald soon informed him—daughters to dispose of. Not far behind were the younger gentlemen, quick to see the potential for suitable associates in the newcomers. For those first few, enchanted days, Aubranael was so busy with greetings and meetings, new friends, rides about the countryside and sports of various kinds that he almost forgot his true purpose in visiting the country in the first place.

When he was recalled to his true aim, only then did the frustrations begin.

He saw Miss Landon once during those heady, early days of popularity. Saw, that is; he was not permitted to speak to her, though he dearly wished to. The shock—the delight—of seeing her all of a sudden, walking in the street with a friend and smiling, had almost overcome him. He had been on the point of greeting her—confessing, perhaps, everything in his haste to restore their former, easy friendship—when Grunewald had intervened. He had all but dragged his wayward friend away, and Aubranael, confused and afraid of acquitting himself poorly, had dutifully left Miss Landon standing there in the street.

He had consoled himself with the notion that it would not be very long before he could speak with her again, and then he might test the power of his new face. He whiled away some hours in pleasant daydreams, imagining all the former easiness between himself and Miss Landon, heightened still further by the charm of his infinitely more attractive appearance.

He soon found that daydreams were all that he was to be permitted, for the present. Wealth and beauty could not buy absolutely anything, he was dismayed to discover, for there appeared to be an endless series of obstacles between him and Miss Landon's society.

As an unmarried man, he could not converse with an unmarried woman such as Miss Landon without the presence of a suitable chaperon (and he had quickly learned that, whatever Miss Landon herself might have permitted in the strange surroundings of Aylfenhame, in England a household brownie most definitely did *not* qualify as suitable chaperonage). He could not talk to her at all without an introduction, but he could not simply introduce himself; the introduction must be of *the proper kind*, performed by a suitable third party. He must find someone else to introduce him to Sophy, which of course meant that he must first become acquainted with someone who had the right of introduction to her. But who? Her father was the obvious choice, but he was never seen outside of church. Aubranael had not been able to think of a plausible reason to visit Mr. Landon at the parsonage and Grunewald had prevented him from merely presenting himself there anyway, saying it would cause talk. And *talk* was absolutely to be avoided, apparently, if one was to be taken seriously by society.

This did not concern him a great deal, at first. Society already seemed to be taking him very seriously indeed, and he could hardly imagine that an occasional departure from the absurd rules they considered necessary would banish him forever from their good graces. But Grunewald assured him that he must be considered *respectable*, if he was to be permitted any access to the likes of Miss Landon, and that too flagrant a disregard for the social mores would soon tarnish his glowing reputation.

In short, he could only rely on his wealth and beauty to carry him so far. He must rely on good behaviour for the rest.

But as Sophy could not be got at through her father, and as she had no mother, no siblings and no friends to whom he could have any access either, his respectability and his good behaviour did him little good. He still could not see her. What was the use of his handsome face if he could not approach the one woman he had hoped to impress? The charm of his newfound popularity soon wore thin after that; he cared little for the good opinion of the neighbourhood if it could not afford him any access to Miss Landon.

His spirits sank lower and lower under this enforced separation, and his patience wore thin. The marks of special favour that had so delighted him several days before began to irritate him instead; he realised that even *he* had been temporarily beguiled into thinking himself of consequence, and that made him a fool.

'This is not what I had in mind, Grunewald,' he said on the morning of his eighth day in Tilby. He had been pacing the drawing-room carpet for some time, having failed to find any occupation to interest him much within the confines of Hyde Place.

'I daresay it isn't,' replied Grunewald cheerfully, 'but it is rather excellent in its own way, is it not? You cannot tell me you are not enjoying yourself.'

'I *was*, for a time. But it is all so absurd.'

Grunewald raised his elegant brows at him from across the room, where he was seated in an armchair. 'What is? Oh, you mean *society!* Yes, of course it is. But it is absurd in an entertaining way, and therefore I shall not hold its inherent ridiculousness against it. Do you not appreciate being universally adored?'

'For no particularly good reason,' Aubranael retorted. 'If they knew what lies under this borrowed face, they would reject me again soon enough.'

Grunewald pondered this. 'No,' he said at length. 'Probably not, entirely. You are still wealthy enough (at least by report) to merit an invitation to any drawing-room in the town.'

'Ah yes; money. Perhaps that is where my mistake lies. Instead of securing a new face, I should have bent all my efforts towards the noble goal of acquiring more *things*.'

Grunewald chuckled. 'How very cynical you are today.'

'It is a cynicism born of years of hard experience.'

Grunewald rolled his eyes and shifted uncomfortably in his seat. 'You are perfectly right, of course, but since neither of us can do anything about it, I suggest you try to enjoy yourself.'

'I cannot. The time for that is past. I care only to see Miss Landon.'

'I am unable to assist you there.'

Aubranael kicked vaguely at a log in the fireplace, too sunk in gloom to reply. Was this how he was to live out his month in England? Fawned over for the things he did not really possess, by people he did not care about? And all the while kept at a distance from Miss Landon?

'How do people usually go about these things?' he asked abruptly.

'I am not sure what "things" you are referring to.'

'Courtship. How in the blazes does anyone ever get married, if they are never permitted to meet with unmarried women?'

'Of course they are allowed,' Grunewald said in a tone of mild irritation. 'I have already told you: once properly *introduced*, and always supposing they are not entirely alone, then conversation is perfectly allowable.'

'Yes, yes, but how do they become *introduced*? Miss Landon cannot be the first young lady with no useful connections in that respect.'

Grunewald did not answer. Aubranael began to suspect him of ignoring the subject altogether, when suddenly he spoke.

'Balls!' he announced.

Aubranael blinked at him. 'Balls...?'

'Balls, parties and assemblies! Social events, you know. Gatherings. There is always someone to whom the duty of general introductions falls. In some places—you will laugh to hear it—there is a *Master of the Ceremonies*. His entire purpose is to manage the awkward business of introducing people to one another! Diverting, is not it?'

Aubranael raised his brows.

'Well, but in this instance it will most likely be a private ball, and the duty of introductions will fall to the hosts.'

'What will be a private ball?'

'Why, the ball that is to be held in our honour! It is quite the obvious thing; I only wonder I did not think of it before.'

'Is there to be a ball held in our honour? I had not heard of any such thing.'

'Not presently, my dear fellow, but there *will be*, of course.'

'When?'

'When I have arranged it.' He smiled and jumped out of his chair. 'The Adairs will do! Young Mr. Edward has been so very determined to become my most intimate friend; he will do anything I suggest. His parents will be very easily persuaded to throw open the doors of their charming house, and make themselves and their riches the centre of attention for an evening. Oh, yes! It will be perfect. And there, you know, you may request an introduction to any young lady you wish to dance with.'

Aubranael began to feel excited. 'Yes! Very good! How long will it take?' Another thought occurred to him and he added: 'Dancing? What manner of dancing?'

Grunewald grinned at him and began to dance on the spot, bouncing on his toes and kicking his feet and turning in tiny circles. 'Awfully complicated, I'm afraid, but since it must take at least a week for a ball to be made ready, you will have some time to practice.'

Watching Grunewald's antics, Aubranael felt faint twinges of alarm. He loved to dance, but he had never danced like *that* before. But he brushed these misgivings aside. 'No matter. Do, please, arrange it! As quickly as possible!'

Grunewald laughed and stopped dancing. 'Very well, I will meet with young Mr. Adair at once. In the meantime, pray follow me to the library.'

Aubranael followed his friend down a short passage into the small library of their borrowed house, and waited while Grunewald dashed about examining the books. At last he cried, 'Aha!' and extracted a slim volume from the shelf.

He handed this to Aubranael with a brilliant smile and said, 'Study it *most* closely! I will be back directly.'

Grunewald left the library at a trot. Opening the book, Aubranael saw the words "The Art of Dancing" elegantly inscribed on the title page. Leafing through, he found pages and pages of written instructions, sketches of dancing figures and strange charts that made no sense to him whatsoever.

With a great sigh, he settled himself in the nearest armchair and began to read.

When Grunewald returned, some hours later, Aubranael was still reading. That is, he was still working away at his book. He had read it through fairly quickly, and then progressed to trying out the steps he had read about, and seen sketched upon the page.

Reproducing the steps of a dance from mere written instructions was more difficult than he had expected; and when Grunewald entered the library to find him dancing about in a space he'd cleared between the chairs, Aubranael found himself heartily laughed at.

'My dear fellow,' said Grunewald, 'I do hope you are not intending to dance in that absurd fashion at our ball.'

Aubranael stopped dancing at once, dropped the book—which he had been awkwardly trying to refer to as he moved—and smiled at Grunewald. 'I take it, then, that you were successful?'

'Oh yes! The easiest thing in the world.' He flopped down into a chair and blew out his breath in an exhausted sigh. 'I hope you are grateful, for I have been obliged to bear a great deal of rather tiresome company.'

Aubranael shook his head, torn between amusement and chagrin. 'I may not approach an unmarried young woman without special leave, but *you* may simply request a ball, and be granted one immediately. What a strange place this is!'

Grunewald laughed again. 'One does not *request* a ball, my dear sap-skulled friend. Had I done so, I am sure I would have been sent packing at once. No, no; it was a mere matter of suggestion. I had only to talk longingly of dancing, and confess that it is many months since I last had that pleasure, and the charming young people were all eagerness to rescue me from this sorry situation.'

'People,' repeated Aubranael. 'Am I to collect that you also saw Miss Adair?'

Grunewald's grin widened, and he nodded. 'Delighted at the prospect of a dance, as one might imagine. All the more so, I'd say, at the prospect of a dance with one—or, very likely, both—of *us*.'

Aubranael shrugged his shoulders. Elizabeth was accounted very handsome, and she certainly tried hard to be agreeable, but he did not find her an appealing partner. 'You will take pleasure in such a duty, I'm sure.'

'Quite so; though I rather fancy *you* are her particular favourite.'

Aubranael raised his eyes heavenward.

'No matter,' Grunewald said hastily. 'The thing is done, the Adairs are all excitement and they have promised *most faithfully* to send invitation cards as soon as may be. All that remains, my good fellow, is to rescue *you* from this intolerable state of ignorance as regards dancing.'

The conversation lapsed for some time as Grunewald lent himself to the task of correcting Aubranael's many mistakes. The steps, once properly demonstrated, came easily to him—he was, after all, extremely fond of dancing, in any manner—but the exertion was more considerable than he had expected. He soon found himself out of breath, and eventually very tired indeed. Since Grunewald was in a similar state, he called a halt to the lesson and ordered refreshments to be brought to the parlour.

These were delivered with pleasing celerity by a young footman. Aubranael was almost sure that he, like all of Grunewald's household staff, was truly a goblin underneath; but if he was, then the glamour upon him was very good indeed.

His friend and host was a quick study, indeed, and when he found that most households in Tilby had brownie helpers in residence, he had even bewitched a few goblins into that diminutive form instead. It was all rather odd. Aubranael had the perpetual feeling that nothing he saw was as he saw it; nothing was real, precisely; and anything might change into anything else at any given moment.

Sometimes, he missed the simplicity of the days before he had met Miss Landon.

'Now,' Grunewald said, after he had suitably refreshed himself with tea and cakes. 'I had better do more than teach you to dance. It is to be a very grand affair, I understand, and so you will need to be well up on good behaviour.'

'More good behaviour?' Aubranael said, with a slight groan.

Grunewald's smile was positively wicked. 'Oh, yes. Dancing is only a small part of the business. There is a great deal more of *etiquette* to be learned; you must know whom to speak to, and how, and when; you must know how to ask a lady to dance, what to do if she refuses, and so on; and there is the matter of dinner, too.'

Aubranael had no intention of dancing with anyone except Miss Landon, and it was on the tip of his tongue to say so. He stopped, however, conscious that Grunewald would probably find a reason why he should not stick to this resolution. Instead, he said: 'A *very* grand affair?'

'The grandest possible, I understand, in so short a time! They wish to make a show, you know, and prove they are up to the standards of wealth and display that they consider us to have brought to the neighbourhood.'

'I begin to understand the workings of this place,' Aubranael said. 'A *very grand affair* will of necessity begin by inviting only the worthiest of guests, will it not?'

Grunewald agreed to this with a spirited nod, his mouth too full of tea and cake for speech.

'And the worthiest guests tend to be the richest, the most well-connected, and, if at all possible, the most beautiful?'

Another enthusiastic nod from Grunewald.

Aubranael sat back, fixing his eyes on the distant ceiling as he considered this. The worthiest guests. He had already learned that Miss Landon was not rich. Nor was she of high "status", as far as he could gather: as the daughter of a clergyman, she did at least rank as part of *polite society*, but as her father was a decidedly impoverished clergyman, she did not rank very highly within it.

Seeing as she was not blessed with any other connections—he had learned that the hard way—he began to fear that she would not be considered very *worthy* at all. The thought prompted a flicker of rage, but he thrust it down and said in a reasonable tone:

'Grunewald. Do you suppose Miss Landon will merit an invitation, on those terms?'

He waited for another of Grunewald's easy assurances, but none came. Instead, his friend frowned—pursed his lips—seemed about to speak—and finally sighed gustily and put down his teacup. He pointed one long finger at Aubranael's nose and said: 'It is fortunate that you are such congenial company, otherwise I might say that you are more trouble than you are worth.'

This odd manner of compliment pleased Aubranael more than it had any right to. *Was* he congenial company? He had never had a close friend before—at least, not one that talked back. Would Grunewald still find him agreeable, he wondered, after Hidenory had taken back his pretty face? He began to think maybe he would.

'I am sorry,' he said with complete sincerity. 'I could not possibly have predicted all these difficulties, otherwise I might never have—'

Grunewald held up a hand, and Aubranael stopped. 'Do not say it, pray. I know very well that you would not have acted differently. Except, perhaps, in being rather better prepared, and therefore you might have made less of a foolish picture later.'

This speech was given in a grave tone, and might have sounded awfully severe if it were not for the merry twinkle in Grunewald's leaf-green eyes. Aubranael smiled.

'I am much obliged to you, truly, and if I can ever be of assistance to you, I hope you will—'

Grunewald held up his hand again. 'Did Hidenory teach you nothing? Beware of promises without limit! If I were not such a good-natured soul...'

His words echoed Hidenory's, and Aubranael felt a moment's uneasiness. But Grunewald was still smiling with every appearance of good cheer.

'Dangerous or not,' Aubranael said, 'I meant what I said.'

Grunewald gave him a long look. 'Very well. I will remember it.' He stood up. 'Now, back to our lessons, I think! I will attend to the matter of Miss Landon's invitation later on.'

'Grunewald! If you can make sure of Miss Landon's friend, likewise—what is her name? The young, slightly silly one—Anne, I think—that would be excellent.'

Grunewald raised a brow. 'Thinking of switching your allegiance? I cannot compliment you on your taste, if so. Pleasant enough girl, but *quite* silly, indeed.'

Aubranael shook his head vehemently. 'Gracious, *no!* Only I feel certain she would enjoy it immensely, and it would be a pity for her to be omitted. And Miss Landon will like to have her friends there, do you not think?'

Grunewald threw up his hands. 'Very well, I shall endeavour to persuade our good neighbours on the topic of Anne Something-or-Other as well. Now, no more kind-hearted requests if you please; you oblige me to enough exertion as it is.'

Aubranael made a cross-my-heart motion, and smiled.

Grunewald laughed. 'Very well, enough delays. On with the dancing!'

Aubranael allowed himself to be led away with only a small sigh. If he was to have not only the pleasure of talking with Miss Landon, but also of dancing with her—actually dancing!—then he must apply himself.

The last thing in the world he wanted was to make a fool of himself in front of *her.*

CHAPTER SIX

Avoiding Mr. Stanton and Mr. Green proved to be more difficult than Sophy had anticipated. Everywhere she went, she heard them spoken of, usually in terms of the strongest praise; everyone was enchanted with them, everyone hoped to become their intimate friend, or to see their daughters distinguished by some particular attention.

Worse, Sophy could scarcely leave her home without encountering them somewhere. If she walked into town, she passed them on the street; if she wandered over the fields or through the woods, she would see them coming back from a ride or a ramble of their own. Mr. Stanton was not again so rude as to stare openly at her, but she often felt his gaze upon her, only to find him looking elsewhere when she turned.

A week went by, and most of another, and still neither Mr. Stanton nor Mr. Green satisfied the hopes of Tilby society by distinguishing any particular young woman. Sophy would have preferred it if they had. If some other—more deserving—young woman caught Mr. Stanton's eye, it would necessarily bring an end to the intolerable speculation that surrounded the two men and their unattached hearts. After ten days of gossip—and Mr. Stanton's odd behaviour—Sophy greeted the return of her particular friend, Miss Isabel Ellerby, with infinite relief.

Miss Ellerby was a few years older than Anne, and considerably more rational. She was also rather prettier than Anne, and certainly wealthier; but she hardly seemed aware of either distinction, treating both her friends with gentle good nature. Having spent a few weeks with an aunt in York, she returned with a great deal of news, and walked up to the parsonage directly in order to share it.

Sophy listened to the tales of Mrs. Grey's household with far more interest than she had ever felt on the subject before. She was delighted to hear of Isabel's engagements abroad, and the doings of her York acquaintance, in any degree of detail, because it bore no relation whatsoever to the tiresome two who had invaded Tilby.

But such felicity could not last. Isabel had not been sitting with Sophy above half an hour before Anne arrived, out of breath as if she had run all the way.

'Isabel!' she cried on entering the parlour. 'I heard that you were returned! I thought I should find you here. Well! You will never guess what has happened while you were gone.' Sophy resigned herself to another interminable discussion of all Mr. Green's and Mr. Stanton's doings, and indeed a lengthy recitation followed. She purchased a few moments' respite for herself by untangling the ribbons of Anne's forgotten bonnet and taking it out into the blissfully quiet hall.

There she met Thundigle bustling through with an armful of cloth.

'Thundigle!' she cried in relief. 'How glad I am to see you! Only tell me there is some emergency in the kitchen and that I am needed at once, and I shall be completely happy.'

Thundigle spread his brown eyes wide and blinked at her. 'Surely you cannot be wishing for catastrophe, Miss Sophy.'

'Indeed I don't, precisely.' She broke off as Anne's voice, raised in rapturous enthusiasm, emanated through the walls to permeate the quiet hallway.

Sophy exchanged a raised-brows look with Thundigle, and the latter nodded gravely.

'I see,' he said, and thought for a moment. 'Mary has just put on a kettle of stew,' he offered.

'Perhaps Mary might spill some of it upon me, obliging me to change my clothes.'

'If not, then I would be most happy to capsize it in your direction, Miss Sophy.'

Sophy began to smile. 'A most obliging offer, but I would need a reason to go to the kitchen first.'

'I might bring you tea in the parlour, in a few moments,' Thundigle offered. 'And I might, in a moment of infinitely regrettable

clumsiness, spill a cup or two upon your gown.'

Sophy laughed at this image, but quickly sobered. 'As tempted as I am, I shall not impose upon your clumsiness. Can you imagine the damage to my poor gown? And I haven't another muslin anywhere near as good.'

Thundigle sighed with apparent regret, though a rare twinkle appeared in his nut-brown eyes. 'Perhaps you might propose a walk instead, to somewhere Miss Anne might find diverting.'

Sophy sighed and shook her head. 'I cannot, indeed, for we would be almost certain to bump into Anne's new beaux! I cannot think how it keeps happening.'

Thundigle greeted this piece of information with a thoughtful look, and ultimately made no reply. 'I must get on,' he apologised, and left again in the direction of the kitchen.

Sophy returned to the parlour just in time to hear Anne say, 'You should have seen how he stared at Sophy! Nothing could be more particular! He is to be at the Adairs' ball, you know, and I am persuaded he will ask her to dance first.'

Sophy, torn between embarrassment, chagrin and mild alarm, knew not what to say. Fixing on the one piece of Anne's speech that was news to her, she turned the conversation by asking: 'Are the Adairs to give a ball? I had not heard.'

'Yes!' cried Anne. 'It has only just got about this morning. Mr. Stanton and Mr. Green are so friendly with Mr. Edward already that they have decided to give a ball to welcome them to the neighbourhood. Everyone is to be invited! Only think how magnificent! They will be hoping that Elizabeth will catch Mr. Stanton's eye, I shouldn't wonder, or maybe Mr. Green's. But I think Mr. Stanton much prefers Sophy.'

Sophy could imagine no such thing, and said so. The Adairs were among the principle families in Tilby, with a large modern house and four or five thousand-a-year in income; their two children, Edward and Elizabeth Adair, were uncommonly handsome, and it was generally agreed that both would do well in marriage. The former was a natural associate for two such young gentlemen, and the latter an equally natural wife for one of them; what could Sophy have to do with any of that?

Anne refused to be swayed, however, and with more loyalty than perspicacity she insisted that Sophy was every bit as handsome as

Miss Adair, and far more agreeable.

Isabel watched this exchange with sharp attention, her dark eyes lingering on Sophy's face. 'I shall look forward to meeting them both,' was all she ventured to say.

Sophy merely smiled, relieved to reflect that she, in all her poverty and her lack of fashion, would almost certainly be omitted from the Adairs' invitation list.

But in due course, a handsome invitation card arrived at the parsonage, and upon seeing it, Sophy's heart sank. Typically an occasion for great excitement, this particular invitation filled her with a mixture of strange, fluttering nervousness (a most unwelcome feeling) and an obscure dread. The ball was to take place very soon, in a mere few days' time. Sophy recollected that Mr. Green and Mr. Stanton had only been said to remain in the neighbourhood for a few weeks; this, she supposed, was an effort to induce them to stay longer.

She briefly considered declining the invitation. Her father would certainly not wish to go, and she might claim any manner of indisposition for herself, without eliciting any true alarm in her friends. But Anne had not confined her speculations about Mr. Stanton to Sophy's parlour; her enthusiasm had, as usual, overridden her sense, and she had spread her ideas somewhat farther abroad. To decline the invitation would, then, invite far too much comment. She resigned herself to an evening of small trials, and wrote to accept the invitation.

But there remained another problem to be resolved: the question of what she could wear. She had, in the past few years, become somewhat notorious for wearing the same yellow silk gown to each and every assembly. Her skill with a needle might ably transform the neckline or the hem, adjust the sleeves or trim it anew, according to the changes in fashion; but nothing could disguise the faded primrose colour, or fool Tilby society into thinking it new.

She hardly knew how it was, but the prospect of wearing this tired old friend yet again filled her with dismay. The silk was beginning to break down under the arms, which must be her excuse; the elderly fabric might fall into tatters at any moment. But she had no choice in the matter, for she had no gown with which to replace it.

She dared not ask her father for the means to buy another. The anxious care he took of her health did not extend to her wardrobe; content with patched and fraying attire himself, he could see no reason why Sophy should be any more concerned with neatness. Blind to the vagaries of fashion and oblivious to the censure and ridicule that Sophy's shabby appearance often brought, he had far rather secure another brace of birds for his table than advance Sophy so much as a shilling for such frivolities as ball clothes. She knew better than to ask.

Her meagre allowance would stretch as far as new shoe-roses and a little trim, but no farther. With a heavy heart, Sophy resigned herself to wearing her old primrose silk.

And why should it trouble me so much? She asked herself. Her wardrobe had been the subject of ridicule before; it had used to pain her, when she was a younger woman, but it could not trouble her very much now. She had learned to care less about such things. Something had changed, however, and left her feeling very differently affected.

Isabel took note of the alteration in Sophy's feelings, it would seem, for three days before the projected ball, she arrived late in the morning, carrying a parcel and wearing a diffident expression.

Sophy, always glad to see her, greeted her with delight; but her pleasure quickly turned to dismay as Isabel continued to hover on the threshold, nervously turning the parcel around in her hands and not quite meeting Sophy's eye.

'Isabel, is anything the matter? Please come in; there can be no call for dancing on my doorstep in such a fashion! Have we not been friends these ten years at least?'

Sophy's warm smile drew a tentative one from Isabel in response, and she took a few quick steps into the room. 'There is nothing amiss,' she said. 'I have brought you something, that is all. That is—if you are minded to accept it.' She held out the parcel, finally meeting Sophy's gaze. 'If you do not like it, you have only to say so; and indeed, Sophy, I would have you know that I mean no slight at all upon your gowns, for they are quite beautiful and you maintain them all so skilfully—if I had half your ability I should have the prettiest clothes in Tilby—'

She stopped, flustered, and Sophy began to understand. She took the parcel and unwrapped the paper, discovering a pile of folded, dark red silk inside. Unfolding it, Sophy discovered that it was a ball-gown, with delicate short sleeves and a gathered neckline.

'It was one of mine,' Isabel said apologetically, 'so it is not new—the merest trifle—I thought perhaps you may wish to make it up new, and so I have brought it to-day. You will have time, I think?'

She paused, and when Sophy still said nothing she added anxiously, 'You are not offended?'

It was not offence that silenced Sophy's tongue, but the opposite. Much moved, she smiled at Isabel and said: 'You are quite the dearest girl there ever was, and everyone shall know it.'

Isabel smiled in relief, and said: 'Oh, no! It is the merest nothing.'

'On the contrary, it is everything. It will fully restore my credit with Tilby society—at least, those parts of it worth the impressing. I will indeed trim it—some ribbons about the hem, I think—and it will require only the smallest alteration to the neck. It will look very well!' After a moment's thought, she added: 'And I can contrive a cap to match, I think.'

'A cap! Oh, Sophy! Must you? It is playing the old maid very sadly!'

'But so I am,' Sophy said, laughing. 'There can be no shame in owning my true state—and it will save the young men from any tiresome sense of obligation when they see me standing by. They will be free to seek more agreeable partners.'

'You should not talk so—especially when Mr. Stanton has been so particular!'

Sophy rolled her eyes heavenwards, and shook her head. 'You must not heed Anne; her fancy runs away with her. How can a gentleman be *particular* to a woman with whom he is not even acquainted? If to stare in a rude fashion is to be *particular*, why, I am sure that Mr. Stanton has been particular to a great many other people besides.'

Isabel smiled, and conceded. 'Perhaps Anne has been imagining a great many things; but still I beg you, Sophy, *not* to wear the cap.'

Sophy eyed her, and would not promise. It was of no use, in her estimation, to put herself forward as a young woman, as a desirable partner, or as a marriageable lady. Better to declare her matronly status at once, with a well-made cap to hide her flyaway hair.

Isabel was not able to prevail on this point. Sophy's gown was made ready, her cap assembled and the whole was elegantly trimmed in no time at all; and on the evening of the ball, the Ellerby carriage conveyed Sophy to the Adair house in finer style than she had ever appeared before, and in only a slight flutter of spirits.

CHAPTER SEVEN

Ye may be wonderin' why I dwell so much on the topic o' the ball. Well! And why not? It's an important event, as ye'll soon see. Fer Aubranael, poor fellow, the promise o' the ball was as the promise o' water to a man dyin' o' thirst. An' t'Sophy... well, she was by no means so indifferent as she pretended. All that faffing wi' gowns an' trim! But who could wonder at it? My Sophy's no more impervious to a little admiration than any other, that's fer sure—no matter what she may say. An' this ball... well, let's just say that nothin' was quite the same after.

Aubranael stood near the great double doors of the Adairs' ballroom, keeping a close eye on the stream of guests as they arrived. Miss Landon was late, he thought; the room was rapidly filling up, and as yet there was no sign of her. The Adairs had spared no expense in turning out their house for the ball: the room shone with the light of hundreds of wax candles, and an abundance of flowers decked every available surface. The effect was undeniably pretty, but Aubranael had no eyes for it. In his estimation, the ball could receive no higher adornment than the presence of Miss Landon, and as yet, she had failed to grace it at all.

Restless, he paced away a few steps and then back again. Grunewald had assured him that Miss Landon's invitation was secured, but as he had seen no direct evidence that it had been sent, Aubranael could not dismiss the suspicion that the Adairs had refused to honour his request after all.

Or perhaps they had invited her, but she had declined to accept!

That was always possible.

Perhaps she had accepted and was on her way, but some mishap had befallen her carriage. Grunewald assured him that she was likely to travel with the Ellerbys—a family wealthy enough to merit an invitation without any interference from Grunewald—so she would be sure to arrive safely. But the light was fading fast; the possibility of their meeting with some danger upon the road did not seem distant enough to Aubranael's mind; and besides, the roads of Tilby were not always very good. He tried not to imagine the Ellerby carriage overturned in a ditch, or held up upon the road by a pair of thieves.

He was not left alone with his fears for very long. His choice of station was not altogether ideal in some respects: he had placed himself where he would be the first to see each new arrival, but that meant he was also one of the first people *they* saw as they stepped into the room. Many paid their respects to the hosts of the evening and then walked directly up to him, with a seemingly endless series of greetings and poor jokes and insinuations to share. They obliged him to exert himself to be sociable, when he wished only to brood; and besides this, they blocked his view of the door.

Worse, he found that Miss Elizabeth Adair was determined to attach herself to him for—he feared—the whole of the evening. She hovered near his elbow, doing her part to welcome guests with many a winning smile and gracious comment, but never moving more than a few paces away from him. And whenever there was a lull in the arrivals, and she found herself with a few moments of quiet, she would invariably direct those winning smiles and gracious comments at *him*.

He was well aware by now that he had been marked out for her by Tilby society, as handsome enough to match her in looks and wealthy enough to match her in importance. She seemed to feel it, too, for she was doing her level best to fascinate him at every opportunity. But as he found her affected, arrogant and cruel, nothing could recommend her to him as a tolerable companion—certainly not the beauty for which she was lauded across the whole of the county. He did his best to suggest to her, by way of a courteous but distant manner, that her interest was by no means returned; but he found that her self-assurance carried her through it all with an unimpaired confidence of winning him in the end. No hint won through to her ear, no subtlety made any impression upon her; she was oblivious to it all.

At length he found that the ball was on the point of beginning. All the company seemed assembled, save that one, precious presence; the orchestra began, in a flurried cacophony, to warm up their instruments; gentlemen began to solicit the ladies for the first dance. He was displeased to notice that no one approached Miss Adair, nor did she seem to expect anybody to do so. All her expectations were fixed upon him, and it appeared that the rest of the guests were equally sanguine in their expectation that Miss Adair would open the ball with Mr. Stanton.

Aubranael ground his teeth together in frustration, and did his best to ignore the smiling presence of Miss Adair beside him.

But the lady was by no means willing to take the hint, and let her prize escape. As the orchestra began to strike up a tune, she approached him directly, opened her pretty blue eyes very wide and directed her most gracious smile at him. 'I can hardly think how it should happen that I should want for a partner—and at my very own ball! Perhaps—just between you and I—I have been saving the first dances for a particular favourite of mine.'

This was a bold speech; Aubranael had learned enough of English manners to recognise that much. But she had been spoiled by too much privilege and admiration, ever since childhood, he would wager. Used to having her own way, and to receiving a great deal of praise and admiration whenever she could desire it, she could not conceive of a world where the handsome young man that she had chosen should not wish to dance with her.

Aubranael stared hard at her. She was looking so becoming in a blue silk gown, rich with embroidery and beads. Her glossy brown hair was perfectly arranged, through the efforts of a very expensive abigail he had no doubt. Her young face looked as though her rich mother and father had simply purchased the most winning countenance for their daughter that the imagination could conceive of.

The whole picture left him utterly cold.

If he had ever hoped to find the people of England less blinded by beauty than those of Aylfenhame, those hopes were long gone. Beauty and wealth; no more powerful combination existed anywhere. He began, just a little, to regret the part he was playing. By masquerading as yet more beauty and wealth, he pandered disgracefully to the superficial attitudes that governed the lives and the opinions of so many of the people around him. He had sought a handsome face, and accepted the appearance of wealth, fully expecting that these things would win him the favour he had never before enjoyed—and so they had. But was he any better than Miss Adair?

And if Miss Landon was moved to bestow her favour upon him because he was now beautiful and rich, was she any better either?

His whole approach began to seem like a colossal mistake. His mouth turned dry, and something like blind panic washed through him. He did not have time to consider these ideas for very long, however, for at that moment there came a little commotion of arrival at the door, and at long last he saw Miss Landon.

She was wearing a dark red gown which was, he thought, very becoming with her slightly brown complexion. The gown was neither so fine nor so richly adorned as Miss Adair's; her face was not nearly so perfect, and not even the silk cap that she wore could disguise the fact that her curling, sun-coloured hair was not at all well arranged.

But she brought with her something special, an indefinable air that Miss Adair wholly lacked. Perhaps it was the way her smile lit up her face, or the way her blue eyes danced with pleasure at the sight of the crowded ballroom. Perhaps it was the way she hung back, diffidently allowing Miss Ellerby and Miss Daverill to enter first. Whatever it was, the sight of her set Aubranael's troubled heart leaping with delight.

She met his gaze, and her sunny smile did not falter.

Miss Adair continued to hover, and he realised he had made no reply to her daring sally. He looked back at her, and smiled. 'That is the greatest coincidence,' he said slowly, 'for I, too, have been saving the first dances for one lady in particular.'

Miss Adair's smile grew satisfied, and she somehow summoned a becoming blush to grace her pretty cheeks. But before she could celebrate what she believed to be her victory, he bowed and said: 'Would you excuse me?'

He walked away without looking back, hoping that he had released himself from her tiresome attentions. He had been rude, he knew that, but he felt that she deserved it. She had probably never received such a set-down before; it was long overdue.

Her mother, Mrs. Adair, was standing not far away. He made his way towards her as quickly as he could, his heart hammering with anticipation. It was time at long last to be formally introduced to Miss Landon.

* * *

Sophy entered the ballroom with the displeasing consciousness of being disgracefully late.

The problem had occurred because of the Ellerby family's generosity. They had undertaken to convey both herself and Anne to the ball, along with themselves and their own children. Some little misunderstanding as to times and places had occurred somewhere along the way, and several little delays had amounted to a rather large one in total. She felt a flicker of embarrassment at seeing the ballroom already crowded with guests, some of them forming up into a set ready to begin dancing.

Her discomfort soon faded, however, in the pleasure of being at a ball. That she had seriously considered declining the invitation was a source of wonder to her now, for the delights of a ball could still enchant her—no matter how much she tried to convince herself otherwise. She lived in such a small way, with so many little trials and troubles to reason away each day—not to mention the large question of her future hanging upon her—that some manner of distraction and delight was absolutely necessary to her happiness. But they did not occur very often.

For a moment, she could not remember why she had been tempted to decline the invitation. Then her gaze fell on Mr. Stanton, standing near the door, and she remembered.

Some oddity about his behaviour, yes; that strange look he had given her when they had passed in the street. But now he stood not far away from her, looking (she must admit) extremely handsome in his evening attire, a rather grave expression upon his face. His friend and joint guest of honour, Mr. Green, was holding court among a gaggle of young women, smiling in high enjoyment and looking ready to dance at least the entire night away, if not more. Mr. Stanton, on the other hand, somehow contrived to be completely oblivious to the attention he was receiving, and the many looks cast his way. He caught no one's eye—until he suddenly looked up and caught hers. It was a fleeting glance, for he almost immediately turned away; but during those brief few seconds his face lit up with a smile of such warmth and delight that Sophy felt a little shocked.

He could not have been thinking of her, she immediately decided. Indeed, he had turned back to Miss Adair, who was lingering nearby. Doubtless he would ask the prettier lady to dance.

But he merely said something very brief to the lady, made her a stiff bow, and walked away entirely.

Sophy was considerably puzzled, but the peculiarity of this behaviour soon slipped from her mind. She was caught up in a little bustle as two gentlemen arrived at once to claim Isabel for the first dance. Her friend departed with one, leaving the other to ask Anne, and Sophy was left alone.

Only briefly, however, for Mrs. Adair approached her immediately afterwards. The hostess of the evening was looking splendid and elegant in ivory silk, her gown sewn over with seed pearls and her shining hair partially covered with a lace cap much finer than Sophy's. She was still an extremely handsome woman, Sophy thought, eyeing her with a little uneasiness. Mr. Stanton was following directly behind her; what could they possibly want?

'Miss Landon,' said Mrs. Adair, her tone slightly stiff.

Sophy made her a curtsey, still mystified.

'Mr. Stanton has requested the honour of an introduction,' she said, sounding none too pleased about it—and no wonder, if the gentleman had ignored her daughter in favour of Sophy.

She made no objection, of course—covering her surprise, she thought, very creditably. The introduction was swiftly performed, and Mrs. Adair as swiftly withdrew. Mr. Stanton did not so much as glance at his hostess's retreating form, dismissing her as thoroughly as he had dismissed her daughter moments before.

But there was no pride or arrogance in his manner. He seemed so entirely unconscious of wrongdoing, as though he had ignored and dismissed them simply because they were unimportant to him. Unimportant! Whereas she, Sophia Landon, somehow ranked as important enough for him to request an introduction.

He gave her another of those warm smiles, held out a hand to her and said:

'It is the greatest pleasure to make your acquaintance at last, Miss Landon. Will you do me the honour of dancing with me?'

Sophy felt too much surprise to venture any ready response. She blinked stupidly at his handsome face, certain she must be misunderstanding the moment somehow.

Propriety obliged him to open the ball with the daughter of his hosts, if she wished it, and she clearly did. And given that the lady in question was beautiful, rich and generally considered charming, it could be no hardship to do so.

Instead he had requested an introduction to one of the least worthy females in the room, and actually wished to dance with her! The all-important first dances, too! Nothing had prepared her for this singular experience; she had shrugged off all of Anne's hints and predictions without a moment's thought, as being far too ridiculous for serious contemplation.

Yet, here it was. So unused was she to being seriously solicited for a dance—let alone by one of the handsomest and most sought-after gentlemen in the room—that she had no idea what to say. She ought to refuse, she knew, for he and his first dances belonged by right to Miss Adair. But her refusal would not make him any more likely to choose instead a woman whom he plainly did not wish to dance with. Besides, that wonderful smile was back as he waited for her reply. How could she resist an invitation delivered with so much warmth, so much apparent delight in her company? Unaccountable as it was, she could *not* resist. She accepted, and tried not to be conscious of the attention she was receiving as Mr. Stanton led her into the set. Much of it would not be in her favour, she knew; her neighbours must marvel as much as she had at her good fortune. She put it from her mind.

Mr. Stanton took his place opposite to her and bowed. His smile had faded, but he continued to look at her with a kind of happy delight that was impossible to explain. She arched a brow at him, and said: 'You appear to me to be in a state of uncommon enjoyment, Mr. Stanton. Do you love a ball so very much?'

'I do, indeed!' he replied. 'Especially this one. It is already my very favourite above all others. And it is a long time since I had the pleasure of dancing.'

'Your favourite, indeed? You enjoy being a guest of honour, and the knowledge that all this splendour and gaiety is for your entertainment.'

Mr. Stanton appeared to be giving her flippant remark some serious consideration. 'No, I do not think that is the reason,' he said, with a twinkle in his eye that she knew not how to interpret. 'Though I believe you have described my friend's feelings perfectly.'

Sophy glanced up to the top of the set. Mr. Green had stepped into his friend's place and asked Miss Adair, and the two were just beginning to go down the dance. Once again, he struck her as being as fully sensible of the attention he was receiving as her own partner was oblivious to it. He played to it, making a fine show, and Miss Adair followed his lead with only an occasional piqued glance at Mr. Stanton and Sophy.

'How obliging of him to take responsibility for some of the more onerous duties,' she said.

He cast her a look of keen appreciation and replied, with a swift grin: 'Oh, he is the most obliging of fellows.'

'You, however, are not very obliging at all.'

'I am known to be, on occasion.' He paused, and smiled. 'This is not one of those occasions.'

'You are resolved upon being entirely selfish, I collect.'

'Entirely, thoroughly selfish, I admit.'

A faint, sardonic smile crossed her face. '*Some* might say that this is the one occasion, above all others, when you ought to be unselfish and obliging, and do as the company expects.'

'Not at all, for if I had been more *obliging* I would have lost the opportunity of securing the most desirable partner in the room for the first dances. This is full reason enough to be selfish, you must agree.'

This was far too much. No degree of eccentricity could explain his finding *her* the most desirable partner in the room, especially on no acquaintance at all. This sort of flattery made sense when it was directed at the enchanting countenances of Miss Adair, or the younger Miss Winbolt, or even Isabel. It could only sound fatuous when directed at Sophy herself.

'You have given that honour away to your friend,' Sophy said pointedly, hoping to recall him to sense.

He refused to understand her, saying instead: 'I was speaking of you, Miss Landon.'

She coloured, feeling more uncomfortable than charmed. 'You mock me!' she accused.

His brows rose and his eyes widened with every appearance of surprise. 'No indeed! How can you suppose it?'

Sophy was not inclined to reply to this. To be forced to enumerate her shortcomings was an intolerable prospect. Besides, to do so was to court further flattery, as politeness would oblige him to contradict every point she might advance. Her pride revolted on both counts, particularly since he must be perfectly well aware of the grave differences between a Miss Landon and a Miss Adair. He was merely being charming, in his odd way, seeking perhaps to put her at her ease. However well-meant she judged it to be, she would not humour him by going along with it.

Fortunately, it was now their turn to go down the dance, and conversation must be over for the present. She put all thought of Mr. Stanton's peculiarities out of her mind, anxious to acquit herself well under the scrutiny she was receiving from those who were not themselves dancing.

And something else occurred to drive the thoughts from her mind. She had not anticipated what it would be like to dance with Mr. Stanton. She could not remember another occasion in her life when she had been so particularly solicited as a partner; she could not recall when she had ever danced with someone who seemed so sincerely desirous of dancing with *her*. Gentlemen had danced with her out of politeness only, or perhaps out of pity, both of which were intolerable. It was this circumstance that had led her to adopt the role of matron, as soon as she had felt herself old enough to carry it off; the caps she wore, and her habit of placing herself with the mothers and older spinsters in a ballroom, had for the last year or so excused the young gentlemen of Tilby from the tiresome duty of dancing with her.

She had never experienced anything like *this*. When their hands met for the first time, she felt a frisson of excitement that took her wholly by surprise. Their eyes met, and she found that his betrayed a surprise, a pleasure, a degree of shock that mirrored her own.

Throughout the dance, he watched Sophy with the intentness of a man who was very much *interested*, and treated her not only with perfect courtesy but also with the kind of *particularity* she had seen bestowed upon others, but never upon herself.

And she found that she was far from indifferent to Mr. Stanton. She knew not how to explain it: perhaps it was merely the experience of being sought-after that had turned her head, or perhaps it was his extreme handsomeness. Perhaps it was even something else entirely, some indefinable characteristic of his, or combination of qualities that shone through his behaviour; for she felt *interested* in him. She wanted to know more of him—his tastes, his opinions, his ideas, his pursuits—and she heartily welcomed that beautiful smile which was, once more, shining down upon her.

Somewhere in the midst of this whirl of emotions, she found a moment to observe that Mr. Stanton danced uncommonly well, with a grace she did not often see. There was a hint of peculiarity about the way he formed the steps, as if he had learned from an unusual source. Perhaps he had been in France.

When their part in the dance was over, they returned to the set and stood in silence for some minutes. Sophy's mind was too full of what had just occurred; the power of speech eluded her altogether, her thoughts too distracted by the racing of her heart, and the flutter of nerves and excitement in her stomach. She regretted that Mr. Stanton had now returned to a more proper distance; she missed the closeness that the dance had briefly rendered allowable.

What occupied Mr. Stanton's thoughts, she could not tell, and she did not dare to venture a guess. He remained as silent as herself, only looking at her with an indescribable expression on his face.

At length, she found her voice. 'Have you travelled much, Mr. Stanton?' It was an insipid enquiry, but it would do for the present.

He looked a little startled at the suddenness of her question, but replied readily enough. 'Why, yes. I suppose you could say that.'

'Now! That makes me quite envious, for I have never travelled anywhere. Perhaps you will be obliging for just a few moments—no longer, I assure you, I have no wish to strain your good nature—and tell me a tale or two.'

His eyes sparkled with amusement at her small—very small— piece of wit, but he shook his head. 'I cannot believe that you have not travelled at all. Perhaps you have not seen France or Italy, but you must have been somewhere beyond the borders of England. Now, have not you?'

Sophy's thoughts turned instantly to Aylfenhame and the village of Grenlowe. This was not an experience she wished to share with a stranger, however, and since Mr. Stanton could not possibly know of it she felt no hesitation in saying: 'No, indeed, I assure you. It is among my greatest regrets, for I should so like to see more of the world.'

He eyed her thoughtfully, and made no reply.

The rest of the dance passed off with no more than commonplace remarks on her side, and his; but she felt that a certain tension persisted between them, lending unusual significance to the familiar motions of the dance. The moment the end of the second dance released them from each other, he immediately bowed and said, 'Will you do me the honour of dancing the next with me, Miss Landon?'

'Sir!' Sophy spluttered, 'You cannot possibly ask me again so soon!'

'No? And why not?'

'It is not proper, as you *must* know. Not after your—that is—you must choose another partner.'

'I will dance with whomever I choose. I see no reason to ask someone else, when I wish to dance with you.'

This was a step too far. Part of Sophy's heart went into an absurd flutter at finding him still so desirous of her company; but the rational part of her nature—always the stronger force—overruled her silliness and drew a firm line. For a man to dance twice with the same partner was undeniably particular; to dance twice in immediate succession with the same woman was *very* particular; to do so having already snubbed the very desirable daughter of the hosts in favour of someone else was enough to excite talk for the next month at least. A flicker of annoyance intruded upon Sophy's happy glow. *He* might be important enough to flout convention and disregard talk, but *she* was not. He might go away at the end of another week, or another month, but she would have no escape from the censure he seemed determined to excite.

'You may think nothing of wagging tongues, Mr. Stanton, but you might give *my* position a little more consideration. I thank you for your kind invitation, but I do not mean to dance any more this evening.'

An expression of concern mingled with confusion crossed his face, and he nodded awkwardly. She waited for a moment, allowing him time to make his apologies if he would. He seemed tongue-tied, however, and so she curtseyed and withdrew.

She found a seat in a relatively quiet corner of the ballroom and claimed it with relief. She was overheated; perhaps that had contributed to her uncharacteristic irritation a moment ago. It was a pleasure to sit quietly and grow cooler, and watch the goings-on from a safe distance. She saw Miss Adair and her brother, both dancing, along with their primary rivals in importance, the Winbolts; Mr. Snelling was present, dancing with Anne but with his eyes fixed upon Miss Adair; Miss Gladwin and Miss Lacey had formed a little huddle in one corner with old Mrs. Snelling and Mrs. Ash; Anne's sisters were giggling around the punch-bowl; Isabel was dancing with Mr. Andrew Winbolt. This last caught her attention for a moment, as they did make a remarkably suitable-looking couple. She wondered if Mr. Winbolt had any intentions.

Mr. Stanton did not immediately seek another partner. Instead he retired to the nearest wall and stood, his eyes turned in her direction. This would not do either! To stand aloof when other young ladies besides herself had no partner—to prefer staring at her to dancing with another—he was thoroughly scandalous! She averted her gaze.

When the dance ended, Isabel spotted Sophy sitting down and made her way over. She quietly took the adjacent seat and said softly, 'I must agree with Anne, Sophy. You have made a conquest there.'

She nodded in the direction of Mr. Stanton and his wall, who seemed every bit as pleased with each other as they had at the beginning of the dance.

'He has certainly paid me a great deal of attention,' Sophy said cautiously.

Isabel was silent. Sophy guessed that she meant to enquire *why* Mr. Stanton had singled her out above every other woman in the room, but would not do so for fear of offending.

'I can account for it no more than you can,' Sophy said.

'I did not mean to suggest—' Isabel began, but then she sighed. 'It is a little strange.'

'Quite, quite strange,' Sophy agreed. *But also agreeable*, she thought privately.

Mr. Stanton chose that moment to leave the companionship and safety of his wall and make his approach.

'Heavens!' Sophy said despairingly. 'Here he comes again!'

He wove his way through the crowd—ignoring several attempts to interrupt him—and stopped in front of Sophy and Isabel. He bowed.

'Mr. Stanton—!' Sophy began, but with a gentle smile he cut her off.

'Perhaps you will introduce me to your friend, Miss Landon?'

Relieved, Sophy did so. She was even more relieved when Mr. Stanton asked Isabel to dance, and they went away. This went some way towards mending matters, and she was pleased that he had chosen to distinguish Isabel. It spoke well of his taste.

The rest of the party passed with little to trouble Sophy. She maintained her seat for some time, until she felt quite cool; then she began to seek out her friends for conversation. Everyone had some remark to make about Mr. Stanton, but since he had, by this time, enjoyed dances with a few different partners and had made no further attempt to approach her, she was able to turn these off with a laugh and a joke.

Only one small disappointment occurred, when Mr. Green approached and asked for her hand. Having told Mr. Stanton that she did not mean to dance again, she was obliged to tell Mr. Green the same. She was sorry for it. The two gentlemen had begun to intrigue her more than she cared to admit, and she would have appreciated an opportunity to converse with Mr. Green as well. But perhaps there would be other occasions.

She travelled home at last with the Ellerby family, at a very late hour and with a great many yawns shared among the company.

'I believe we shall soon be wishing you joy, Miss Landon!' said Isabel's mother, with her usual liveliness. 'I like him the better for it, I do indeed. Although I must own that I think he and my Isabel looked very well together, do not you think?'

Sophy agreed to this without hesitation. They *had* made a very fine couple, and if Mr. Stanton had any sense at all he would cease his odd pursuit of herself and transfer his attentions to her sweet-natured and far more beautiful and eligible friend.

This would be the logical thing for him to do, certainly, but in spite of her love for Isabel, Sophy found she could not truly wish for it in her heart.

CHAPTER EIGHT

Now, I'm a troll o' few words. I can no more manage eloquence than I can dance a quadrille, an' believe me, I've tried. So ye'll no doubt excuse me if I say only that I was right proud t' hear o' my Sophy's triumph, an' don't try to tell ye how much. Ye may draw yer own conclusions as t' that.

But I'll admit: as fond o' Sophy as I am, I also know full well that she don't usually "take", in the way the gentry-folk say; not like that! She ain't usually pestered wi' invitations and solicitations an' the like. Just between you an' me, I think it's as much because she don't put herself forward. She hangs back, an' lets herself be eclipsed by bolder types—like that Miss Adair.

But anywho, I got curious about this Mr. Stanton. He must be a gentleman o' rare perception if he caught hold o' my Sophy's merits in so short a space o' time. I'm not sayin' it's an impossibility, mind! No, indeed! But I were curious, as I said, so I made a point o' lookin' into the matter, didn't I?

'Mama would like you to come and spend a day with us again soon, Sophy. Do say you will come! We would all be so glad of your company!'

Isabel Ellerby stood in the centre of Sophy's parlour, wearing the pretty lavender silk gown she had previously worn to the ball. She would not normally be so attired in the middle of the morning, but in the crush of the ball her gown had been trodden upon, and the delicate fabric had torn. Sophy was on her knees at Isabel's feet, her hands full of silk and needles and her mouth full of pins as she attempted to mend the tear.

Taking the pins out from between her lips, she shook her head and replied, 'I am not at all sure I shall have time. Papa has a great deal of mending for me to do—as ever—and I must at least *try* to be of use to poor Mary and Thundigle.'

'What a shocking untruth! Of course you have time. It is only that you do not *wish* to come.'

Sophy sighed inwardly. It was not that she did not like the Ellerbys; she did, very much. But their goodwill was sometimes overpowering, and she had so little to offer in return. She hated to feel like a charity case, and the extreme kindness of Mrs. Ellerby made her feel like an object of pity.

Furthermore, the lively family life that Isabel enjoyed made her feel her own lack the more keenly. It was best to keep her visits infrequent, she found.

'I am very much obliged to you for the invitation,' Sophy said, giving her friend a warm smile to show her gratitude. As she did so, the sharp tip of her needle somehow found its way into her finger, and a tiny spot of red blossomed on Isabel's fine lavender silk.

'Oops,' Sophy said, absently scrubbing at it with a scrap of cloth. 'Please convey my thanks and regards to your mother, also. She is far too good.'

'But the answer, I collect, is still no,' Isabel said, craning her neck to see what Sophy was doing behind her. 'Has something gone amiss?'

'Nothing of any great moment.' No one would ever see the tiny speck of red, Sophy assured herself, though resolving at the same time to pay a bit less attention to the conversation, and a bit more to the whereabouts of her needle.

Isabel smiled ruefully down at her, shaking her head. 'I will need you next Tuesday, for Anne is to come to us. You know she will tease poor Charles until he is quite out of patience if you are not there.'

Charles was Isabel's elder brother, and the pride of the Ellerby family. He was heir to their small but worthy estate, soon to take orders and become a clergyman. And he was, as yet, unmarried. Naturally, this made him a great favourite with Anne.

He was a favourite with Sophy, too, though more on account of his manners, which were courteous and amiable, and his interests, which constituted reading and walking more than the sporting and card-playing which pleased most other young men. Isabel had once hoped that her brother would take a more direct interest in Sophy; but Sophy knew well that her parents, in spite of all their kindness to her, had been a little relieved when he had not.

'I can hardly prevent Anne from teasing Charles,' she said.

'No, but you may occupy him for some portion of the time, so he is not left entirely at her mercy.'

'As a programme for a day's activities, that is not very enticing; that you *must* acknowledge,' said Sophy, laughing. 'Charles is very well able to manage himself.'

Isabel sighed deeply. 'I do wish you would not shut yourself up so. How can you possibly expect to meet anyone if you will hardly go into society—and when you do, you pass yourself off as an old matron?'

'Perhaps I do not wish to "meet someone".'

'Do not wish…? But what will you do if—when—if, I mean…' Isabel broke off, her pink complexion turning pinker.

Sophy understood her perfectly well. What Isabel was trying *not* to say was that she would be quite alone when her father died, and she must therefore do all in her power to secure a husband before this sorry event occurred. And her father's health was not good, that she could see all too well.

But Sophy's pride revolted at the notion of *husband hunting*, or going *on the catch*. And to shackle herself for life to any man who would take her, no matter what his character, his ideas and his interests may be! The notion was too hideous; she could not contemplate it without a shudder.

'Well, but there is Mr. Stanton!' Isabel continued, having recovered from her confusion. 'You *have* met someone, in spite of your attempts to put everyone off with those caps of yours.'

For a moment, Sophy considered this notion. It would be a different matter if the man who would take her proved to be agreeable, generous and good-hearted, of course. But she had no particular reason to believe that Mr. Stanton was any of those things, except that he could be agreeable when he chose. Was it his handsome face which encouraged her to credit him, far too soon, with all the rest?

Amused at herself and blushing at the direction of her thoughts, Sophy quickly dismissed these reflections. Two invitations to dance most certainly did not amount to an imminent proposal of marriage!

Even if it did, she could hardly accept him on so little real knowledge of his character. One dance and a little conversation were by no means sufficient. How she had come to think so favourably of his character she could hardly imagine, especially given that his behaviour had, at first, struck her as odd. There was something about him, she supposed, that set her at ease and encouraged her to trust him; some quality which rendered conversation easy, and banished awkwardness between them.

But she was being foolish. She had felt nothing of the kind until the ball, and their interaction on that occasion had still been slight. A small, desperate part of her mind—that corner which held all the doubts and fears for her future that she dared not confront—had broken free of its confines and run away with her. She was attaching huge importance to trifles, seeing portents where none existed, and beginning to live too much in her own fancy.

That was quite enough of *that*. She resolutely packed every absurd thought and foolish idea back into the dark spaces where they belonged, and summoned her usual sunny smile for her friend. 'There, your gown is quite healed! You may change now, if you wish.'

Isabel bent to examine the silk. 'I can barely see it at all! You are a marvel. I had given up my poor gown for lost.' She picked up her skirts and stepped carefully out of the room, leaving Sophy alone with her thoughts.

This was dangerous in her present mood. She occupied herself with tidying up her scissors and pins and thread, and so busy was she that she did not hear Mary come in.

'Mr. Stanton, Miss,' said Mary.

Sophy jumped, and turned quickly around. There he stood indeed, immaculately dressed in a dark red coat and freshly tied cravat, his hat in his hands. Her heart thumped a little uncomfortably. *People as handsome as that*, she thought, *should not smile too much, and certainly not in that* particular *way. It is very hard on the rest of us.*

Mary talked on. 'I am sorry, Miss! I couldn't find Mr. Landon and I didn't know what else to do.'

'It is perfectly all right,' Sophy assured her. 'You were quite right to bring him to me. Is there any possibility of tea, do you suppose, and perhaps something to eat?'

Mary nodded vigorously. 'Oh, to be sure. There's an apple tart, fresh from the oven. I'll send it in directly.' She turned to leave, casting a sly wink at Sophy as she did so.

Sophy suppressed a smile, torn between amusement and mortification. Mary had heard the news, of course, and would be sure to tease her about the visit later.

'Will you sit down, Mr. Stanton?' she said, mustering a calm smile for her visitor. She felt reasonably confident that her momentary flutter had not been perceptible; now she must ensure that her manner remained friendly and composed.

Mr. Stanton seated himself in the proffered chair, and proceeded to study her face rather intently. The conviction that he was registering all of the faults of her face took hold of her mind, sweeping away all her composure. It was very possible that she was actually *blushing* with mortification.

This would not do at all.

Lifting her chin, she said: 'Does something displease you in my countenance, Mr. Stanton?'

He looked surprised. 'Of course not. Why should you suppose it?'

There was no simple answer to that question, and Sophy would not attempt any. She should have confined her conversation to the commonplace, of course. Hastily she said: 'I am sorry that my father was not able to receive you. He often sleeps at this time of the morning. His health is not the strongest, as you may have heard.'

Mr. Stanton nodded thoughtfully, his dark brown eyes still fixed immovably on Sophy's face. 'I had heard, and I am sorry to hear it. I do hope his health will improve. I had not set out to visit the parsonage with any thought of seeing your father, however.'

Here was more of that awkward particularity. Did the man know nothing of small talk? Torn between pleasure and irritation, Sophy hardly knew whether to smile or frown. Deciding on attack instead of avoidance, she said: 'Oh? What was the nature of your errand?'

'I wished to hear your opinion on a matter of some importance to me.'

He said this in such a serious tone that Sophy began to feel a little fluttered—a little afraid that the silly daydreams she had indulged in only moments before may actually come to pass. Unable to suppress the colour that rose in her face, she managed only, 'Indeed?'

'Indeed.' The smile returned to his face and he said, 'What do you think of this coat?'

Sophy blinked. 'I beg your pardon?'

'This coat! It is new, and an entirely new colour for me. Mr. Green says it is altogether too military, but I cannot agree. The shade is much darker than the traditional *redcoat*, as I am sure you will observe.'

Struck by the incongruity between his manner and his subject matter—between her flights of fancy and the truth behind his words—Sophy lost control of her dignified composure and began to giggle. Mr. Stanton laughed too, and at once the slight tension in the room eased and disappeared.

'I had no notion that gentlemen worried over such things,' Sophy said, when she had regained her breath. 'A difficult problem, indeed! I can only assure you that it looks very well.'

'Ah! Then I shall not mind Mr. Green's opinion. He cannot abide red, you know, but then it would not do at all with his hair.'

His serious manner was back, but now Sophy could see the gentle self-mockery that lay behind it. 'No, indeed,' she agreed, mimicking his gravity. 'Too much red all in one place! It cannot be good for a person's health.'

'That is a possibility I had not considered,' said he seriously. 'Do you think it will be of detriment to mine?'

'No, for you are not at all red.'

He smiled and leaned a little forward. 'I have been learning all manner of things about you, Miss Landon. The neighbourhood has a great deal to say, since the ball. For instance, you are a terrific seamstress! Is my information correct?'

'I cannot agree with the term chosen; modesty forbids it, you know, and there can be no more awful prospect than an immodest young woman. But I do sew a great deal.'

He nodded wisely. 'By which I understand you to mean that you *are* a terrific seamstress, and you are also very dutiful as regards the expectations of society.'

'Not *very* dutiful. Society places so many and varied demands upon a person; it would be far too tiring to keep up with them *all*.'

'Oh, quite! I am exhausted with it myself. For instance, I should like nothing better than to invite you to walk with me; but that could never be considered proper, and so I must resort to subterfuge.'

Her brows rose at the word *subterfuge*. 'What manner of deviousness did you have in mind?'

He thought for a moment. 'If, say, you were to walk in Tilton

Wood one morning—say tomorrow, for the sake of argument—and if you were to walk just a little too long, and find yourself suffering under the affliction of a head-ache—and if, by the most complete chance, you happened to encounter me there as you turned towards home—why, common decency would oblige me to see you safely home, would it not?'

Sophy pondered this for a moment in silence. Judging, from his smile and his gentle manner, that he meant nothing objectionable by it, she returned his smile and said: 'It would not be wholly out of character for me to do so, certainly.'

'I would, of course, offer you my arm, so that you may lean upon it. I would not wish to see you faint from over-exertion and the pain of the head-ache. And if anyone should happen to observe us, I may disarm any prospect of *talk* by claiming mere gentlemanly good behaviour. May I not?'

The picture he painted was an attractive one. The prospect of walking through Tilton Wood on a sunny morning, her arm linked with Mr. Stanton's, her time whiled away by pleasantries and amusing nonsense, charmed her immensely. But dare she do so by prior agreement? Such behaviour would be considered intolerably bold, were it known.

But her social standing was already very low. Her likelihood of marrying had already been largely written off by Tilby (as well as herself). Her social credit, then, could hardly grow worse; and since she had no particular position to protect, no prospects to guard and no connections to offend, she might think herself free to consult her own pleasure.

'I imagine I will wake tomorrow morning with every intention of walking in Tilton Wood,' she said. 'And it would be the very height of courtesy in you to rescue me from the ill effects of the head-ache which, I feel sure, must inevitably strike.'

This won her a smile of genuine delight; but he had not time for more, because Isabel at that moment returned to the room, now properly attired in a morning-gown. 'Oh!' said she, on perceiving Mr. Stanton. 'I do beg your pardon! I had no idea that Miss Landon had a visitor.'

'It is of no moment, Isabel; do please sit down! Mr. Stanton called to consult with father, but unluckily he is at this moment laid down upon the bed, and I am reluctant to disturb him.'

Isabel cast her a sharp look which proclaimed that she did not for an instant believe Sophy's story; but as Mr. Stanton went along with it, she was obliged to likewise. She took a seat near to Sophy's, arranged her skirts tidily, and proceeded to be entirely silent.

Sophy began to talk of the weather, of the roads, of the markets—anything, in short, that she could seize upon to fill up the silence. Mr. Stanton obliged her with a number of sensible comments, proving that he could indeed manage the delicate art of small talk; but the charm of their earlier conversation had gone. The entrance of a third party put paid to the easy intimacy which was beginning to grow between them, and the conversation was stilted. Sophy was not surprised when Mr. Stanton rose to depart.

'I will look forward to seeing you both very soon,' he said in parting, with a swift look at Sophy bespeaking his dependency on seeing *her* very soon indeed. She smiled her assent, and bid him goodbye with, she flattered herself, a very convincing calmness.

Isabel was not at all convinced. As soon as Mr. Stanton's steps had retreated beyond their hearing, she turned to Sophy, her eyes shining. 'Why, Sophy! What a Banbury tale! He came to see *you*, I am sure of it.'

'You are fully as bad as Anne,' Sophy said, with an attempt at severity; but she could not contain her smile. It *would* return, no matter how she tried to suppress it.

Isabel clapped her hands together in genuine delight. 'Now, Mama will have to stop teasing me about him! I will tell her so directly. I only hope Mr. Green may prove as enchanted with Anne, as she is quite wild over him. I fear it is rather improbable, however.'

It was like Isabel to think of everyone else's prospects, and omit her own. 'Come, now,' Sophy said, regaining her seat. 'The likelihood of Mr. Stanton's paying *me* any attentions was highly improbable, too.' She picked up the cooling cup of tea which Mary had provided—pouring the tea for her, even, in the knowledge that Miss Landon would be sure to spill it—and sipped. It was cold, but the apple-tart was delicious; as Isabel declined any, she finished Mr. Stanton's neglected slice as well as her own.

Later that day, Sophy sat alone with one of her father's shirts in her lap, diligently mending the fraying seams, when Thundigle came trotting into the room. He made her a hasty bow, with none of his usual fastidious courtesy, and gasped out: 'Mr. Balligumph wishes to talk to you, Miss Sophy! He says it is important.'

This came as a considerable surprise to Sophy, for Balligumph had never summoned her before. He prided himself on not being a *needy* acquaintance, as he put it, leaving it to Sophy to decide when she wished to visit him.

What could he possibly have to say that was so important? Sophy had no notion at all, but she would not trifle with Balli's concerns. She rose at once, folding her mending neatly and leaving it upon a side-table. 'Thank you,' she said to Thundigle. 'I am much obliged to you for bringing me the message. Do you have any idea at all what Mr. Balligumph wishes to discuss?'

Thundigle looked grave. 'Not very much, but it relates to that Mr. Stanton, and his friend.'

A small feeling of disquiet invaded Sophy's heart, spoiling the sunny mood she had been in ever since Mr. Stanton's visit—ever since the ball, in truth. 'Is there some manner of trouble?'

'I couldn't say, Miss, though Mr. Balligumph was awfully serious.'

Balli, serious? This was unlike him indeed! Sophy's heart began to pound with alarm. 'I will go at once,' she said to Thundigle.

It was the work of mere moments to collect her bonnet and spencer, and then she was out of the door, walking as fast as was seemly on her way to the bridge. Thundigle did not accompany her, and so she had no one to distract her from the unpleasant reflections that passed through her mind as she walked.

Balli was extremely knowledgeable about local business. *Gossip,* one might even say. He extracted many a secret from Tilby's citizens as they passed over his bridge, and he maintained something of a network of observers among the brownie helpers of the town, and other fae. Sophy occasionally consulted him, if there was something she wished to know; but when she had asked him about Mr. Stanton and Mr. Green some days before, he'd had only commonplace information to give. Had he uncovered something new? Thundigle's manner suggested that the news was poor.

She arrived at the bridge somewhat out of breath, her heart beating rapidly from exertion as well as trepidation. 'Balli?' she called.

The moment her foot touched the bridge, he appeared. 'Ye're a good girl, Miss Sophy,' he said at once. 'I knew you'd come.'

The familiar twinkle in his eye was absent, and Sophy's alarm deepened. 'Of course, why should I not? What is it that you have to say to me?'

Balligumph sat down on the bridge—a sight which always worried Sophy a little, for fear that the hefty stone bridge would collapse under the troll's considerable weight—and folded his hands over his stomach. 'What do ye know of them two fine gents as are up at Hyde Place?' he asked. 'Mr. Green, Mr. Stanton? Do ye know much o' them at all?'

'No, no at all. No more than all the neighbourhood knows, that is: that they are of good family; that they have been friends since they were up at Oxford together; that they are both of good fortune—'

'Yes, yes,' Balli interrupted, waving a meaty hand. 'They told me all o' that themselves. But I cannot find out that any of it's the *truth*.'

'What do you mean?'

'I can't find anything to contradict it, precisely, but there's nothing in support of it, neither. No one's heard o' these two, not so much as a whisper. An' there's some mighty strange things about the way they conduct theirselves, too. For instance, did you know there ain't a single brownie in that house?'

Sophy frowned, puzzled. 'No? I am sure I heard otherwise—that they were adopted remarkably quickly, in fact, as soon as the house was opened.'

Balli shook his great head. 'Whatever's in that house, it's not brownies. They just *look* like brownies. Got a glamour on 'em, I'd wager.'

'A glamour!'

'Quite so! I don't know who in that house has a way wi' the fae-magics—whether it be your Mr. Stanton or Mr. Green—but sommat's not right. An' it makes me wonder: what else might be lurkin' under them glamours?'

Sophy's heart instantly absolved Mr. Stanton of guilt in the matter. He seemed too…too *normal*. It was Mr. Green who possessed a certain fey quality: something in his air at times, in his wild red hair and his leaf-green eyes.

'Does it matter?' Sophy asked. 'Say that Mr. Green *does* know some of the fae-magics; is it so very bad?'

Balli eyed her with evident misgiving. 'There's sommat not right in a house wi' no brownies,' he stated bluntly. 'I can't get a straight answer out o' the brownie-folk, neither, as to why they're avoidin' the place. They say only there's no need of 'em there, or suchlike. An' you know what else? Not a single local chap or girl was hired to work at the house. It's like the two of 'em brought their own staff along. Unheard of!'

Sophy's puzzlement only deepened. For sure, it was unusual for a gentleman to use the arts of glamours, or at least to own to it; but it did not imply any particular villainy if they did. Nor did it seem all that terrible for them to staff their own household; it was a shame for the locals to lose the prospect of a job there, for certain, but Sophy could see no other harm in it. 'Is there something in particular that you fear, Mr. Balligumph?' she asked. 'For my part, I can see no great harm in anything that they are doing, or said to be doing.'

Balli sighed gustily. 'Not in so many words, Miss Sophy. Only, I hear as ye're quite the favourite wi' that Mr. Stanton, an' I would be happier to know the household's all right-and-proper in that case.'

'I am much obliged to you for your kind solicitude, and I have no wish to dismiss your concerns. If you hear of anything more specific, I trust you will inform me?'

Balli nodded. 'That I will, Miss.'

Sophy smiled her thanks. 'In the meantime, I shall not be too alarmed. Mr. Stanton is one of the most agreeable gentlemen I was ever in company with, and I cannot believe anything too awful of him.'

'Ye're that impressed?' Balli said, his thick brows disappearing behind the brim of his hat. 'I heard the talk, but I didn't know ye were sweet on him.'

'Sweet on him! Gracious, no. It is far too early to think of such things. But that I find him very *agreeable* I shall not deny.'

Balli's blue eyes twinkled down at her, something of his customary joviality restored. 'I want to like him meself,' he admitted. 'If he can see the merits in my Sophy, he must be all right! I'd only be glad to be assured of it on more impartial grounds.'

'Try not to be too concerned,' Sophy told him. 'I feel perfectly easy about it, myself.'

Balligumph eyed her severely. 'Aye, but bein' none too concerned about things is your way, Miss Sophy—even when ye *ought* to be thinkin' differently.'

It wasn't the first time that Balli had alluded to the difficulties of her situation, and Sophy knew he was right. But she saw no merit in worrying about troubles she had no power to change. If trouble came, *then* she would worry about how to solve it. In the meantime, the only way she knew to get from one day to the next was to fret as little as possible, and take pleasure in the good things she did possess.

'All will be well,' she said to Balligumph. 'I feel it in my heart!'

'That heart o' yours is a mighty powerful piece o' magic, then,' he told her in a laughing tone. 'Ah, well. I'll trust it, 'till I have reason to think otherwise.'

CHAPTER NINE

When Sophy arrived at Tipton Wood, she found Mr. Stanton awaiting her in a little clearing near the centre. He was seated upon a fallen tree, with his hat in his hands and the top two buttons of his waistcoat undone. He had the air of a man who had been waiting for some time, but who minded it not at all; he appeared relaxed and in fine spirits. The smile he directed at her when she approached suggested that the one thing that could improve the day for him had now arrived, and her heart beat a little faster.

He said nothing, however, by way of greeting. He merely moved over a little on the tree, making room for her to sit down. After a momentary hesitation, during which she suffered more than a few feelings of awkwardness, she accepted his unspoken invitation—although she did take care to leave a few clear inches of space between herself and Mr. Stanton.

The next few minutes passed away in a companionable silence. Sophy sat quietly, enjoying the warm sunshine, the flourishing greenery of Tipton Wood and the birdsong drifting down from the canopy overhead. She allowed her eyes to rest on patches of spring flowers, and velvet-green moss, and the gleaming feathers of the birds that sailed merrily by, breathing deeply of the delicious fragrance of the woods in the height of May.

The silence was so comfortable that her awkwardness soon faded, and she began to feel as relaxed as Mr. Stanton looked.

At length he broke the silence by saying: 'Do inform me when your head-ache reaches intolerable proportions, Miss Landon, or I may not be aware when it is time for me to escort you home.'

Sophy smiled. 'I will be sure to do so. It is not yet an insurmountable affliction.'

Another few moments' silence ensued. Sophy's mind wandered back to the topic of her recent conversation with Mr. Balligumph, and the doubts he had raised about Mr. Stanton's household. She had resolved on making some enquiry with him, in order to set Balli's mind—and her own—at rest, but she was reluctant to break the comfortable mood that existed between them. Nor could she think of a subtle way of raising the topic—some manner of approaching the subject that would give her the information she wanted, but without making him feel interrogated.

She began by asking him questions: perfectly ordinary ones about his family, his background, and his pursuits. He seemed equally desirous of learning more about her, and so for some minutes they engaged in an amicable exchange of information. Sophy learned that, like herself, he had no siblings; that both of his parents were gone; that he had grown up in a small village in Nottinghamshire, and he had hopes of soon making a permanent home for himself through the purchase of an estate.

His lack of relatives went some way towards explaining how he and Mr. Green had come to settle at Hyde Place without a lady to do the honours; though it was undeniably peculiar that both Mr. Stanton and his friend should find themselves with no one to call upon. But she gave this barely a moment's thought. He was even poorer in connections than she was herself; and as he talked about this, she detected a degree of loneliness in him that echoed her own. He desired to build a settled home for himself; to rectify his solitary state through the happy additions of a wife and children. These, too, echoed her own secret wishes, and she felt drawn ever closer to him.

But Balli's doubts remained unaddressed, and so she began to turn the conversation towards the topic of domestic arrangements, and the difficulties most households faced in securing suitable help. She led the way with an honest appraisal of her own lack of housekeeping talents, and warmly praised Thundigle's inexhaustible energy in assisting Mary.

This gambit failed, for he was far more interested in her lack of proper help than the subject of household brownies. He asked her a number of questions about Mary, and her father's income, and her own inability to assist. His questions became so particular, and he laughed so heartily at her recounting of her own clumsiness, that she began to feel a little offended; but he instantly noticed the fact, and began to praise her fortitude instead.

This was almost as bad. 'Oh!' she said hastily, 'I deserve no such praise, for really, Thundigle makes everything easy. I am sure you are aware of the very great difference a dedicated brownie or two can make to a household.'

'Oh, well, as to that, I hardly know what to say,' he said, laughing. 'I admit, I have always left such matters up to my housekeeper to arrange; but I daresay my friend would agree with you.'

'Mr. Green?'

'Yes, for he handles everything of that kind at Hyde Place—as far as it is necessary. I am left with nothing at all to do.'

This was not quite the information Sophy was hoping to receive, but it interested her nonetheless. If Mr. Green was primarily responsible for the house they shared, then he was very likely the person responsible for any unusual arrangements within it—as she had suspected before, though without nearly so substantial a reason. She was pleased, for this news would give direction to any enquiries Balli might wish to make—and that direction would be *away* from Mr. Stanton. His careless statement seemed to absolve him of any collusion in Hyde Place's peculiarities.

Sophy did not feel inclined to press him any further, and the conversation lapsed. Mr. Stanton soon broke the renewed silence, however, by turning to her with an expression suddenly intense, and saying: 'Miss Landon! I do wish—that is, if there were some way that I could—if only it were possible to—to assist, somehow, with the difficulties you have just now described! You should not be left with so little assistance—with so many troubles—it is not right.'

Sophy began to feel rather uncomfortable. In recounting her experiences, she had only been seeking a way to draw him out on the subject of his own arrangements; but she now saw that her candour may have appeared to him as a plea for sympathy. His offer was an odd one, given their very new acquaintance, but as a response to her apparent complaints his good wishes did him credit.

Unfortunately for him, they also violated Sophy's sometimes delicate pride. She stiffened, and said in a cool voice: 'I am very ably assisted, I assure you. Please do not suppose that I intended to solicit your aid in any way.'

He held up his hands in a pacifying gesture, his expression of warm solicitude turning to mild alarm. 'Please forgive me: I meant no offence. I am fully convinced of the merits of your Mary, and Thundigle also. I am equally convinced of your own merits in the case, though you did not, perhaps, intend to convey them to me. I only meant to express a general wish that your circumstances might be... a great deal easier than they are at present.'

'Thank you,' Sophy said, relaxing slightly. 'I too wish for that, sometimes.'

'And if there should ever be a way in which I might assist you—'

'Pray, don't,' Sophy interrupted. 'There can be no way in which a gentleman such as yourself, so wholly unrelated to my father or to me, can be of assistance to us.'

She had meant to put a stop to his embarrassing solicitude, but the moment these words left her mouth she regretted them. To him, her statement may appear as a coy way of saying that he must first render himself a close relation before he could seek to assist them, and she would not have him think her encouraging any such notions for the world.

'I feel a head-ache approaching,' she said abruptly, jumping to her feet so fast that she almost toppled herself. 'And my father will be expecting me soon; I must return home at once.'

Mr. Stanton rose likewise, though with considerably more grace, and offered his arm. 'Allow me to escort you home, Miss Landon,' he said softly, and judging from the concern in his eyes, he was quite convinced that her head-ache was not real.

Sophy was not convinced of it, either. She felt tense, and pressure beat behind her eyes. If she did not altogether have a head-ache yet, she would soon.

But why? Having begun so promisingly, the comfort of his company had gone, giving way to a disagreeable awkwardness. That tended to define their relationship, Sophy reflected with an inward sigh, at least on her part: she went from quiet pleasure to awkward self-consciousness in an instant, and it took very little to effect the change.

Perhaps it was merely her awareness that a handsome, agreeable and highly eligible gentleman appeared to be interested in *her*. She still found it impossible to reconcile this fact with her knowledge of herself, her life, and her circumstances, and so she expected at any moment for the flattering signs of interest to disappear. And then she would lose not only the brighter prospects which his particularity began to suggest, but also a friendship: for she had begun to think of him as a friend, though she knew not precisely when.

'I did not mean to appear ungrateful,' she said as they walked. 'I am fully sensible of your kindness, and I do thank you for your friendly concern.'

'It is not the concern of a friend,' he began, and then stopped. 'Not the concern of a friend *only*, I should say.'

This statement seemed to augur something serious, and Sophy was at a loss for a reply. She waited in silence for more; but he seemed paralysed by some inner turmoil, made a few further attempts to speak, cut himself off repeatedly without managing a full sentence, and finally lapsed into silence. They walked back to the parsonage without any further conversation, and Mr. Stanton left her on her doorstep with only a mumbled platitude by way of parting.

He did, however, kiss her hand before he departed.

Sophy watched him go in a tumult of conflicting feelings. What could he mean by such strange behaviour? Did he intend to offer for her, or had he meant something else entirely? In some ways, she fervently hoped he might: for he was, without doubt, the most agreeable man she knew. In other ways, she was equally fervent in hoping that he would not, for their acquaintance was so new—and she herself had so little to offer—that she struggled to understand on what his regard might be based.

A moment later, she progressed from wondering to berating herself for her absurdity. He might never make the offer; if he had been thinking of it half an hour ago, he had apparently changed his mind; and until he did, there was no sense in wondering about whether or not she might accept him. It would be far more reasonable, more practical, and more logical to bend her thoughts in the direction of those prospects which did not rely upon the interest of a man, however slim they might appear.

She made a mental note to visit Mr. Balligumph again very soon. She wanted to relay Mr. Stanton's comments on the subject of his household, and she made a resolution of asking him some more questions about Grenlowe at the same time. Try as she might, she could see little future for herself in England, after the passing of her father; but Grenlowe might offer her an entirely different set of prospects. It was, at the very least, worth the enquiring.

* * *

Aubranael arrived home to find that Grunewald had company.

He was sitting at his ease in the study, smoking something that smelled strangely sweet. In an oversized chair to his left sat Mr. Frederick Winbolt, eldest son of the Winbolt family. His slight frame was half buried in the enormous chair, and Aubranael could only see the top of his blond-curled head. In a rather less comfortable-looking chair to his right sat Mr. Edward Adair, his dark hair immaculately arranged—putting Winbolt's tousled locks rather to shame—and his handsome face fixed in an expression of discontent. All conversation ceased as Aubranael walked in, and three heads turned to regard him.

'Stanton,' Grunewald said lazily. 'Thought you were never coming back.'

'Oh?' said Aubranael, advancing into the room. 'It is not so very late, I thought.'

'But as you went to see Miss Landon, I fully expected to see nothing of you until dinner-time at least.'

To his annoyance, Aubranael felt heat rush into his cheeks. Hastily he walked to the window, putting his back to the room so that they wouldn't see his confusion. He couldn't help wishing that Grunewald had held his tongue about Miss Landon, when they weren't alone.

Predictably, it was Adair who took up the subject. 'Miss Landon,' he repeated in a mocking tone. 'Oh, surely not, Stanton! To be sure, the ball gave every appearance of a *special preference* in that direction, but I could hardly believe it of you!'

Aubranael turned around, just far enough to catch Adair's eye. The young man was flushed with something—it looked like drink, but at this time of the day it was probably just swaggering overconfidence—and he met Aubranael's stony gaze without flinching.

The boy was still piqued on his sister's account, Aubranael decided. But understanding the motive did not make him feel much more inclined to forgive the ill-will that was offered as a result, and he turned back to the window without saying anything at all.

The silence stretched, until Winbolt spoke. 'She is a fine woman,' he offered, with a little too much cheer.

Aubranael appreciated this show of support, but as it resulted in a derisive snort from Adair, he felt that it had somewhat misfired. Not contented with this small show of contempt, Adair went on. 'I have never seen a woman so absolutely without countenance!' he declared. 'And not a penny to her name, either! I must say, you do have the most extraordinary taste.'

'Steady on, Adair!' said Mr. Winbolt.

'I suppose you mean to offer for her,' continued Adair, and laughed. 'Prefer an easy target, do you? Don't like to have to compete for a lady's favour? You've chosen well.'

Aubranael clenched his teeth together so tightly that his jaw hurt. Only by such uncomfortable means could he keep back the retort Adair so richly deserved, but which would debase him to deliver. Another awkward silence followed—Grunewald apparently preferring to stay out of the ruckus he had started—before Winbolt once again broke it.

'*Do* you mean to offer for her?' he asked.

'I have no thoughts of such at present,' Aubranael replied.

'Shame,' Winbolt said mildly. 'It would be a very good thing if you did.'

That, Aubranael thought, deserved his full attention. He turned around, ignoring Adair, to regard the open, friendly countenance of Frederick Winbolt.

He was a few years older than Adair, Aubranael judged, though his smooth-skinned face looked youthful. His blue eyes held a pleasant expression and his manner was artless and cheerful. Of all the connections he and Grunewald had made since their arrival in Tilby, Frederick's company was the most congenial.

'Why do you say that?' Aubranael asked.

'Oh! Well, she is a charming woman, you know, and a very good sort. But her circumstances... ah... well, she deserves more than she's got, that's all.'

'Would she thank me, do you think,' said Aubranael with a slight smile, 'if I offered for her purely to improve her prospects?'

'Heavens, no! Not what I meant,' said Frederick easily. 'But if you did happen to like her—and for my part, I can't see that it is so very unlikely—why, she would make you a fine wife.'

Here Adair thought it appropriate to interject with another vulgar snort, which Aubranael and Frederick both ignored.

'Why didn't you offer for her then, Winbolt?' said Mr. Adair.

Aubranael was confused by this sally, until he remembered that Mr. Winbolt had recently engaged himself to an acquaintance from Derbyshire. A fairly wealthy acquaintance, if the rumours were to be believed.

'Oh, well—as to that—' Frederick began, but Adair cut him off with a wave of his hand.

'You had more sense than to offer for a plain, penniless woman, no matter how "charming" her character,' he said. 'I understand you completely. I only thought Stanton would follow your example, but I suppose he is without sense after all.'

Aubranael tilted his head, regarding Mr. Edward Adair without expression. All the anger he had felt moments earlier had dissipated, for the boy made himself so ridiculous, it was not worth the effort of despising him. 'I ought to thank you,' he said with a faint smile, 'for making up my mind. You too, Winbolt. I had not thought of making Miss Landon an offer, but now I quite see the merits of the idea.'

Frederick looked pleased and gratified at the same time, as though Aubranael's beginning to think of Miss Landon on such terms was entirely in compliment to his opinion. Adair merely looked incredulous.

'An excellent plan,' said Grunewald, choosing to involve himself in the conversation at last. 'There may be a few difficulties in the way, but I am sure they will not signify.'

There were, indeed, difficulties in the way of this otherwise wonderful plan. The fact that he had no home to take her to, for example, and no means to purchase one; the fact that his identity was fabricated, and everything Sophy knew of him in this world was a lie; the fact that his real face would soon be restored to him, and though she had not seemed to object to it when he stood in the character of a friend, he could hardly imagine that she would ever accept him in the character of a lover.

A few small difficulties, indeed.

In spite of this, Aubranael felt energised and strangely elated. He had spoken at first out of a desire to put Adair in his proper place; but as the words left his mouth, he realised that meant them. The prospect of securing Miss Landon's company to himself forever—of winning her love, not just her friendship—transformed all his ideas about his own future. His existence of lonely isolation would be over forever, and so would hers; he would ensure that she was never lonely, never slighted, never overlooked again.

Winbolt was right: she deserved better, and one way or another, he would find a way to provide it.

He thought back to the precious hour or two he had spent in Miss Landon's company that morning; how easily they had talked together, how comfortable even the silences had been. As a pattern for his future life, he could hardly conceive of anything more perfect.

But how to bring it about? The obstacles Grunewald had hinted at were considerable; insurmountable, at first glance. But there had to be a way out of his difficulties, and he swore to himself to employ every means he could think of to overcome them.

All of this passed through his mind over the course of two or three minutes; minutes that he spent staring sightlessly at a spot on the study wall and looking, he was sure, like a half-wit. He returned from his reverie to find three faces staring at him in silence: one wearing a pleased expression, another looking perfectly disgusted, and the third looking lazily cynical.

He smiled upon them all and said: 'Would you excuse me?' Offering a careless half-bow by way of parting, he strode quickly from the room without a backward glance. He needed some considerable time by himself, he judged, in order to get all of his thinking done.

CHAPTER TEN

'Tell me about Grenlowe.'

Sophy sat beside Mr. Balligumph on the edge of the old stone bridge, her legs folded beneath the fabric of her gown, her bonnet lying discarded upon the stone slabs beside her. The mid-day sun shone warm upon her smiling face, and the fresh breeze seemed to take all her cares sailing away with it.

The troll had taken off his hat, too, though he chose to cradle it in his lap. He sat near to Sophy, idly stroking the crown as he spoke. 'Grenlowe, is it?' he said, with a toothily smug smile. 'I take it ye're pleased wi' the place, to be askin' me that.'

'One should not form judgements too quickly, I know,' replied Sophy, 'but I could not help myself. Grenlowe was charming.'

Balli's smug smile vanished and he turned serious. 'Aye, well, I won't deny I had hopes ye'd like it. But ye must not get too carried away wi' such notions, Miss Sophy. T'ain't all charming, to be sure.'

'That is certainly the truth! For I was awfully pulled about in the market-square; I have never seen anything so busy. And almost knocked off my feet entirely, by such a *careless* gentleman! But I hardly minded it at all.'

Balligumph chuckled heartily, nodding his great head. 'Oh, it's a busy place. The Grenlowe market is famous, did ye know? Folks journey from all over Aylfenhame to spend an hour or two browsin' the wares.'

'Truly? But Grenlowe seems such a small place. Barely larger than a village, I thought.'

Balli winked at her. 'It's a mite bigger'n ye'd think, Miss.'

The consciousness of having walked from one side of Grenlowe to the other with Aubranael, and in less than an hour, puzzled Sophy immensely. 'But how? What I mean is, where do they keep the rest of it?'

'Down below, above ground, an' in hidden ways and corners.'

'Enchantments! Very well. I will take your word for it, for I hardly know when I shall ever be able to return.'

'Do ye wish to return?'

Sophy thought of the market, the ribbons, the food, the trees, the meadows, the strange purple cat and Aubranael. 'Yes!' she said. 'I should like it above all things.'

'Yes? An' what will ye do there?'

'I should like to explore a great deal more, as I have evidently missed a great deal. I should like to buy one of those very beautiful ribbons from the market. And...' here she hesitated a moment, 'There is someone I would very much like to see again.'

Balli tilted his great dead downwards in a listening gesture, but some strange reticence discouraged Sophy from elaborating. Instead she said: 'Do you suppose—that is, I was thinking—if I wanted to be part of the market, how would I go about it?'

Balli blinked down at her in palpable confusion. 'Part o' the market? I can't understand you.'

Sophy hesitated. 'Well... I know it is hardly proper to think of selling things—awfully vulgar, some would say—but in my position—and it is Aylfenhame, you know, where the rules are *quite* different—'

'Ye wish to sell at the market?' Balli interrupted. 'Is that what ye're saying?'

Sophy felt a faint blush crawl into her cheeks. 'I... why, yes, I suppose I am. Is it so very awful?'

A huge grin wreathed Balli's round face and he chuckled. 'Very awful indeed, if ye were to consult those whose opinions ain't worth havin'. For my part, I think it a grand idea. Only, what are ye minded to sell?'

'There was something I noticed in particular about the people I saw in Grenlowe,' Sophy said, smiling in relief. 'They do love their finery! Much as Thundigle does.'

Balli nodded vigorously. 'Finery an' garments and sundry! Very well. 'Tis a fine plan.'

'Only, I have no notion at all how to go about it. It would require materials, of course, and no doubt there would be other difficulties.'

'Oh, plenty. But that don't mean it's hopeless, by any stretch. Ye'd be leavin' England altogether, though; is that the plan?'

Sophy sighed, feeling a momentary pang of regret as she looked out over the green fields of Lincolnshire that stretched away before her. 'It is not that I am unhappy here,' she said, 'only I can see so little place for myself, in the future.'

'Ye're not minded to take that fancy fellow ye danced with at the ball, then? Even wi' all his money and fancy suits?'

Sophy laughed at this picture of Mr. Stanton, though a note of disquiet sounded within her mind. 'Is that the talk? No, I am not at all minded to throw myself at a fortune! Besides, he would have to ask me first, and I am very sure he never will.'

'That ain't what I heard.'

The disquiet grew. 'Oh, dear. Is there a great deal of gossip? That is very embarrassing.'

'Embarrassin', ye call it, t' have yer name linked with so fine a gentleman?'

'Awfully! We are barely acquainted, after all.'

Balli sat in scowling silence. For all his levity, he was still suspicious of Mr. Stanton and Mr. Green; but his efforts to find out more about the two gentlemen had, so far, failed. To Sophy's mind, this merely indicated a lack of buried secrets to uncover, but Balli remained unconvinced.

'Of the two plans,' said the troll after a while, 'I like yours the best.'

Sophy supposed he meant the market over the marriage. 'I like it much better, too,' she smiled. 'But I fear I will find it even more difficult to achieve.'

'Yer friends will be pleased to help, Miss Sophy, never fear.'

Sophy smiled up into his dear face and uttered her sincerest thanks. Balli's eyes, however, were fixed on something behind her, and he did not meet her gaze. 'Now,' he muttered, 'What's Mary in a flap about?'

'Mary?' Sophy repeated in surprise, and turned to look. There indeed was Mary, coming towards them at a dead run, her hand clutching the cap that threatened to fly off her head, her face red with exertion. Sophy watched her approach with growing dread. What in the world could have sent her patient, long-suffering servant running after her like this?

When Mary reached them, she was at first too out of breath to speak. She stood with her fine, greying hair flying in the wind and her chest heaving with the effort of drawing in as much air as possible. But her eyes spoke eloquently, the expression in them one of alarm and extreme dismay, and no hint of a smile leavened her wrinkled face.

'Oh, Miss Sophy,' she gasped after a minute or two, 'I'm that glad I've found you! You must come at once!'

Sophy felt the beginnings of a fine panic flare to life within her. In a voice of forced calmness she said: 'What is it, Mary? What has happened?'

'It's your father,' Mary panted. 'Thundigle has gone for the doctor, but he has been gone above half an hour and no help's come! I thought, if only Miss Sophy was here, she'd know what to do, right enough.'

Sophy had jumped to her feet at the beginning of this speech. Now she briskly tied her bonnet back into place, ignoring the shaking in her fingers. 'You were right to come and find me, Mary; thank you.' She took only a few moments to bid goodbye to a patently worried Balligumph, and then she set off. She began at a brisk walk, but the fluttering concern in her belly blossomed into full-blown panic and she broke into a run.

Late that afternoon, Sophy sat on the threadbare sofa in the parlour that was no longer hers. She was in such a state of exhaustion, she could barely think.

The last few hours had been, without contest, the worst of her life. She and Mary had arrived at the parsonage to find that Thundigle had returned with Doctor Howard—but too late. Her father had already gone.

When she had left the parsonage that morning, she had done so in a state of good cheer, her mind full of ideas and better hopes than she had enjoyed in some time.

She returned to it to find herself bereft of all familial connections and without a home, for her father's living had been secured to another long before. In effect, the living passed into the hands of her father's successor on the very moment of his death; and that included the parsonage.

The comfort of her father's presence had been meagre, certainly; he had often vexed her, and habitually neglected her, and his passing did not leave her as heartbroken as she felt she ought to be. But still, she was not without compassion for him: he had been eating himself into the grave, she supposed, from the moment of her mother's death, and his sudden, complete absence still affected her deeply.

That it had occurred so suddenly was a source of extreme concern to her. She had only just begun to think about the wider plans for her future that her visit to Grenlowe had encouraged; she had as yet had little time to give the matter any serious consideration, or to begin to make the necessary arrangements. Her future stretched ahead of her in her mind's eye, empty of solid prospects and empty of companionship. It would not be long, she supposed, before the new parson of Tilby would arrive to claim the living and the house, and she would have to ensure she had removed herself and her life from the premises before that occurred. But where would she go? To whom could she turn for help? She felt lonely and frightened and helpless, and was for the present so overpowered with it that she could only sit, and stare out of the window.

The news would travel across the town in a matter of hours, she knew. Already they would be talking about her over their evening meals, and sitting in their parlours afterwards; they would talk of her lack of relations, her lack of husband, her lack of money, tutting and shaking their heads over her father's conduct, and reflecting on how she must, inevitably, sink forever beneath good society. And in a very few days, the subject would be over—hurried off, in favour of the next shocking piece of news. Sophy and her plight would be consigned to history, and what became of her would interest no one at all.

Such dark thoughts were unproductive, but her exhaustion was so complete that she knew not how to shake herself free of them. She felt that she had been deluding herself for years; hiding from the truths she did not wish to think about, setting them aside in favour of finding some little enjoyment, some small piece of comfort in her life; setting herself up, in short, for the terrible predicament in which she now found herself.

But it had not been in her power to do very much more than she had. She could, perhaps, have followed the well-meant advice of such persons as Mrs. Ellerby, and Anne, and even Isabel, and tried harder to *catch* a husband. But such a course of action had always struck her as so very repellent—so absurd in *her* in particular, to throw herself at eligible men in the hopes that she might *take*. Even if she had been able to see into her future, and been forewarned about the terrible situation she now found herself in, she could not have acted differently.

Sophy became aware of soft footsteps approaching, and looked up to find Isabel stepping quietly into the room. She was carrying a tray set out with tea-time fare, and a steaming pot of tea.

'Dear Sophy,' she said, with a sympathetic smile. 'I do not know if you can find it possible to eat? Poor Mary is quite overset, so I have sent her to lie down and made up a few things for you myself. Please, do, try to eat a little. Mamma has left you some of her very best tea, in the hopes you might be persuaded to try it. She swears it is quite fortifying.'

Sophy managed a tremulous smile, ashamed of the tears that sprang to her eyes at Isabel's words. Cold meat and tarts and tea! As if such things could help her now! A towering ingratitude took hold of her heart—an irritation, even, with such ineffectual assistance, no matter how well-meaning might be the givers—and she had to swallow the retort that rose to her lips. To be impatient, angry, *waspish* even, was not her way, and she would allow the impulse to overpower her now.

'Thank you,' she said softly. Isabel's concern was real, no matter the form it took, and she managed to find a little gratitude in her heart that *someone* cared for her fate. 'Perhaps I can eat, a very little.' She felt sick through-and-through, from mind to heart to stomach, and the prospect of food revolted her. But to neglect her meals altogether would only weaken her further—perhaps even turn her into one of those wretched *fainting misses* in novels, whose lack of fortitude had always irritated her profoundly. So she took the food and nibbled at it as Isabel watched with all the anxious concern of a mother overseeing a sick child.

'Mother wished you to know...' began Isabel, and then hesitated. 'If there is ever anything that we can do to assist you, you need only ask.'

Sophy fully understood the reason for Isabel's hesitation. She knew very well—as did her mother and father—that she was beyond the mere commonplace kind of help that they could offer. This kind of assistance had been offered to her many times already over the course of the afternoon, and she was exhausted with the effort of thanking people for words that were uttered mostly as a matter of form. They knew she was beyond their help, and that they would not be expected to carry their promises through into actual assistance; as such, the words came cheaply and were easily given.

Wearily, Sophy thanked Isabel anyway.

Isabel seemed on the point of speech once more, changed her mind and closed her lips, and then shook her head. After this little display of indecision, she finally said: 'Charles has... expressed a great deal of concern for you, Sophy. He has stayed away, he said, because he feels sure you must be overrun with visitors at present, but he will be sure to call on you very soon.'

Sophy began to laugh, a mildly hysterical, empty piece of mirth born of exhaustion and despair. 'Charles! My dear Isabel, he is *certainly* not going to relieve me of my troubles. You must put that idea out of your head. No gentleman is going to ride to my rescue! I am perfectly reconciled to it!'

Isabel opened her mouth to speak, and Sophy held up a hand. '*Don't*, I pray, mention Mr. Stanton's name to me! I am sick of hearing it! *He* will have no inclination to rescue me either, I have no doubts at all on that score; and even if he were—or dear Charles, or anyone—I am not at all minded to accept. To do so out of desperation, because I have no choice! I cannot conceive of anything more humiliating! No, I will find my own way out of my troubles.'

Isabel subsided, and sat in silence while Sophy ate through the repast she had provided. The silence continued as Sophy sat motionless, her head aching, her eyes sore from weeping, her heart empty of all hope. The sun continued to shine outside, which seemed an insult to Sophy's tired mind: the beautiful, golden sunshine that had blessed the happiness of the morning, now shone down with equal vigour upon the despair of the evening.

'Isabel,' she said abruptly.

'Yes?'

'Would you be willing to stay here tonight?'

Poor Isabel seemed energised at the prospect of some service she could perform for Sophy, and answered almost rapturously: 'Of course I will stay! I am so glad you asked, for I was not at all looking forward to leaving you here alone.'

Sophy's loneliness eased, just a little, at the prospect of having company for the night. She had never before spent a night alone at the parsonage, and she did not feel equal to it today of all days. 'Thank you,' she said with real gratitude, and pressed Isabel's hand. 'I will feel better in the morning, I am sure. A night's sleep will restore me to my usual self, and leave this cursed wretchedness behind.'

CHAPTER ELEVEN

There's a sorry state to be in, an' no mistake. Miss Sophy was in a deal o' trouble, poor lass, but she's no fine lady as wilts at the drop of a hat.

As if to illustrate this point, Balligumph drops his fine hat into the dust of the road—and then hastily scrambles to pick it up again. He winks broadly, and with a throaty chuckle, continues:

Ye may be thinkin' this is all gettin' a mite complicated-like. People pretendin' to be someone else entirely, an' poor Sophy not knowin' who she's talkin' to—nor me neither! Ye'd be right, but I warn ye: that's nothin'. Here's where everythin' really gets complicated.

I had another visit from Miss Sophy, an' she was all rarin' to put her plans into action. Didn't have the first idea o' where to start, mind, but that never stopped her!

Three days after the death of Mr. Landon, Sophy made her way once more to Balligumph's bridge. She was in a calmer state of mind, though still troubled and sorrowful. Wearing borrowed mourning-clothes, and with a black ribbon hastily applied to her summer bonnet, she knew she made a sorry sight in Tilby.

This concerned her little, however, for her goal was now to leave Tilby as soon as she could possibly arrange to do so.

'There's my favourite lady,' said Balligumph when she arrived at the bridge. Every feature of his great round face spoke of sympathy and compassion, and his voice was full of warm affection. It was enough to bring a lump into Sophy's throat.

'Good morning!' she said in a cheery tone. 'Dear Mr. Balligumph, it is always such a pleasure to see you.'

He looked kindly upon her for that statement, and winked. 'Aye, that I know! I'm thinkin' this is no social call, however; ye've that purposeful look in yer eyes.'

Sophy smiled ruefully. 'How disappointing to be so transparent! You are perfectly right, however. I am come with a request.'

Balligumph leaned closer to her, tilting his great head in a listening gesture.

'It is about Aylfenhame,' Sophy said, feeling curiously nervous as she said it. 'I meant what I said before. My prospects are limited in every direction: I must make my own living, I fear, but I have few means to do so. Sewing must be my rescue; but to take up that profession *here!* It would be insupportable.'

'Now, it may not be so very bad! Why should you say so?'

Sophy sat down upon the bridge, taking care not to dirty or tear her borrowed skirts. She leaned against Balligumph for comfort as she spoke. 'To make one's living with the needle is not a respected profession in England; that you must know! And to sink so far beneath society—to do so *here,* where I have always lived, always been known—it would be an endless source of misery to me. And I hardly know how I would contrive to support myself. But in Grenlowe! Their regard for finery seemed to me to be so *very* considerable, I have some hopes of better prospects there.'

'An' ye liked Grenlowe, that I recall,' said Balli, nodding thoughtfully. 'It ain't a simple matter, that's the truth, but it may be managed. Let me think a moment.'

He sat in thought for some minutes. Sophy felt no impatience; she was too tired for that. She closed her eyes, enjoying the feeling of warmth on her face and the fresh breeze against her skin, until Balli spoke again. 'I think I may know someone who can help,' he said, a statement which set Sophy's heart leaping. 'I can't promise, mind! But if ye wish to pursue it—'

'I do, I do!' Sophy interrupted eagerly.

He chuckled, and patted her head. 'Aye, very well. I can send ye back to Aylfenhame—though it won't be so easy nor so pleasant as the last time—an' a guide will take ye to the friend I have in my mind. Ye must put the case to her, and I can't promise she will help, but she may, if she likes ye. An' if ye mention my name, that might not be an awfully bad idea neither.'

A relieved, joyous smile came to Sophy's face—the first real, unfeigned one in days—and she thanked Balligumph with all the most fervent language at her disposal. He actually seemed embarrassed, and waved her gratitude away with a few muttered syllables as the blue skin over his cheeks darkened a shade or two. 'No promises, remember that!' he said. 'I wouldn't like ye to be too disappointed, if it weren't to come off.'

Sophy agreed to it; she would have agreed to anything, if it furthered her aim.

'Do ye wish to go right away?' Balli asked.

Sophy considered this. She was tempted to say yes, to leave at once; the sooner she secured some future to herself that she could welcome—that she could even tolerate—the sooner her troubled mind would be at peace. But there remained some matters that required her attention. She could not in conscience simply abandon Mary and Thundigle without notice, not even for a few days.

She relayed this to the troll, and he nodded wisely. 'Well, now,' he said when she'd finished. 'Given our last conversation, I had a thought that you might be needin' this.' He fetched a little glass sphere from a pocket—the same as the one he had given her before—and offered it to her. 'So I put my hands on another. Here, take it. Ye may use it whenever ye feel ready.'

Sophy took it, with more profuse thanks which Balli waved away. She tucked the little sphere into her reticule, and drew the string tightly to secure the precious object inside.

'I will find a way to repay you, someday,' she said to Balligumph.

He found that amusing, or perhaps he was merely delighted; an enormous grin split his face and he gave a great, rumbling laugh. 'Ye're a good woman,' he pronounced, administering another heavy pat on the head. 'Ye'll be all right.'

Sophy fervently hoped so. The flutter in the pit of her stomach suggested otherwise, but she was growing used to ignoring it.

* * *

Aubranael stood in the library at Hyde Place, pacing about among the bookshelves and pausing at intervals to stare moodily out of the large windows. Their house was situated on the edge of the Lincolnshire Wolds, and the library windows afforded a pleasant view of fields and hedgerows and, in the distance, rolling green hills.

He saw none of it; not even when the sun came out from behind a smattering of clouds and cast a golden glow over the countryside. He was too absorbed by his own concerns, and the problems he faced.

Mr. Landon's death had come as no surprise to anybody but him, he had discovered. The neighbourhood was more inclined to feel surprised that it had taken so long. The good reverend's health had been in decline for years, and while people's opinions as to the cause differed—some spoke romantically of heartbreak following the long-ago death of his wife, others spoke more disparagingly of selfishness and gluttony—all agreed that his time had come, fair and square.

Few seemed concerned about the fate of his daughter. Most talked very comfortably about her imminent fall from society, and speculated about the probable character and appearance of the new reverend in the same breath. Even those who expressed concern for her could think of no way to help her.

To his chagrin and anger, he found that there was no longer any expectation that he, Mr. Stanton, would seek to claim her as his wife. Now that she was penniless in fact rather than merely in prospect—and homeless into the bargain—it was generally agreed that he would give up all thought of her. Did they think him so shallow, or were they merely projecting their own feelings onto him?

He had paid her a visit as soon as he had heard the news. She had been subdued, exhausted, and in pain, and despite her attempts at composure he had detected more than a hint of fear behind her eyes. It angered almost as much as it frustrated him; she should not have been left in this situation! Her pain had hurt him far worse than any misfortune of his own; shocked at how deeply he felt, he had wanted to hold her until she was smiling once again.

He could do no such thing, of course, so he had merely hovered, exchanging awkward pleasantries with Miss Landon until he judged that it was time to withdraw. The meeting had taken barely fifteen minutes, and he had gone away with so many things unsaid...

If he could, he would have settled the matter once and for all, there and then. But there remained the problem of the mess in which he had embroiled himself. He could hardly ask her to marry him in the character of Mr. Stanton, when she had no idea who she was truly engaging herself to, and he had no home to take her to, nor the means to acquire one. And so, as the days passed, the neighbourhood took his inactivity as confirmation of their expectations. Edward Adair had even had the effrontery to congratulate him on his escape! On his having, as the revolting boy put it, "come to his senses"! It was intolerable.

But he had only himself to blame. What had possessed him to begin this ridiculous masquerade? Where had he expected it to end? The truth was, he hadn't thought that far. Seduced by the prospect of beauty, he had succumbed to the temptation with the greatest of ease. At the beginning, it had all seemed so easy; by the time his month was up, he and Miss Landon would of course be on such good terms that she would accept the truth about him with equanimity.

Almost four weeks had passed, and he had only a few days left before Hidenory's enchantment expired. It no longer seemed so easy, and he could only curse the appalling naivety—and insecurity, and fear—that had got him into this mess. He was stuck, and he could see no solution that would end in the way he wished.

'Aha!' came a cry from behind him. 'Got you!'

He turned to find Grunewald standing in the doorway, holding a household brownie by the ear. It took Aubranael a few moments to shake off his preoccupied daze and fully register the scene before him. When he did, he frowned. Grunewald appeared to be searching the creature.

'What are you doing?'

Grunewald flashed a brief glance at him, his leaf-green eyes shining with anger. 'It seems we have a visitor,' he said lightly. 'Though uninvited visitors are usually given less courteous names, are they not? Intruder, perhaps? Or *spy*?'

The brownie stared up at Grunewald with calm passivity. She was dressed as most of her kind, in ragged clothes stained with dirt and dust; her hair was a mass of flyaway brown curls, and the expression in her dark brown eyes was gentle. She showed no signs of fear or alarm at Grunewald's treatment, however, merely staring up at him with flawless calm.

'I don't understand,' Aubranael said. 'Is not this one of your people?'

'Why, no,' Grunewald said. 'This one is a *real* brownie.' He finished his search, apparently finding nothing interesting or incriminating about the person of his "visitor", and frowned down at her. He was a great deal taller than she and wearing such a fierce expression that Aubranael felt quite sorry for her.

'Certainly I am a real brownie,' she said, calmly smoothing herself down.

'And why are you here?' Grunewald demanded. 'I thought I established that this house was not to be infiltrated.'

It was a curious choice of word, Aubranael thought. *Infiltrated*, as if a brownie helper might be expected to have some ulterior motive in moving into the house.

The brownie smiled gently up at Grunewald. 'I am here to help.'

Grunewald smiled nastily back. 'As I am sure you have had ample opportunity to observe, I am in need of no help.'

'Indeed, sire, for your entourage is considerable.'

Aubranael blinked. There was that word again: *sire.* He'd thought he had heard it before, at Grunewald's house in Nottinghamshire, but he could have been mistaken. This time, he was sure he had not misheard.

Grunewald was scowling in annoyance. 'My name is Mr. Green,' he said shortly.

The brownie merely nodded and said, 'Of course, sire.'

Grunewald sighed and released her. He muttered something under his breath, of which Aubranael could just catch the words *interfering trolls*.

'You may tell Mr. Balligumph that his surmise is quite correct, that we are all awfully impressed by his cleverness, and that he will certainly be the first person I will ask should I be requiring information at any time in the future,' Grunewald said severely. 'You may also inform him that he is *not* welcome to send his spies and snitches into my household and that any further incursions will be greeted with the *utmost* severity.'

The brownie smiled gently at him again, and bowed. 'My name is Pharagora,' she said politely. 'In case you were interested.'

'I was not.'

She bowed again. 'Very good. I will take your message to Mr. Balligumph.' She walked calmly past Grunewald—her head barely reaching his knee—and disappeared.

Grunewald smiled sunnily at Aubranael. 'Now that that's cleared up,' he said, and turned to leave.

'A moment,' Aubranael said. 'What was that about?'

'Nosy, self-appointed bridge guardians prying into our business,' Grunewald replied. 'In other words, nothing at all of any import.'

'Oh? But you were quite angry with her.'

Grunewald's green eyes glittered dangerously. 'I dislike spies.'

Aubranael smiled faintly at him. 'You have many secrets, sire.'

Grunewald pointed one long finger at him and said, 'Do *not* call me that.'

'Why not? If that is what you are.' Aubranael spoke calmly, but the revelation that his suspicions might be correct—that Grunewald was the Goblin King—rattled him somewhat. He had heard all manner of strange stories about the king of the goblins. That he was famously eccentric was patently true, and not terribly alarming; but he had also heard tales of a poor temper, a tendency to tire quickly of other people, and occasional forays into shocking violence when he was thwarted.

Grunewald smiled a slow, not very pleasant smile. 'Whatever I am,' he said coolly, 'you will find me a much more congenial companion if you do *not* attempt to pry into my secrets.'

'That is evidently true,' Aubranael said with a smile, and a slight inclination of the head.

Grunewald sighed, and further disordered his wild red hair by running a hand through it. 'Complications,' he muttered. 'I suppose it is better than boredom.'

With that slightly mystifying comment, he disappeared into the corridor. But a moment later he was back. 'Aubranael?' he said.

'Yes?'

'Will you please, for the love of my sanity, make a decision? And then *act upon it?*'

Aubranael opened his mouth to reply, but Grunewald had gone. He sighed, and ran a hand through his own hair.

Grunewald had thought only of his own secrets when he had caught Pharagora, but Aubranael spared a thought for his own. Mr. Balligumph was, he knew, friendly with Miss Landon. Had Pharagora discovered anything about Mr. Stanton's real identity? Was that news even now on its way to the troll? If so, he knew it would not be long before Sophy was informed of it.

A flutter of panic shot through him, turning his knees to water. He was not a worldly gentleman, and he could at times be astonishingly naive; but even *he* knew that if Miss Landon was informed of his true identity by anybody but himself, she might not react well to the revelation at all. All thoughts of the mystery of Grunewald's true identity fled from his mind, in the wake of the realisation that he had run out of time. He had no way of confirming how much Pharagora had discovered, but she only needed to have heard Grunewald call him by his real name, and that was by no means impossible.

He glanced at the handsome library clock, and learned that the hour was already past four. He would have time to see Miss Landon this afternoon, if he hurried; and he had better hurry. The time for indecision was past; he would have to do as Hidenory had insisted, and tell Miss Landon the truth. Whether or not she would forgive his deception remained to be seen—his heart thumped uncomfortably at the prospect that she might not—but if she *did*, then he would do his utmost to win her over entirely.

Given the desperation of her circumstances, perhaps she would be grateful for his timely appearance, and not be too hard upon him.

Perhaps.

* * *

Ye may be able t'imagine my feelin's when Pharagora came back wi' the news. The Goblin King! In my town, messin' about wi' Miss Sophy! An' that Mr. Stanton bein' somebody else entirely! I don't like to leave the bridge unattended, as a rule, but what could I do? Miss Sophy had t' know! Off I went wi' barely a second thought. I caused a bit of a stir rampagin' through Tilby, but it ain't like anybody'd dare to stop me, now is it?

Aubranael was in too much of a hurry to walk—or even to wait for the carriage to be prepared. He called for his horse to be saddled with the *utmost* urgency, and within ten minutes he was astride and on his way to the parsonage.

It was an anxious ride. He barely noticed the beauty of the golden sunlight filtering through the leaves of the roadside trees, or the sweet, cooling breeze that swept over the fields; his mind was too busy with the problem of how to tell Miss Landon that he had lied. The short journey stretched interminably, and he could have sworn he had covered three times the distance before he finally came within sight of Miss Landon's home; but he had no better idea of how to confess than when he had started.

He pulled up his horse just outside the parsonage, jumped down and hastily secured the bridle to the house's gate-posts. All the while his eyes searched the house for any signs of Miss Landon. What would he do if she was away from home? He would have to sit and wait for her to return.

He all but ran up to the front door, and, seizing the brass knocker in a hand that shook, he hammered it against the solid wooden door several times. When no one answered after a few seconds, he hammered again; and he was just about to begin for the third time when the door swung open. On the other side stood a shortish, stoutish woman of middle years with untidy, grey-brown hair. She wore the plain, practical clothing of a servant, along with an expression of alarm on her lined face.

'Mary!' he gasped. 'Is Miss Landon at home?'

Mary shook her head, and his heart sank. 'She went out more'n an hour ago,' Mary said.

'When will she be back?'

'Oh,' said Mary cautiously, eyeing him with some suspicion. 'Reckoned she'd be gone a while, so she said.'

Aubranael blinked. A while? What did that mean? A few hours— or days? He asked, but Mary merely shrugged. If she knew the answer at all, she was not inclined to tell *him*.

'Is something amiss?' Mary asked.

He sighed, leaning his shaking hand against the doorframe. 'Somewhat,' he said bitterly. 'It is most important that I see her. I need to speak to her on an urgent matter.'

Mary softened slightly, her suspicious manner relaxing. 'I cannot invite you in, not with the mistress gone,' she said apologetically.

'Certainly I would not presume to intrude,' he said hastily. 'Perhaps I might leave her a note, or something of the like?'

'I suppose you could,' Mary said doubtfully. She began to look flustered—Aubranael guessed she was trying to think of where to find paper and pen, and coming up blank—but before she could resolve her dilemma, Aubranael heard a great shout from behind him and the sounds of rapidly approaching feet.

Whoever owned those feet was rather large, he judged. Was he imagining it, or did the entire street shake with every pounding step?

He turned around, and beheld Balligumph.

He had already met the bridge guardian, of course, on his arrival in Tilby. He had also *heard* of Mr. Balligumph; he was a minor legend in Aylfenhame.

Neither this previous meeting, nor any tale he had heard, could have prepared him for the sight that now met his eyes. The troll was in a high temper—a burning rage, Aubranael would have said—and given his height and considerable bulk, this was no trifling matter. The troll approached the parsonage at a dead run, his eyes blazing fury and fixed upon Aubranael.

Aubranael swallowed.

'Hi!' yelled the troll, as soon as he was close enough to be heard. 'Hi! If it isn't the so-called *Mr. Stanton!*'

If Aubranael had been entertaining any hopes that Mr. Balligumph had yet to hear from Pharagora, those hopes instantly evaporated. He stood a little straighter, took a deep breath to quell the fresh surge of panic in his gut, and straightened his shoulders.

'I am called that, sometimes,' he said calmly.

Balligumph kept on coming. For a moment Aubranael suffered a paralysing certainty that the troll meant to crash straight *through* him and into the parsonage, perhaps taking poor Mary with him along the way. Instead, he came to a thundering halt a mere few feet away from Aubranael, and stood glaring down at him, his huge chest heaving with exertion.

'And?' the troll demanded. 'What have ye to say for yerself?'

'On which topic?' Aubranael replied.

Balligumph's great blue eyes blazed anew, and he actually spluttered with indignation. 'On—on the topic o' Miss Landon, and yer *friend*,' he bellowed. 'What have the two o' ye been gettin' up to wi' Miss Sophy?!'

'Nothing at all, I assure you,' said Aubranael.

'Ha!' roared the troll. 'I like that! "Nothin' at all", says he, as cool as can be! But it will not do. There's more to *ye* than meets the eye, that's fer certain; and do ye deny that yer friend *Mr. Green* is a great deal more than he's pretendin'?'

Aubranael held up his hands in a pacifying gesture. 'I deny nothing,' he said in a low voice. 'But I never meant any harm to Miss Landon—nor did Grunewald. You must believe me.'

Balligumph glared down at him. 'I don't *have* t' believe anythin' ye've got t' say.'

'I know, but it is the truth! If you will give me a moment to speak, I will explain.'

The troll shook his enormous head and actually stamped one of his enormous feet, sending a tremor through the ground. Aubranael winced and hastily backed away, expecting a blow to fall upon him at any moment.

Before he could collect his scattered wits and find some way to defend himself, however, Mary waded into the fray. 'See here!' she shouted at Balligumph. '*I'll* tell you what won't do! It won't do to run about terrorising the townfolk, just because you're bigger'n everyone else!' She actually shook a fist at the troll—a pitiful gesture, given the huge discrepancy in size between the two of them—but the fervour in her voice apparently made some impression, for Balligumph looked taken aback. 'That's better,' Mary said firmly. She adopted an aggressive, no-nonsense stance: feet planted wide apart, hands upon her hips, and glared up at the troll. 'It's disrespectful to Miss Sophy, carryin' on like this on her own doorstep! You ought to be ashamed.'

To Aubranael's mild disbelief, Balligumph actually did look ashamed. He backed off a step or two, then took off his hat and held it in his two hands in an unquestionably remorseful gesture. 'Sorry, Mary,' he said contritely. 'Ye're right at that. I meant no harm.'

Mary nodded crisply and relaxed her battle stance. 'Very good,' she said. 'Carry on.'

She returned into the house, though she continued to hover near the door—probably to keep an eye on Balligumph, Aubranael supposed. Relief mixed with anxiety and more than a little panic weakened his knees, and with a deep sigh he sat down upon the parsonage step.

Balligumph stared down at him, all the wind taken out of his sails. Perhaps Aubranael's obvious dejection softened him a little further, for he said kindly enough: 'Ah well, lad, ye cannot blame me fer bein' concerned, can ye? What is it that ye're doin' in these parts? Tell me everythin' that ye can.'

So Aubranael began at the very beginning, from the day that Miss Landon had entered his life in Grenlowe, and spared no detail. The tale took some time, but he resisted the temptation to hurry and skip over things. Balligumph's obvious concern for Miss Landon seemed to warrant a thorough and honest narration (quite apart from his terrific size), and besides, he had nothing else to do but wait for Sophy to return.

Balligumph was kind enough to refrain from interrupting. He said nothing at all until Aubranael had finally finished, after which he spent a few minutes in silent reflection.

'Well then,' he said at last. 'The next thing t' ask is: where's Miss Sophy got to?'

Aubranael shrugged his shoulders hopelessly. 'If you have no idea, I am sure I do not.'

Balligumph directed an enquiring glance at Mary, but she had no more information to give.

'I'm afraid she's gone through, then,' said the troll.

'Gone through?' repeated Aubranael. 'To where? You mean Aylfenhame?'

'Aye. She came to me a day or two ago, wantin' the means to return. I gave it her, naturally!' He eyed Aubranael suspiciously and said: 'She spoke o' havin' met someone in Grenlowe. I got the distinct impression she was off in hopes o' seein' him again. I suppose she meant *you*.'

'Did she?' Aubranael said, his pulse quickening. She had liked him well enough to go in search of him again? This was news, and very welcome news at that; but she would not find him in Aylfenhame, of course, and he still had a few days left before Hidenory's enchantment wore off.

Curse it all! What had *possessed* him to engage in this absurd masquerade? If he had only had the patience to wait, Miss Landon would have come to him!

'I had better go after her,' he said, jumping resolutely to his feet.

'Had ye?' Balligumph said. 'How do ye plan to find her?'

Aubranael blinked up at him. 'I… well, if she is looking for me, perhaps she will return to the places we visited together before?'

'That she may,' the troll conceded. 'An' when she doesn't find ye there, what then? Will she stand about an' wait for ye, day after day? No, not Miss Sophy! She has other business there.'

'What other business?'

Balligumph launched into a tale of his own, regarding Sophy's stitchery and her hopes for a shop in Grenlowe. A shop! In Grenlowe! She actually intended to settle in Aylfenhame, for good! This news electrified Aubranael, flooding him with a mixture of unlooked-for hope and renewed remorse and self-recrimination. The more he learned about Miss Landon, the more his masquerade seemed wrong-headed and ill-advised.

No matter. It was too late to regret what he had done: he had to focus on how to set matters to rights.

'Then I *must* go after her,' he declared when Balligumph had finished talking. 'She will need help, perhaps, and guidance.'

'I have arranged fer both,' said the troll bluntly.

'It cannot hurt for her to have *more* help and guidance,' Aubranael said stubbornly. 'Especially if she is looking for me!'

'Aye, an' so I'll ask ye again: how are ye goin' to find her?'

Aubranael opened his mouth, and closed it again, stumped. Balligumph had a point, damn him! 'But I cannot simply sit here and await her return!' he protested. 'Who knows how long she might be?'

'Not all that long, I reckon,' Balligumph said confidently. 'She has business still to finish in Tilby.'

Aubranael pondered the question of simply *waiting* for Sophy's return. He was sorely tempted to ignore Balligumph's advice and charge after her; but the situation was complicated enough. Miss Landon had gone in search of Aubranael, never knowing that she had left him behind in the person of Mr. Stanton; if he followed her and failed to find her, she would return to Tilby only to find that Mr. Stanton had also left. They could go on forever, narrowly missing each other, and the task of revealing his duplicity would fall to someone else—Balligumph, or Pharagora, or even Mary—and she would probably never forgive him.

As much as it tried his patience, he had to trust that she would soon return, and wait for her in Tilby.

'I will wait,' he said heavily. 'Though it is hard.'

Balligumph clapped him on the shoulder, knocking all the wind clean out of him. ''Tis the wisest course,' he nodded. 'Ye can keep me company at the bridge, an' tell me all about yerself and yer plans to marry my Sophy.'

Aubranael was relieved to note a gleam of approval in the troll's eyes as he said this, though there was an edge to his voice that suggested Aubranael still had some talking to do.

Very well, so be it. If he could win over Miss Landon's self-appointed guardian, perhaps the troll would be able to help him in winning over Miss Landon herself.

It gave him something to do for the next two days, anyway.

CHAPTER TWELVE

Sophy's second journey through to Aylfenhame was considerably less pleasant than the first.

Previously, the crossing-over had been as simple as walking. A mere few steps had carried her over the invisible threshold between the worlds, and a mere touch of the gates had returned her to England.

The process was no more complicated, the second time; she had dropped the crystal Balli had given her, it had turned into a will-o-the-wyke and she had followed along, with none of the doubts that had assailed her before.

She had not been expecting pain, or the sensation of being *squeezed,* as though she was attempting to fit herself between two very solid gateposts placed a bare few inches apart. When she had emerged, panting and shocked, on the other side, she expected to find her clothing in shreds and her skin in ribbons. To her surprise and relief, however, she was intact; the sensations had *felt* physical, but perhaps they were not.

Now she understood Balli's previous insistence that she travel on Beltane. There were days when the barriers between Aylfenhame and Sophy's world disappeared, she concluded, and travellers did well to time their visits accordingly.

She wondered when the next such day would be.

She had dropped the crystal sphere directly outside of her house, this time, so she emerged into Aylfenhame in a different place, too. For a moment, she stood confused, taking in the rows of jumbled, mismatched cottages without recognising anything. But, there: a shop sign announcing a cobbler's establishment caught her eye. The sign depicted a pair of glittering shoes, one clear and apparently made of glass, the other deep black as if wrought from obsidian. She recognised that sign. And there was the funny, twisted tree with purple bark and silver leaves; she had passed it with Aubranael.

She was in Grenlowe, then, some distance from where she had first stepped through—and some distance from the place where she had met Aubranael, too. But that was all right.

Having established her whereabouts, she was keen to get started; but how? Where would she go? Balligumph had promised her a guide, but the streets were largely empty, and those who did pass by seemed in a great hurry and did not stop. She waited for a little while, watching as a succession of gnomes, hobs, trows, dryads, goblins, brownies, Ayliri and even an occasional ogre stepped briskly past. Where was Balligumph's promised guardian?

The wind blew, a mighty gust that carried with it the scent of flowers and the distant sounds of bells. It also brought a quantity of dust, some of which settled in Sophy's eye. She devoted herself to removing it, with many a flutter of her eyelids and a great deal of moisture seeping from her eye. When at last her sight was restored to her, she noticed a newcomer.

Before her sat an enormous, purple-furred cat. She recognised it at once as Aubranael's mischievous companion, and, delighted, she stepped forward with a joyous greeting on her lips.

'Felebre, I believe?' she said with a sunny smile. But the cat did not react, and her certainty faltered. It *looked* exactly like Aubranael's companion, but what did that signify? If there was one purple cat in Aylfenhame, of course there were probably more.

'Is it not Felebre? I am sorry,' she said. 'Even if you are Felebre, you may not remember me. I spent precious little time with Mr. Aubranael, after all.'

The cat stared at her with unblinking eyes.

It occurred to her that this may be Balli's promised guide, whether or not it was the same cat she had met before. 'Are you a friend of Mr. Balligumph's?' she asked. 'He did promise me a guide and helper, and perhaps you are it.'

Still the cat did not react, but nor did it leave. It sat, staring at her with wide golden eyes, and Sophy began to feel unnerved.

'Very well; my mistake on both counts,' she said. 'I am sorry to have bothered you.' She made the cat a curtsey—feeling just a little silly as she did so—and made to leave.

But as soon as she showed signs of wanting to wander off, the cat's manner changed completely. It—she?—got in Sophy's way, blocking her departure. To Sophy's surprise, the cat bumped her head against Sophy's waist and rubbed her ears over her gown. The gesture seemed friendly—affectionate, even—and Sophy was instantly charmed.

'Well, then!' she laughed. 'Perhaps you are Felebre after all. I hope you will not mind if I address you by that name, at least until I am given a different one.'

The cat made no objection.

'Very well, and are you here to assist me?' Sophy enquired.

Felebre gave a great purr and, with one more affectionate bump against Sophy's hip, she turned and began to walk away. She looked back at Sophy, twitched her tail meaningfully and took another few steps.

Sophy understood. 'I am coming,' she said, and followed. She was unsure precisely who had sent Felebre—if anyone had—but it seemed very likely that this was Balli's promised help; or if not, perhaps the cat would take her to Aubranael! Privately hoping for the latter more than the former, Sophy followed along as Felebre wove her way through the streets of Grenlowe and out of the north gate.

After walking for an hour or more, she began to feel a little concerned. Felebre had led her through meadows and woods, over bridges and across streams, and at quite a brisk pace; where could she possibly be going? The town of Grenlowe had been left far behind, and Sophy had seen no sign at all of any other settlements. For a while she enjoyed the tour, for Aylfenhame had many beauties to offer: the streams were covered with lily-pads and water-blossoms, the meadows strewn with fragrant grasses and vividly-coloured flowers; the woods were dense with ash and rowan and oak trees, and many more she did not recognise, their varicoloured bark and leaves a delight to the eye.

But as time wore on she began to feel tired, and wondered with rather more urgency where Felebre was bent on taking her. She tried to enquire a few times, but Felebre made no attempt to answer.

At last she stopped, panting for breath, and sat down upon the trunk of a fallen tree. Felebre went on for a few moments; then, realising that Sophy had stopped, she came stalking back, her fur rising along the back of her spine and her tail lashing angrily.

'I know,' Sophy panted. 'I am sorry, but I must rest for a moment.'

Felebre continued to bristle and lash her tail for a while, then—with an almost audible sigh—she curled up at Sophy's feet, tucked her nose beneath her tail and went to sleep.

'Lovely idea,' Sophy muttered. She was hungry and thirsty as well as tired, but she could see no way to remedy these complaints. Not that she should, perhaps, even given the opportunity: Thundigle's warning about food sounded in her mind, loud and alarming, and she tried to persuade herself that she was not in urgent need of water and sustenance. But, she realised, that warning had been given some time ago, when she had been only a visitor; if she planned to settle in Aylfenhame, it need not apply, perhaps?

This realisation cheered her, and she looked around herself in case a handy crop of fruit or a clear stream might conveniently present themselves. They did not, however; it was too early in the year, yet, for fallen fruits, and no amount of wishing could conjure up a steam of water.

'I hope we are not going very much further,' she said to Felebre. 'Not that I am not grateful for your kind assistance, but I am *quite* tired and rather in need of refreshment.'

The cat slept on.

Suddenly and incongruously, a shriek of laughter reached Sophy's ears. It sounded far away, but another, much nearer laugh followed immediately afterwards. Sophy stood up and turned about in circles until she saw the source: a large table set among the trees some way off, its surface covered in a neat white table-cloth and crowded with tea-things. Chairs were crammed up and down the length of the table, or at least as much of it as Sophy could see, for only one end was visible. The chairs were all occupied, but she had not time to observe who the picnic guests were, for a gust of wind sent the trees into a brief paroxysm, blocking her view. When the wind calmed once more, the table had vanished.

Felebre remained inflexibly asleep, and Sophy sat beside her for some time, pondering what she had seen—or thought she had seen. The whole scene had faded away like a dream upon waking, and she was by no means certain that she had not imagined it. Perhaps hunger and thirst had unbalanced her mind a little.

At length she sighed, and stood up. 'Very well, let us carry on. The sooner we arrive, the sooner I may rest properly.'

Felebre uncoiled herself, stood up, and stretched luxuriously, curling her back and her tail. Then she padded off, without even the briefest of glances at Sophy.

They walked for another two hours. Sophy managed to quench her thirst, but her hunger remained, eating away at her insides and sapping her strength. When at last Felebre stopped, she felt ready to drop with weariness.

The day had waned, the hour now early in the evening, Sophy judged. The sun hung low and heavy on the horizon, casting a rich golden light over the deep, tree-studded valley Felebre had taken her to. She saw nothing to suggest that her journey was over; no sign of a house, let alone a village or a town.

'Where are we?' she said to Felebre.

The cat said nothing.

'Are you sure this is the right place?' Sophy turned in a few anxious circles, taking in tree after purple-barked tree, shining leaves of silver and gold and shades of green, a luscious carpet of grass and nothing whatsoever to suggest the presence of another living soul.

What had she been doing, following this strange golden-eyed cat? Just because she had seen Aubranael keeping company with the same creature, or a similar one! She deserved her predicament. These reflections did not help her to decide what to do, however, so she banished them, straightened her shoulders and began to think more productively.

Before she had got very far with this, however, a voice split the air. 'Who is at the door!' said the voice merrily. It sounded like a woman.

Sophy cleared her dry throat. 'Um, I... Miss Sophia Landon,' she answered. 'And Felebre.'

'Excellent!' sang the voice. 'Come in!'

To Sophy's surprise, a door opened in the centre of an enormous tree, or what she had taken to be a tree. Light shone from within, and Sophy was glad enough to step inside.

The room beyond was far too large to fit into the trunk of any tree. It was a sumptuous room, luxuriously decorated and furnished, dripping in silver and jewels. The air smelt of herbs and spices and fruit, and she could hear the rippling notes of a harp.

The music stopped abruptly, and someone—the owner of the

merry voice, presumably—stepped into the room. Given the beauty of her voice, her music and her home, she was not what Sophy had expected to see. She was an elderly woman, dressed in shrouding layers of homespun fabric in drab colours. Her skin was a map of wrinkles, her hair a mess of rough, tangled grey-and-white strands. Only one of her rheumy eyes focused on Sophy; the other looked off in a different direction, rolling sometimes in its socket. The woman even had warts on her face, three that Sophy could see.

Flustered, Sophy tried to hide her surprise behind a polite curtsey. 'I am sorry to intrude upon you like this,' she said, keeping her eyes fixed on the floor. 'Felebre has brought me to you; I hope I was not mistaken in coming.'

'Ohhh,' said the crone. 'No, not at all mistaken. Miss Landon! You are very welcome. I will give you tea.'

'Thank you,' said Sophy. The woman's courtesy made her still more ashamed of her reaction, and she forced herself to meet her hostess's gaze.

'And something to eat,' said the crone. 'You are famished, I should imagine!'

'Thank you,' Sophy said again. 'I am indeed. We walked for some hours.'

The woman nodded and patted Felebre's sleek head approvingly. Then she raised her beautiful voice and called: 'Pharagora!'

A small door opened in the wall and a brownie appeared, her ragged skirts dragging on the floor and her brown hair flying out in a hundred directions. 'Madam?' said the brownie.

'Tea, please, and refreshments! The usual.'

The brownie nodded and began to bustle about. Within minutes a little tea-party was spread upon a low table, and Sophy sat down to take tea with her new friend.

'I am called Hidenory,' said the crone, catching Sophy's inquisitive gaze. 'You were not expecting to meet me, I think?'

'No. That is, I knew that Mr. Balligumph had arranged for some kind of assistance, but he did not say who I should expect.'

'Ah yes! Mr. Balligumph. He speaks very highly of you.' Hidenory sipped daintily at her tea, her good eye fixed on Sophy's face. 'Perhaps you will tell me what you are looking for?'

So Sophy recounted her problems and her hopes. Hidenory listened avidly, interrupting with an occasional question. How had her prospects in England become so limited? Was there no other way to resolve her difficulties? No gentleman in the question?

Blushing, Sophy shook her head "no" to the last question. Mr. Stanton flitted through her thoughts—his height, his athletic build, his handsome face and his kindness—but she pushed the image away. She would *not* fall into the trap of relying on a proposal of marriage to solve all of her problems—and then, when none came, of falling into hysterics or into despair and having no notion what to do with herself. Mr. Stanton and his intentions—if he had any—were entirely irrelevant.

Hidenory appeared to realise that she was not telling the whole truth, for she gave Sophy a long, considering look and smiled a sly smile. 'Oh, very good! I applaud your resolve. Why should we rely on men, hmm? I enjoy your plan much more.'

Sophy hesitated, suspecting mockery, but Hidenory's expression was pleasant and apparently sincere. 'Can you help me?' Sophy said. 'Perhaps you may know somebody already in the business—someone who may need an assistant? I only need somewhere to *begin*, you see, and I will see to the rest myself.'

Hidenory nodded wisely. 'Quite, yes. Oh, I have the very thing for you.'

She lapsed into silence, no longer looking at Sophy. Her reverie seemed to be a thoughtful one, and Sophy did not wish to interrupt, so she turned her attention to the food. It was excellent, of course, beyond anything she had ever taken at home; fruits so rich and full of juice she could scarcely believe they were real, tarts bursting with flavour and colour, and tea heady with a rich, spiced fragrance that was almost intoxicating. So busy was she in sampling and enjoying that, for a time, she forgot about Hidenory and her deliberations. By the time she had finished, the light outside had faded, night had fallen and Pharagora began to light twinkling lamps to lift the gloom.

When Sophy looked up, she received a shock. The chair opposite to her was still taken—she would have sworn that Hidenory had not moved from it for an instant—but it was no longer Hidenory sitting there. The woman sitting opposite to her was younger—*much* younger. She was of Sophy's age, or thereabouts; her grey-white, tangled hair had been replaced by shining golden locks; her eyes were no longer rheumy, and both were fixed on Sophy's face, gleaming with amusement. Her features were perfect, her skin was perfect, her clothes were perfect. She sat with perfect grace, sipping from her cup with the same dainty manner as before, only now it suited her.

Sophy blinked, and stared. 'I…' she began. She looked around for Hidenory, the crone, but saw no one else in the room—not even Pharagora. 'I don't understand,' she said. 'Hidenory?'

The beautiful woman smiled delightedly, and nodded. 'It is still Hidenory,' she said, and laughed. 'I promise.'

'But how…? Why?'

'Why indeed?' said Hidenory, and her face darkened with momentary anger. 'That is a long tale.'

Sophy considered that for a moment. 'Which is the real you?' she asked.

Hidenory cast her a sharp look. 'A very good question,' she murmured. 'Both, and at the same time, neither.'

Sophy frowned. 'Are you… a witch?'

Hidenory smiled wickedly. 'One of the best, my dear. What do you think of my handiwork?'

'But then… why would you…?' What Sophy wanted to ask was *why* someone with the powers of glamour would suffer the indignities of the crone's shape, when she could be as beautiful as she desired. But the question was appallingly rude, and in spite of her extreme curiosity she could not bring herself to say it out loud.

She did not have to. Hidenory's face darkened with anger again, and she set down her tea cup with such a clatter that it broke. 'Curses,' she said. At first Sophy thought she was referring to the broken cup, but she repeated the word much more fiercely and Sophy realised she was talking about herself. 'Curses! I am an expert in the art of Glamour, Miss Landon, but *some* arts remain beyond my ability. I made a mistake, long ago now, and a curse was my reward.'

A curse. Sophy's thoughts turned to the stories Mary had told her when she was a child, tales of Aylfenhame and the folk who lived there, and the strange things they did. She distantly remembered something along these lines: the Korrigan's Curse, it was called. The Korrigans were young and beautiful by night, but haggish by day.

'Can you not…?' Sophy enquired. With a vague gesture of her hand, she sought to illustrate her question: could Hidenory not hide her crone's form behind a glamour?

'Do you think I would hesitate, if that were within my power?' said Hidenory, with great indignation. 'No! That comfort is denied me. No power of mine can alter my shape during the daylight hours.'

Sophy felt desperately uncomfortable. Her own troubles seemed inconsequential beside Hidenory's, and she pitied the woman terribly; but there was nothing she could do, and little she could say.

'Is there a cure?' she said at last.

Hidenory smiled slowly. 'Oh, all curses have conditions. It is a peculiarity of the art: if one wishes to do one's very *worst*, one is obliged to provide a way out. It does not have to be an achievable way out, however.'

'Is yours not achievable?'

Hidenory stared hard at Sophy, her eyes tracking every detail of her face, her hair, her body, her clothes. 'I thought not,' she said slowly. 'But I begin to believe otherwise.'

Sophy waited uncomfortably.

'It has to be a *man*,' Hidenory said with great disgust. 'A man! And he must love me in both my forms, night and day. Then I will be restored to myself.' She smirked, her expression one of bitter mockery. 'But I ask you,' she said in a conspiratorial tone, 'you know men as well as I do, I am sure. Can you imagine the sort of man who could love the hag that I am by day? The very thought! That is the clever thing about curses: one must provide a means of escape, but if the caster can think of something *utterly impossible,* the curse can remain in place forever.'

Sophy sat mute. She longed to be able to reassure Hidenory somehow, but she could not. Had she not been overlooked and unwanted all of her life, she with her youth and her health and her strength? Her features may not be *very* pleasingly arranged, but her skin was smooth, her hair only unruly, not decaying. Her figure was not perfect, or even near it, but she was a vision beside Hidenory-the-hag. If even *she* had not attracted a single proposal of marriage, what hope had Hidenory?

All of a sudden, her qualms about her own appearance seemed absurd. What right had she to repine, because she had not been born a beauty?

But Hidenory's expression had turned speculative, and there was a light in her eyes that began to disturb Sophy. 'I have been thinking,' she said confidingly. 'Perhaps it is not so impossible. What kind of man could love a hag like me? Why, a damaged one. A man whose own appearance is little better than mine. A man who is lonely, and desperate for companionship. Where would I find such a being, thought I? Such a creature does not exist in Aylfenhame.'

'But Felebre has given me the answer,' she smiled. 'Felebre, and you, Miss Landon.'

Sophy's thoughts rushed to Aubranael, an Ayliri with a ruined face. She had seen the loneliness in him; it had spoken to her own, drawing them rapidly together. Or so she had thought. But weeks had passed since her afternoon with him, and she had heard nothing of him. He had known where she lived; he could have found her, if he had wanted to.

The prospect of his curing Hidenory, however, left her feeling strange. She did not begrudge the poor woman her chance at a cure; how could she? On the contrary, her own feelings of inadequacy and loneliness left her feeling deeply sorry for the beleaguered witch, and eager to help if she could. But Aubranael? She did not begrudge him the companionship either, if he could love Hidenory. So why did the idea leave her feeling so wretched?

'There is a name that leaps to mind,' Hidenory said, watching her knowingly. 'But, unfortunately, he has become distracted. He has gone elsewhere for his bride. A trifling inconvenience.' She stood up, the conversation apparently over, leaving Sophy to feel confused. *Was* she talking about Aubranael? If so, where had he gone for his bride? Who had he chosen? Her spirits sank even lower at the idea, and she toyed restlessly with her frayed cuffs as she fought to get her emotions under control.

'Enough of that,' said Hidenory merrily. 'Let us return to the problem of Miss Landon and her difficulties. You will want to be on your way, I imagine, as soon as may be?'

Sophy pulled herself together, lifted her chin, and nodded. 'I am grateful for any assistance you can provide, of course.'

'I know just the thing,' Hidenory said with a dazzling smile. She pointed to a door in the far wall—a door which, Sophy would have sworn, had not been there before—and at her gesture, it swung slowly open. It was too dark outside for Sophy to see what lay beyond it.

'Now then, the one you want is Tut-Gut. He will be very willing to put you to work. Step that way, and when you are quite through the door, call his name. He will soon find you.'

Sophy turned to thank Hidenory, but the words died on her lips.

Hidenory had changed again, and it took Sophy a horrified instant to realise what was so wrong with her new image.

Sophy stared, taking in Hidenory's tumbling blonde hair, messily tucked under a faded straw bonnet; her skin slightly browned from the sun, and dusted with freckles; the laugh lines around her wide mouth; the nose that was the wrong shape for her long face. Hidenory was wearing an old, much-repaired cotton print gown and a green spencer, in good condition except for the fraying cuffs. Scuffed and worn half-boots clad her feet, and a lovingly hand-stitched reticule dangled from her left wrist.

Sophy was looking at *herself.*

'What?' she gasped. 'Why would you...?'

Hidenory looked down at herself critically. 'I can *hardly* imagine,' she said frankly, 'but for some reason, our friend has taken a liking to you. If this is what pleases him, who am I to argue?'

Sophy stood speechless as her brain fought to interpret Hidenory's words and actions. 'You mean *Aubranael?*' she said at last.

Hidenory's smile grew a little bit wider.

'But he—I do not see how—we hardly—I mean, we met only once! Why should you imagine he is enamoured with me?'

Hidenory shook her head. 'It will come to you in time, my dear.'

'But then you intend to—to *trick* him!' Sophy said with great indignation.

'Only a little bit,' Hidenory smiled. 'And why not? He likes this shape, and I am *very* eager to please.'

Sophy opened her mouth to object, but Hidenory interrupted her. 'Do not think to object!' she said sternly. 'A chance was offered you, and you have passed it up. It is now *my* turn.' She smiled once more, much more kindly, and added: 'I will make him happy, fear not. Now, off you go.'

Sophy did *not* intend to go! She had a great deal more to say to Hidenory, and besides that a strong inclination to abandon her errand and find a way to warn Aubranael. But Hidenory smiled kindly at her and delivered a swift, sharp, shocking push to Sophy's shoulders. Never very graceful on her feet, Sophy's balance was instantly overset, and she stumbled in the direction of the door. A second push sent her sailing through it.

She landed on her hands and knees in wet grass, panting. Before she could gather herself and turn, the door swung shut behind her and she was alone.

Pulling herself slowly to her feet, she stood for a moment, shaking with shock and confusion and breathing deeply of the crisp night air. Once she had gathered herself, she conducted a thorough search for the door; but she was not surprised to find that it had vanished. A tree stood in its place; it was to all appearances a real tree, with no manner of door in its wide trunk at all.

The moon was full and high in the sky, but she was standing beneath a number of very tall, very leafy trees, and little of the silvery moonlight reached the forest floor. It took her a few minutes to realise that something was wrong with her hands: they did not seem quite as she expected. Holding them close to her face, she was shocked to discover that they had, apparently, aged at least fifty years in the course of a few minutes. They were lined and spotted and shrivelled with age, and as soon as she noticed this she realised that they continued to shake, perhaps not with shock but with a kind of palsy.

A series of other realisations quickly followed, each one equally mortifying. Her cotton-print gown had vanished, in favour of the drab homespun garments that Hidenory had worn in her crone form. Her bonnet was gone, her head crowned only with a bird's nest of thin, brittle hair. Putting her hands to her face, she felt skin soft and sagging with age, and adorned in several places with warts of princely size.

Hidenory had turned her into a crone.

It was of little comfort to her to realise that the shape she wore was merely external; she did not *feel* old. She was not afflicted with the aches and pains of the elderly, nor did she feel weak or frail. She felt the same as always; only she knew that she *looked* utterly different—and utterly repellent.

Vain it was now to wish for her old body back; hopeless to realise how much beauty she had possessed before. She stared in horror at her twisted, shrivelled hands and, to her shame, a tear crept down her cheek.

What was she to do now? How long would Hidenory's glamour last? Perhaps forever! Perhaps it would never wear off, never be withdrawn. How could she continue with her plans, in this wretched shape? Who in Aylfenhame would want to go anywhere near her?

And how could she warn Aubranael? Even if she could find

him—and without Felebre's help that seemed impossible—he would have no idea who she was. Her tale sounded ridiculous; how could she convince him of her identity, or of Hidenory's plan?

Even worse, what if he did not *wish* to be warned? He might welcome Hidenory's plans for him. He would have the companionship he had wanted—even if it was won through somewhat questionable means—and why would anyone pay any attention to Sophy?

But no, this was not right. Hidenory was wearing Sophy's image: she would win Aubranael's attention by impersonating her. Aubranael may well believe he had met the real Sophy Landon again; why would he doubt? But he should not be duped so! Briefly she wondered why Hidenory would want to be loved in such a way— taken for someone else, loved under false pretences. But she was desperate, of course: she would grasp at *anything* if it held the possibility of an escape from the Korrigan's Curse.

She could not leave Aubranael to fall victim to it, however. She suspected that Hidenory deserved better; she *knew* that Aubranael did.

She had to find him, somehow. But how? She was alone, lost somewhere in Aylfenhame, with no idea where she was and no idea where to go or how to get home. And Aubranael could be anywhere.

Taking a long, deep breath, Sophy stilled the wobbling in her lower lip by biting down upon it—quite hard indeed. Feeling thus strengthened, she began to walk. First she would find a way out of this forest; *then* she could consider the problem of where to go next.

CHAPTER THIRTEEN

I did not send Felebre to Sophy! Ye'll have guessed that much, I imagine. Funny bein', that cat. I reckon there's more there than meets the eye, but try as I might, I cannot find out what.

No matter. 'Twas a full day before I knew that the guide I sent hadn't found my Sophy, and by then... well, a single day can make a lot o' difference, can it not?

Two days after Miss Landon's departure for Grenlowe, a note arrived in the morning's post.

Mr. Stanton,
I will be attending the Alford Assembly on the evening of the 8th of June. May I hope to see you there?
Miss Sophy Landon

The 8th of June was today—and today was his last day as Mr. Stanton. Thank goodness! He was being given a chance; one last chance to set things right and make everything well with Sophy.

But when he showed the note to Grunewald, his friend conspicuously failed to share his elation. The Goblin King (if that was what he was—he had yet to either confirm or deny it to Aubranael) held the note with the tips of two fingers, as though it was dirty, and curled his lip at it.

'What is it?' Aubranael asked anxiously. This was not the reaction he had expected, at all.

Grunewald looked at him as if he was stupid, and said: 'Miss Landon sent this?'

'I—well—apparently?'

Grunewald's eyes narrowed, and then he smiled a smile of pure, malicious glee. It made Aubranael nervous.

'Is that... bad?' Aubranael faltered.

'Bad?' Grunewald said, blinking at him incredulously. 'My dear boy, have you learned nothing?'

Aubranael could only blink back at him, mystified.

Grunewald beamed. 'It is the rules, my dear fellow. A lady and a gentleman may not correspond unless they are married, closely related or engaged to each other. That goes doubly if neither party is married to someone else.'

Aubranael thought that through.

'Are you engaged to Miss Landon?' Grunewald prompted.

'I... no.'

'Indeed. In which case, Miss Landon knowingly breaks all the conventions of polite society in sending this note to you. In doing so, she runs a great risk; for if it became known that she had sent you a note, her reputation would be considerably tarnished. It is a serious matter for single young ladies, and Miss Landon's situation is already delicate.' He grinned widely again and added, 'I never would have thought it of her.'

Clearly he intended this reflection as a compliment, but Aubranael could hardly view it as such.

'Perhaps that is why...' he began weakly.

Grunewald raised a brow.

'Perhaps she is pushed to desperate measures by... because circumstances...'

'That will not do as a defence,' Grunewald said with a malicious twinkle in his eyes. 'You are suggesting to me that she is desperate enough to go "on the catch", as I believe the charming phrase goes, and risk everything in order to 'land' a rich husband. In this instance, you.'

Aubranael frowned. This did not sound like Miss Landon at all. But that the note came from her, he did not doubt; who else would have sent it, and signed it with Sophy's name? He could only shrug helplessly, and put the matter from his mind. The more important problem was that he had only a few hours to prepare for the Assembly, since the journey there would take up the rest of the afternoon.

He spent a great deal of time at his looking-glass; it took more than an hour for him to realise that his borrowed good looks would shortly be withdrawn, and therefore what was the use of attempting to please Miss Landon this way? He would only be giving her an example of what she would not, henceforth, be enjoying. A spasm of dread twisted his stomach; he was *not* looking forward to going back to being Aubranael. It had not taken him long to get used to being sought-after instead of avoided. He could relinquish the extreme popularity of a Mr. Stanton, he thought; much of it was based on purely superficial considerations, and he had little value for that. But the universal acceptance he enjoyed was a different matter. He could go anywhere without being ashamed of himself, knowing that the people he met would be pleased to meet him—or at least, that they would not be horrified and uncomfortable as soon as they saw his face.

With a deep sigh, he abandoned his looking-glass and left his dressing-room behind. He ought not to indulge such reflections. Instead he should focus on Miss Landon: hers was the only opinion that really mattered. If she would only accept him as he was, everyone else may treat him as badly as they desired and it would not matter at all.

Grunewald let him take the carriage without a word of complaint or censure. His eyes, though, gleamed with something like contempt as he watched Aubranael settle himself inside, dressed in the very best of his clothes and wearing his nerves like a cloak.

'Enjoy yourself,' Grunewald said drily as the coach began to move.

Aubranael made no reply. Enjoying himself was probably out of the question, as his friend well knew. All he was concerned about was acquitting himself without embarrassment, pleasing Miss Landon, and surviving the evening without catastrophe.

But the promise of catastrophe seemed to hang in the air over the carriage, following him all the way to Alford. When he got out of the carriage before the Assembly Rooms, it settled about his shoulders, weighing him down and dampening all his best efforts at good cheer. He went inside with leaden steps and a heavy heart, suddenly gripped with a paralysing fear that Miss Landon had not sent the note at all and she was not here.

But she was. She was waiting near the door—just as he himself had done a few weeks ago, on the occasion of the Adairs' private ball—and she stepped forward to meet him. Her face was alight with pleasure, her face lit with the sunny smile he loved so much, and his heart eased a little.

'Miss Landon,' he murmured, making his very best bow. 'I am so pleased to see you safely returned from your journey.'

She curtseyed, and smiled on him some more. 'How very kind of you!' she declared. 'Perhaps it was naughty of me to go off unattended like that. I ought to take a gentleman with me, next time.'

She smiled at him archly as she spoke, and the implications of her little speech were clear even to *him*. She held his gaze too long, and his cheeks flushed with warmth. What was she doing? He felt out of his depth.

Clearing his throat, he managed to say: 'May I claim the next dance?' with tolerable composure. She acquiesced gracefully, and they had only a few minutes of conversation—arch on her side, awkward on his—before the dancing began. He led her into the set with relief; at least for the next half-hour or so he could focus on getting the steps right and not on the strange verbal fencing-match that appeared to be going on with Miss Landon.

But he was soon relieved of this comforting expectation. It wasn't only her manner that was different; so was her dancing. She came closer to him than was strictly considered proper; she stroked his fingers when he took her hand; she looked up at him from beneath coyly lowered lashes, held his gaze for long, long moments, and blushed frequently. Nothing could be more unlike the gracious, dignified warmth of her earlier behaviour.

'You are different, Miss Landon,' he ventured to say after quarter of an hour.

'Oh?' she said with a pleased smile. 'In what way am I different?'

Aubranael stared at her, at a loss to know what to say. How could he describe her behaviour? He did not know the words—and besides, it could not be considered gentlemanly to throw her unseemly manner in her face in such a fashion. So he stuttered something incoherent, and she laughed. Was he imagining the glint of cruel enjoyment in her eye?

'You know what people say of Aylfenhame,' she said lightly. 'It *changes* you.'

Had it changed her? She had been gone only two days. Remarkably fast work, if so. But did he disapprove of the changes? Grunewald's reaction to her note had given him a bad feeling, and if the stares and whispers at the Assembly were anything to go by, the good folk of Alford did not approve of Miss Landon's behaviour either.

But what did it really mean? Naïve as he undoubtedly was, even he recognised that it signalled a very definite interest on her part. Previously, he had been left in considerable doubt as to the nature and strength of Miss Landon's feelings towards him; she was always friendly and obliging, always seemed at least a little bit pleased to see him, but she had never given him anything that he could call *encouragement*.

Now every word, every movement seemed designed to do just that. She was encouraging him with all her might, and no one could mistake it.

A flutter of pleasure ran through him at the thought. She liked him! Liked him a very great deal, in fact, and she wanted him to know it! He might venture to guess that her business in Grenlowe had not worked out as she had hoped; but since she had not confided her business to him herself, he felt he was not in a position to enquire after it.

He suffered a note of discomfort at that thought; was she, as Grunewald had put it, trying to 'catch' at him because she had no other option? That was hardly flattering, and he would not wish such a desperate situation upon her for the world—not even if he was the eventual beneficiary of it. But nonetheless, her manner began to please him. They danced again and again, with no objection at all from her, and he began to feel increasingly elated. She adored him; she would forgive him anything! Everything would be well after all.

Relief and delight soon drowned out his misgivings, and for the first time he allowed his extreme partiality for her to show. The rest of the ballroom was a blank to him; he saw nothing of anyone else's doings, had no interest in anything they had to say. All he saw was Sophy.

Late in the evening, when they had danced as much as they could desire, Miss Landon cast him a significant look, smiled invitingly at him and took his hand. 'Come with me,' she whispered, and drew him towards the door. Unhesitating, he followed.

She led him out of the ballroom—oblivious to the mutterings they left behind—and through the corridors beyond until she found a quiet, dark nook away from the bustle of the assembly. She drew him close to her, and still closer, until her face was only inches from hers; only then did she release his hand.

'Mr. Stanton,' she breathed. 'Aubrey…' She slipped a hand behind his head, twined her fingers in his hair, and drew his face down to hers.

Her lips were incredibly soft. He returned her kiss—only the second of his life—with fervour, holding her soft, warm curves close to him. She kissed every bit as well as Hidenory; better, even, because this was *Sophy* and he would give anything at all—the whole of Aylfenhame, if he had it—if she would only accept the gift of his heart.

He grew breathless, but Sophy continued to kiss him and he couldn't let go of her. His knees grew so weak he could barely stand, and his hands shook as he held her to him. When she finally pulled away, he could only rest his face against her neck and gasp, 'Sophy… marry me?'

She beamed up at him. 'I thought you would never ask,' she whispered.

He gripped her. 'Is that a yes?'

'Yes! Of course it is.'

For a few minutes, Aubranael entirely lost control of his emotions. He could only cling to her and smile and kiss her again and again, his whole body shaking with relief and excitement and desire. His heart swelled with happiness and he could barely breathe.

At length, however, some unwelcome recollections pierced his cloud of happiness and he was obliged to calm down. She had said yes—yes! She was *his* Sophy at last—but she had done so without knowing the whole truth about him. His promise to Hidenory rang in his ears, and today was the eighth of June.

'Sophy,' he said in a serious tone, gently disengaging her arms from around his neck. 'Before we… I mean, there is something I must tell you. I should not have asked you before I had… that is, please listen to me for a moment.'

She said nothing, only smiled up at him with such a sweetly loving expression that his heart spasmed and his stomach jumped with fear. Would she take back her beautiful *yes* once she knew? Would that loving expression turn to hatred?

His shakes were back. Taking a small step away from her, he hid his trembling hands behind his back and opened his mouth. But he couldn't speak. The words would not come. All he could see in his mind's eye was Sophy's sweet face turning white with horror; of her rejecting him, storming away, never consenting to see him again. If *he* had been in her position he would probably have done the same. How could he claim to love her when he had lied so deeply, and for so long?

She watched him for a long, awkward moment, her smile faltering. Then in a whisper she said: 'What is the time?'

Aubranael blinked, confused. He was on the brink of making a confession—he had prepared her for something very important indeed—and she was asking about the time?

'I hardly know,' he said. 'Late.'

She smiled. 'Almost midnight.'

Midnight! It had not occurred to him to wonder exactly *when* Hidenory's enchantment would wear off. He had not expected to be standing with Miss Landon when it did. He had thought that he would go to bed on the night of the eighth, and wake on the morning of the ninth with his own face restored. But midnight was the precise end of the eighth of June—it would make perfect sense for the enchantment to be over on the stroke of twelve.

As the thought formed in his mind, he heard the church bells beginning to chime the hour. One, two, three chimes... quickly, he had only seconds to make his confession! Four, five, six, seven, and he could only stare dumbly at Sophy, his stomach churning with dread as eight, nine, ten and eleven sounded...

Twelve.

The deep chiming of the bells faded away on the night air, leaving silence in its wake; silence broken only by the distant babble of talk and laughing voices from the assembly rooms. He stared at Sophy and she stared back. Her face didn't change, and he began to feel confused. Was he still Mr. Stanton? Was he back to himself?

He glanced down to find that his fine evening clothes were still there. But of course they were: Grunewald had given them. They were not part of Hidenory's enchantment.

Slowly, he reached up a shaking hand and touched his cheek. His fingers met the rough texture of his ruined, twisted flesh, and his heart broke.

'I'm sorry...' he whispered. 'I'm so sorry.'

But Sophy did not look horrified. She watched him calmly, and when he began to apologise she actually smiled.

'So,' she said. 'I knew you had a secret.'

He stared, stunned. 'Wh-what? How?'

'It is funny,' she said thoughtfully. 'When one lives with a secret, it becomes easier, somehow, to sense when others are hiding something.'

'I cannot understand you,' he stuttered. 'You... have a secret?'

'Yes! A very important one! And I will tell you what it is, but first you must tell me who *you* are.'

So he explained everything, and now it was suddenly easy. He talked and talked, relief making him almost incoherent. At length, Sophy stopped him by placing a gentle hand over his lips.

'Enough,' she smiled. 'I think I understand everything. I have only one question.'

He lifted his brows to show that he was listening.

'How did you come by this curse?'

She removed her hand, inviting him to talk, but this time it was not easy. He took a deep breath, and another, trying to order his thoughts. The tension of the evening—the excitement, the elation, the fear, the relief—had sent his thoughts into chaos and it took him some few moments to summon the clarity—and the resolve—to answer Sophy's question.

'I grew up in a palace,' he began at last. 'That sounds wonderful, does it not? But in truth I was one of several stray children. My mother had been a servant; she probably died in childbirth, but no one seemed to know. And my father was rumoured to be one of the gardeners, but nobody could say for sure.

'I had many friends, however, as there were other children like me; belonging to no one, living wild in the grounds. But the person I loved best was Lihyaen. I should have had nothing to do with her: she was the princess, and I only a wild boy. But how could I help it? She was perfect.'

Sophy had turned white, but he hardly noticed, so involved in his story was he. 'We were the same age, we loved the same things... her nurses kept trying to chase me away, but we were too cunning for them.

'Then one day...' His throat tried to close and he was forced to stop and clear it. 'One day,' he continued, 'Well, even now I hardly know what happened. Lihyaen had asked me to wait for her in the second potting shed—we had a secret way in and out, and we often used to crouch there, telling each other stories. She had a way with the flowers—truly remarkable. Anyway, she did not appear. I went looking for her.'

He took a deep breath. 'I found her in the nursery. She was lying in the cot she had used as a baby; it was too small for her by then, and she was all twisted up inside it. Her face was blue, and her eyes stared blankly at the ceiling.

'I realised someone else was in the room, someone I didn't recognise. He or she was wearing a white cloak that covered everything—face, body. I had no idea who it was, but I *knew* that he or she was an enemy. I threw myself at them—I don't know what I expected to achieve, but I was distraught. I got a face full of dark magic for my trouble, and when I awoke I was like this.' He touched his face.

He could not bring himself to tell the rest of the story. Ayliri lived for a very long time, ordinarily, but Lihyaen's family had been dogged by tragedy. Soon after Lihyaen's death, her mother had died as well; some said she had died of sorrow. Then scarcely a year later, her father disappeared. He had left behind a document abdicating the throne of Aylfenhame in favour of his next heir, whoever that might be—even he did not know. He had never again been seen in Aylfenhame.

Since then, there had been no monarch. Many had laid claim to the throne, but none had been able to prove their right to it above any other. There had been many years of turmoil and instability, and people often spoke of the king's return with longing.

Aubranael cared nothing for that. All he cared for was Lihyaen, and she was gone.

He was so far buried in his memories that he failed to notice Sophy's silence for some time. At length he looked up to find that her face was bone-white and she was staring at him with a stricken expression.

'I'm sorry,' he said quickly. 'Gracious, you ask a simple question and I tell you the whole tragic tale…' He talked on in what he hoped was a soothing way, stricken with remorse. What had possessed him to trot out the entire sorry story? No one had ever asked before. Perhaps the thrill of this new closeness—of having someone to confide in—had temporarily disordered his wits.

At length Sophy seemed comfortable again. Her smile wobbled a little, but it held, and she slipped her hand into his in a gratifyingly trusting way.

'Perhaps you had better tell me your secret another day,' he suggested. 'I have shocked both of us enough for one evening.'

Sophy nodded. 'It will be better if I show you,' she said cryptically. 'Come to the parsonage tomorrow, early.'

He nodded. 'Are we...?' he began, then hesitated. He couldn't tell what she really thought of his tale. Finding out that Mr. Stanton and Aubranael were the same person had obviously shocked her, but he couldn't tell what she really thought about it. Did their engagement stand?

She smiled warmly enough to banish his fears, and nodded. 'We are,' she said quietly. 'I can understand why you lied.'

He felt such a glow of satisfaction, affection and relief, it was as though he was filled with sunshine from head to toe. He had never dared hope that Sophy would be so very understanding; that there would be no interval of dismay and distrust, no misgivings to explain or soothe away. She was perfect, he decided, and made a vow to himself then and there: he would never, *ever* let anything happen to her. He had failed Lihyaen, but he would never fail his Sophy.

These heroic reflections were interrupted by the sound of approaching footsteps in the passage behind him, and he was abruptly brought back to reality. Here he stood in the Alford Assembly Rooms with his own face! Mr. Stanton's palatable good looks were gone, and he stood in danger of exposure.

Sophy grasped the situation instantly, and took his hand. Rapidly she led him back through the passages—hurrying past the person whose footsteps had alerted them—and out the front door. When she climbed into his carriage after him, he was too distracted to notice the impropriety of it. He called to the driver from within the coach, hoping that nobody would glance in and see his face.

They did not. The carriage moved off, and he was able to relax for the journey home. Miss Landon's presence helped, for they had much to say to one another—and a great deal else to share, besides.

It was not until the following morning that Aubranael began to feel really curious about Sophy's secret. So much had happened the night before that he had hardly taken her announcement seriously.

She had said it was very important, but her manner had not suggested that she was worried or troubled. What could it possibly be? Perhaps it was even a good secret; though he struggled to imagine why anyone would hide something like that.

He was obliged to use Grunewald's carriage, in spite of the beautiful weather. Hidenory's enchantment had gone, absolutely gone; not only was his real face restored (nothing like Mr. Stanton's) but so was his real hair (long, loose and nothing like Mr. Stanton's) and his real skin (dark brown and nothing like anybody else's in Tilby). He travelled the short distance to the parsonage with the blinds drawn, amusing himself on the way with speculations as to the nature of Miss Landon's secret. Perhaps she had discovered that her father had *not* left her entirely penniless after all. That would be a pleasant discovery for her, and it would save his dignity a little, too: she would not be accepting him purely about of desperation.

Or perhaps she wished to tell him about her scheme of settling in Grenlowe and opening a shop. He had learned enough about English society to know that *opening a shop*—even in faraway Aylfenhame— would never be considered a respectable thing to do, and so of course she would keep it secret. This second theory made so much sense that he accepted it as the truth at once, and felt much more comfortable. He would not let on, perhaps, that Mr. Balligumph had already told him about it. Better to let her explain it in her own words.

When the carriage drew up at the parsonage, he paused only to ensure that his hat was pulled low over his face and his coat was buttoned up over his throat, and then he stepped down. He went up to the front door as quickly as possible, hoping that Sophy would be waiting for him.

She was not. He knocked, waited and knocked again, and there was no sign of her. He began to grow concerned. The parsonage was tucked away behind the church in a little nook of its own, with trees lining the walls that separated it from the road; but still, it could not be long before somebody passed this way, and in spite of his excellent disguise they could hardly fail to notice that there was something odd about him.

Just as he began to grow alarmed—had something happened to Sophy?—the door opened. He began to smile; it was immediate on seeing Miss Landon and he couldn't help it. But the smile faded when he realised it was not Sophy at the door.

An old, old woman stood there instead, stooped over with age. Her brittle white hair all but obscured her wrinkled face, and her clothes were ragged and dirty.

'I... I am looking for Miss Landon,' he said uncertainly. 'Is she here?'

Gripped with a sudden alarm, he cast a long look about himself at the other houses, then back at the one before him. 'This *is* the parsonage, is it not?'

The woman cackled—actually *cackled*, the way old women tended to do in stories—and opened the door wider. 'Yes, and yes,' she said. Her voice did not match her appearance; instead of the feeble, quavering notes he had expected, she spoke in firm, vibrant tones.

Aubranael stepped inside, feeling oddly wary. 'Would you be so kind as to tell her I am here?' he asked politely. 'I am expected, I believe.'

The old woman shut the door behind him, then looked him in the eye and smiled. 'She knows,' she said.

She did? Was she here somewhere, watching? Aubranael turned about, but did not see her. The old woman beckoned him into the parlour and he followed her inside, expecting to find Sophy waiting, but she was not there. He stared at the woman, confused.

'I told you I had a secret,' she said softly.

Realisation dawned, and horror with it. '*Sophy?*' he said incredulously. 'Wha—how? Why?'

A spark of irritation flashed in the old woman's eyes. 'A curse, of course,' she snapped. 'Or did you think that you were the only one?'

Aubranael swallowed his distaste—ashamed that he felt it at all— and met her gaze squarely. 'Tell me about it,' he said in a gentle tone.

'No.'

'Please,' he said softly. His reaction had been shock, and nothing more; now that he'd had a few seconds to absorb the truth, his heart broke for poor Sophy. He felt anger begin to simmer somewhere inside. Who could have done this to her? She was sweet and kind-hearted and caring and... and *unthreatening*. What could possibly have happened?

Sophy sighed, chewed one of her old woman's lips and looked up at him. 'I have no wish to recount the whole story,' she said firmly. 'I am sorry—especially since you were so sharing last night. But I can't... bear it.'

He made desperate soothing motions, anxious to convey that he had no wish to pressure her at all. He would have spoken but she rushed on.

'It happens... once a month,' she said, with some small hesitation. 'For a few days, and then I am restored to myself.'

'A few?' he repeated. 'How many is that?'

'A *few*,' she snapped.

He made another apologetic gesture. It was unlike Sophy to be irritable, he thought distantly; but no doubt it was the pressure of confession, and the prospect of rejection. He had felt awful himself, only a few short hours ago.

There was only one question he would venture to ask, in the face of her obvious reluctance to speak. But he had to know. He could already feel it eating away at him, burning in his mind.

'Sophy,' he said. 'Who did this to you?'

Whoever it was, he wanted to hurt them. He felt the same way he felt whenever he thought of Lihyaen and the white-cloaked person who had disappeared into the night, leaving her silent corpse behind.

Sophy stared up at him, despair in her rheumy green eyes. 'I don't know,' she whispered, and the hopelessness in her voice convinced him that she spoke the truth.

He opened his arms, inviting her to walk into them. But she straightened her spine, lifted her chin and smiled a weird little smile. 'I am not in need of affection,' she said. 'What I need is a *promise*.'

'What kind of promise?'

'That you still want me, in spite of *this*.' She grabbed handfuls of the revolting rags she wore and shook them in sudden fury.

Aubranael stared at her in surprise. 'Do you need a promise?'

'Of *course* I—' she began.

He held up a hand to cut her off. 'What I mean to say is: that goes without saying. Does it not? How could I possibly reject *you?*'

Sophy stared at him in amazement, and he realised that her irritation stemmed from despair. In spite of his circumstances, she had been truly afraid that he would forsake her.

'Are you certain?' she said.

'Yes. I promise.'

A smile of pure happiness crossed her face, and for an instant he could almost see his Sophy beneath the veneer of age. But as seconds passed her smile gradually faded, and she looked down at herself, perplexed.

'Say it again,' she ordered.

Aubranael took both of her hands and held them between his own. 'Sophy Landon,' he said gravely, 'I promise to love you every day of our two lives, *including* the cursed ones.'

A spasm crossed her face—annoyance? Despair?—and she said: 'Could you say that again, but leave out my name?'

Puzzled, he nonetheless obliged.

She stared down at herself, at her ragged skirts, withered hands and knotted hair, and something like a suppressed howl of frustration tore from her throat. Pulling her hands free of his, she stared wildly at him. 'Maybe we need to be married,' she said feverishly. 'Yes! That must be it. Merely *saying* that you promise cannot be enough, or anybody could do it. You have to marry me to prove it!'

Aubranael began to feel alarmed. 'We will be married,' he said. 'Soon, if you like—though perhaps you will like to wait until the cursed days are over for the month.'

'No!' she shrieked. 'We must be married as soon as possible! Today!'

'We cannot be married today. Tilby has no clergyman, remember? And it will take longer than today to make the necessary arrangements.'

To his horror, Sophy began to claw at her face. Her nails were sharp and broken, and they left long, red welts on her skin. 'Stop!' he said in horror, grabbing at her hands. 'Sophy, what is this about?'

'I am a *korrigan*, you fool!' she cried. 'You are supposed to break the curse!'

Korrigan! He knew the tale. How a korrigan had ended up *here*, the daughter of a country clergyman in an out-of-the-way town, he had no notion at all. But he understood her panic.

'Consider the good!' he said, making another attempt to capture her clawing hands. 'You must be right: it is marriage that will break the curse, and we *will* be married. You will be free very soon.'

She began to calm at last, and he was able to smile into her eyes. 'It gives me so much pleasure to know that I can free you from this,' he said gently. 'Do not fear, love.'

She eyed him with suspicion, but to his relief she did not fly into another rage. Instead she patted his hand a little awkwardly, and sighed. 'I had tea prepared,' she said. 'I had hoped to partake of it curse-free, but however.'

She led the way into the parlour and offered him a seat, all trace of her frustration gone. Mindful of her aged hands, he attempted to take over the duty of serving the tea, but she waved him off with a little return of her irritability.

'I may be ugly but I can still pour tea,' she said frostily.

'Of course,' he murmured, puzzled. He would not have said that irritability was part of Sophy's character, and she could not still be worried about rejection. Where had she been hiding that trait?

Not that it mattered; nothing could dim his delight in her company. But it wounded him a little, and worried him. Was she concerned about anything else?

He watched absently while she poured the tea, gracefully and without spilling a drop. Accepting the proffered cup with a smile, he said, 'Where is Mary today? I had fully expected to meet her at the door.'

Sophy cast him a quick, sharp look. He would have sworn she looked... *shifty*, if he didn't know better. 'She has the day off today,' she said quickly. 'She will be so sorry to have missed you.'

Aubranael nodded and took another sip. 'And how is Thundigle getting along?'

Sophy looked blank. 'Oh... very well,' she said.

'Yes?' he said. 'I shall see for myself soon enough, no doubt! He cannot bear to leave the tea-things uncleared for more than a very little while.'

Sophy gulped tea. 'He has the day off as well,' she said in between gulps.

'Oh! My word, I had not thought they would leave you alone all day, especially at this time.'

Sophy smiled vaguely and muttered something about important errands. He watched her quizzically, unsure how to interpret her behaviour. That she was hiding something from him was obvious, but what could it be? Perhaps there was something amiss with either Mary or Thundigle or both, but she did not like to tell him. Perhaps they had left her! The very thought of it angered him, and he forced himself back to calmness. He could not believe that either of them would desert Sophy, let alone both. There must be some other explanation.

He opened his mouth to talk of something else, but there came a rattling from some other part of the house, and the sound of footsteps.

'Ah, here is Mary back again,' he said with a relieved smile.

Sophy, however, looked horrified. She jumped up, paused only long enough to set her teacup neatly down upon the tray, and all but ran to the door. 'I must not be seen!' she hissed.

Aubranael was surprised that so loyal a servant as Mary knew nothing of Sophy's condition, but he could not blame her for keeping it a secret. He would have done the same, given the chance. He jumped up, too, and followed her; he had forgotten for an instant that he, too, was a stranger to Mary in his current form, and a potentially horrific one at that! It gave him pain to have to creep from the house like a thief, but he did so. There would be time later to break the news to Mary; for now, he was happy to escape her notice.

Sophy had preceded him out of the parlour, but when he reached the corridor beyond there was no sign of her. He dared not call her name in case of attracting Mary's attention, but her sudden disappearance bothered him. Where could she possibly have gone?

No time to consider the matter; here was Mary coming back again! He made his way to the front door with extreme haste and slipped outside. He had better hurry: he had a wedding to arrange, and no time at all to lose.

* * *

Hiding in a parlour drawer would not rank among Thundigle's favourite pastimes, he decided. It had taken him less than two minutes to grow tired of it; his neck was twisted at a strange angle in order to fit his head inside, and the rest of his body was curled into an uncomfortable ball. But the discomfort had been worth it.

He had not been able to discover exactly *who* was the person currently occupying the parsonage, but that it was *not* Miss Landon was abundantly clear. But where was the real Sophy? What had this woman done with her? He did not know.

His confusion was increased by the appearance of Aubranael in Miss Landon's parlour. He had not known that Sophy had remained in contact with him since her return from Grenlowe, nor that matters between them had advanced to such a degree as to warrant a proposal of marriage. Perhaps that was why she had not encouraged Mr. Stanton—and where was Mr. Stanton anyway? The neighbourhood gossip reported that he had vanished, but no one seemed to know where he had gone.

Either way, something had happened to Miss Landon and Aubranael was mistakenly preparing to commit himself to someone else entirely. Having liberated himself from the drawer, Thundigle spent several minutes in frantic contemplation. What could he do? How could he find Miss Landon, or warn Aubranael? How could he discover the identity of the imposter?

Nothing came to mind. Badly out of his depth, Thundigle did the only thing he could think of.

He went to see Mr. Balligumph.

CHAPTER FOURTEEN

Sophy wandered for a time, hoping that she might encounter some manner of village or town, or a landmark that would help her find her way back to Grenlowe, or even some helpful soul who could set her on the right path. An hour or two passed in this fruitless endeavour, during which time the deep blue twilight darkened into night lit only by the waxing moon.

The nervous flutter in her stomach grew stronger and stronger, in spite of her attempts to quieten her alarm. When her foot caught something ropy and solid in the dark—a tree root, perhaps, or a fallen branch—and she almost went tumbling to the ground, she was forced to stop. An injury would turn a difficult situation into a catastrophe; if she was hurt, she would be entirely helpless.

She stood for a few minutes, catching her breath and considering her options. Dearly she wished for another of Balligumph's guides; local wisdom insisted that to follow a will-o-the-wyke was fatal, but Balli's friends had always done well by her.

Any guide at all would be welcome, she thought bitterly, even a treacherous one. At least it would give her some kind of direction.

Abruptly she remembered Hidenory's words—before the witch's theft of Sophy's face and form had driven all other thoughts from her mind. *Tut-Gut*, she had said. He would be willing to 'put her to work', had those not been her words?

Sophy considered that. The comment had seemed innocent enough at the time, but in light of Hidenory's later actions it began to sound far more sinister. Who was Tut-Gut really, and how would he put Sophy to work? Had this piece of advice been sound, or was Hidenory seeking to lead her ever further astray?

It was impossible to know, of course, without seeking him out. Sophy wavered for some time, assailed by misgivings, but at length she gave in. She had no other options; none except to continue wandering in this dark and lonely forest until she either fatally injured herself, starved to death, or found her way out.

Taking a deep breath, Sophy opened her lips and called, 'Tut-Gut! I am in need of your assistance, if you are at leisure to come to me.'

There; that was polite. He could hardly be offended by so courteous a request, surely? But no answer came and no one appeared, and Sophy's fledgling hopes died away.

'Tut-Gut?' she called.

Nothing.

But in the stories—the ones her mother had told her as a child— one had to call a fae-being's name three times to attract his or her attention. Perhaps there was some truth to be found in tales.

'Tut-Gut!' she called once more.

'What is it, now?' said a creaking voice, and Sophy jumped.

A light appeared in the darkness, so bright that Sophy's night-blind eyes shut tight against the glare. When she could open them again, she found that the forest had gone and she stood inside a wooden hut.

It was fairly large, and around the room were arrayed the paraphernalia of a simple lifestyle. A little wooden bed stood in one corner, a rough-cut table and chairs stood on the opposite side of the room, and a small bookcase proudly bore three worn-looking bound leather volumes of miniature size. A strong fire burned in the centre of the floor, over which an iron pot hung. Sophy could smell something delicious cooking, and her stomach tightened with hunger.

In a tiny rocking-chair before the fire sat a hobgoblin. He looked a little like Thundigle, though his skin was even darker, almost black. He was two or three feet tall, with spindly limbs, a pronounced belly and a smile that looked far too big for his face. His clothes were ragged and much-mended. He held a pair of wooden knitting needles in his hands and he was knitting at terrific speed. He fixed his dark green eyes on Sophy and stared, but his knitting did not pause, or even slow, for a second.

'Are you Mr. Tut-Gut?' Sophy said, offering a hasty curtsey.

'Who else am I like to be?' he said grumpily. 'When ye've been bandyin' me name about like it was a toy or some such.'

Sophy blushed and hastened to apologise. 'I am sorry, only your name was given to me by someone who thought you may be able

to help me, and I am in a terrible situation and I was quite, quite desperate.'

Tut-Gut raised shaggy black brows at her, still knitting furiously. 'Oh? An' who is it as advised the likes o' *ye* to bother me?'

This was not the welcome Sophy had been hoping for; but nor had he made any move to harm her. Her confidence growing a little, she said: 'Her name is Hidenory.'

Tut-Gut's face darkened and he muttered something.

'I beg your pardon?' Sophy said politely.

'Witch-woman!' he said loudly. 'Owes me a favour, and instead o' repayin' me like any person of honour she sends me a beggar! An old croaky! A hag!' He threw his knitting aside, jumped out of his chair and began to pace in circles, tugging at handfuls of his wild black hair and pounding himself on the forehead with his fists. 'It's a slight, that's what it is! An offence! An insult of the very lowest kind! I have a good mind to put this old croaky in my dinner, that I do.' This last was directed at Sophy, delivered in a dark voice as he glowered at her from beneath thunderously lowered brows.

Sophy did not like being referred to as an old croaky, and she certainly did not enjoy the suggestion that she might be turned into dinner. 'A moment,' she said hastily. 'I had no idea that Hidenory was in your debt, but perhaps I may be able to repay it somehow.'

That brought him up short. He stared at her, and his anger turned to calculation. 'Oh?' he said slowly. 'Have ye any idea *what* the witch-lady owes me?'

'None whatsoever.'

'Tis a dangerous offer to make, then, old croaky! Could be years you'd be slavin' away in the home o' good old Tut-Gut. Years!'

Sophy's heart sank. Slaving away in Tut-Gut's house for years was a better prospect than being made into stew, but not very much better. Careful to keep her dismay from showing on her face, she said calmly: 'Very well, if so.'

Tut-Gut's glee abruptly faded and his shoulders slumped. 'Twas not so great a favour as all that,' he admitted. 'A mere triflin' business, if I *must* tell the truth.' He glared at Sophy again, as if it was her fault that he felt compelled to be honest. 'Can you cook?' he demanded.

Sophy shook her head. 'I always burn the food.'

'Can you clean?'

Sophy shook her head again. 'I am certain to break something.' He did not appear to possess many breakable objects, but still she was hesitant to risk it.

'Hmph. Useless old croaky. It will have to be dinner.' He gave a firm, decisive nod, and patted his stomach. 'Same old stew, day in, day out!' he said cheerfully. 'Not today, no, not today!'

'But I am a very *old* croaky,' Sophy said quickly. 'Old and tough and stringy! My meat would not be at all appealing, I am quite sure.'

'She should've sent a juicy young bit o' dinner, that's true enough,' said Tut-Gut, 'but I makes do.'

'I can sew,' Sophy said desperately, backing away from Tut-Gut's fire and swinging stew-pot. 'I am very skilled with a needle. I can knit, too.'

'That I can do meself,' said Tut-Gut with a smile, indicating his discarded needles.

'Oh, but together we might accomplish a great deal more!'

Tut-Gut paused to consider that. 'Such as?'

Desperately, Sophy glanced around his odd little house. He had curtains put to the windows, she noticed, but they were crooked and misshapen. A few rugs lay across the rough wooden floors, each one threadbare and falling into holes. She looked back at him. 'Your clothes are falling into pieces,' she said. 'Your curtains do not fit the windows, and they are hanging much amiss. Your rugs are in very poor shape indeed, and that chair you are sitting on has no cushion to comfort you. I can mend all of these problems.'

Tut-Gut followed her gaze to his curtains, his rugs, his chair and his own self. ''Tis more than I'm owed,' he said doubtfully.

'That is of no concern to me.'

He looked back at her with a cunning gleam in his eye. 'I accept!' he said. 'I like you *much* better than Hidenory.'

His manner had wholly changed, all trace of suspicion and anger gone in favour of a sudden overflowing goodwill. He beamed at her with his too-wide smile, his eyes twinkling in the firelight.

'I have something else to add,' Sophy said.

'Go on with it, then!'

'It must be, oh, five or six hours until the dawn, am I right?'

'I reckon so.'

'Well, then. I will do all that I have said before the first light hits your windows. If I do, then you will be in *my* debt.' She delivered this offer as confidently as she could, hoping that she had not miscalculated. He seemed to her a being who took favours and debts very seriously indeed, and who was likely to enjoy a deal—and a bet.

Perhaps she was right, for his eyes began to shine. 'A game! A very good one at that,' he said in delight. His cunning eyes fixed on her gnarled old hands, and he smiled. 'But there must be something else. If ye do not do all that ye've said in the allotted time, what then?'

Sophy swallowed and said: 'Then you may make me into stew.'

He cackled at that, and beamed again. 'Very good! Ye may begin.'

'I will need materials,' Sophy said promptly.

'That was not part o' the bargain!'

'Of course it was. How do you expect me to make up your home anew without anything to sew with?'

Tut-Gut grumbled, but he could not deny the logic of her argument. He began to circle the room, opening chests and looking under and behind furniture, pulling all manner of bits and pieces of cloth from each hiding-place he consulted. It was a motley collection, and Sophy stared at the growing heap in some dismay. She saw cotton and linen and silk, some dusty and aged, some bright and shining new; she saw red and green and blue and purple and every other colour besides. What could she do with such a mismatched pile of scraps?

But she was not designing somebody's drawing-room, she reminded herself: she was in a hut in the woods, surrounded by rags and fading fabrics. She took a deep, steadying breath, accepted the long bone needle Tut-Gut offered to her, and set to work.

She had never sewn so much or so quickly in her life. Again and again she blessed Hidenory: the witch had betrayed her, but how fortunate it was that her glamour was only skin-deep! Her hands may *look* aged and twisted and stiff, but beneath the unpromising appearance, her fingers were as young and strong and supple as ever. It had been an unfair trick to play on Tut-Gut, she supposed; to his eye she was incapable of working at speed, and he had counted on that when he had accepted her game. But since the alternative was to end up in his stew-pot, she was unconcerned.

It did not take him very long to realise that he had been tricked. She set to with such furious speed, and kept it up for half an hour without faltering in the slightest. He watched her quick, deft movements as she plied the clumsy needle and his face darkened. 'Old croaky, ehh? Not so, not so at all!'

Sophy made no reply. She was unconcerned by his discovery: the rules of Aylfenhame were strict, and once a deal had been made, no fae-creature would go back on his or her word. Tut-Gut did not attempt to renegotiate, nor did he waste very much time raging at her duplicity.

Instead, he began to interfere. When Sophy reached for a new piece of fabric to stitch into the curtain she was sewing, he stabbed her with his knitting-needle.

'Oops!' he declared. 'Now, how could I be so clumsy? I beg your pardon, croaky.'

When she got up to hang the curtain at the window, he stuck out a foot and tripped her. 'Now! Clumsy again. Must be my advancin' years.'

When she turned back from hanging the curtain, half of the pile of fabric had disappeared. 'Where is the rest of the red cotton?' she demanded.

'Red cotton? Red cotton?' said Tut-Gut. 'I never saw such a thing!'

But Sophy had been expecting such tricks. Coolly she removed a length of red cotton that she had hidden inside her grubby old robe, and began to sew. Each time Tut-Gut turned his back, she secreted more of the remaining pile of fabric, until she had plenty inside her robe to finish her projects.

This went on hour after hour. Tut-Gut tried every piece of trickery his wily brain could come up with, and Sophy had to work hard to out-think him. By the end of the night, her hands were covered in little wounds, she had fallen over three times and bruised her knees and legs, and her temper was wearing thin.

But Tut-Gut's tricks were in vain. Sophy sewed and sewed until her fingers hurt and began to bleed, and by the time the first rays of morning began to filter into the room, she had completed her labours. New curtains hung at every window, neatly stitched out of coloured patches; the rugs had been mended and renewed; cushions padded not only Tut-Gut's rocking chair but his bed as well. He had a new shirt, trousers and cloak: they were not at all refined, but they were much better than the rags that he was wearing. She had even made a little patched throw to cover the blankets on his bed.

Tut-Gut spent a long time going over everything that she had done, looking for anything that would invalidate their agreement. But he found nothing. Sophy waited in the centre of the room, her nerves steady and her temper calm, knowing that she had done well.

'Oh, very well,' Tut-Gut said at last. 'Same old stew for Tut-Gut.'

Sophy lifted an eyebrow. 'Is that all that you have to say to me?' she demanded. 'Your house has never looked so wonderful, I would wager, and you will be comfortable for years to come. I have done all that I promised, and more besides.'

The hobgoblin glowered at her, but then his frown faded away and his disturbing too-wide smile was back. 'Good with yer hands, yes, you are.' He picked up the clothes she had made for him and spun about, too fast for Sophy's eyes to follow. When he stopped, his rags had vanished and he was wearing the new garments. He bowed low, and chuckled. 'What's it to be, then? Is it youth yer after? Beauty? Riches? 'Tis always one o' those type o' things.'

Sophy wondered for a moment whether he was actually able to grant any of the things he had mentioned. He did not look as though he possessed such powers as that. 'Nothing so difficult,' she said with a smile. 'I merely want to find my way to Grenlowe.'

'Well, now!' he said delighted. 'Tut-Gut is the one to ask! I can find anything and anybody, don't you doubt it. But Grenlowe is a long way.' He eyed her. 'What business have ye there?'

'My business is my own.'

Tut-Gut waved a hand and pulled a face. 'Very well, keep yer secrets! Off we go.' He galloped to the door, leaving Sophy feeling a little startled at his sudden speed. She was bone-tired, her hands and legs hurt and she was desperate for a little rest, but she would not chance her luck by requesting any delay. Tut-Gut's moods changed with the winds, it seemed, and she had better capitalise on this sudden good temper. She sighed, and dragged herself after him.

Sophy walked with Tut-Gut for some time, as the sun rose higher in the sky and its rays began to shine strongly down between gaps in the tree-cover overhead. The day grew warm, and she began to regret the layers of heavy rags she wore. Despite her tiredness and discomfort, the bright sunshine and the delicious scent of summer flowers, flourishing foliage and rain-damp earth refreshed and cheered her. She had always loved being outdoors; there were few complaints which could not be cured by a long walk.

One of those few was the death of her father. She realised she had not gone for her customary walk ever since she had received the sorry news, and now she regretted that very much. Perhaps her spirits would not have sunk so low, had she taken better care of her own health and taken her exercise.

She began to think of her father, with less pain but more real regret than she had ever done before. His story had been a sad one, and she was sorry that she had never been able to make him happy after the death of her mother. She saw now how the heart had gone out of him all those years ago, and he had done little since then but mark time, taking little pleasures where he could. If he had done so with no regard for his health, well, that was because he had little use for his remaining days on earth; it was of no moment to him if those days were shortened.

He had, perhaps, expected that Sophy would marry soon after she came of age. He had been fond of her, in his own way, and could not have predicted that others would not find sufficient value in her person and her company to make her an offer. As such, he had made no provision for her of any kind; he had not expected to need to. It was short-sighted of him, and he had been neglectful when Sophy had needed him desperately. But it was of no use clinging to old regrets; Sophy tried, in the silence of this strange journey, to forgive his shortcomings and remember only the good.

But Aylfenhame did not smile upon such noble reflections, it appeared, for the sky clouded over and the forest quickly became gloomier than her thoughts. A few cold droplets of rain fell, catching her cheek and forehead, and she sighed. Now she would have to be stoic.

The atmosphere continued to darken, and soon her disgust with the rain gave way to the first stirrings of fear. The light drained away as though night had fallen, but that could not be! It was not possible. They had walked for only two, perhaps three hours. She would swear it.

'Tut-Gut?' she said nervously.

'Aye,' he said grimly. 'Somethin's afoot.' He had acquired a gnarled stick from somewhere, a solid-looking branch almost as tall as he was. He gripped this like a quarterstaff, ready to swing it should something untoward materialise.

Nothing did, however, and for several long minutes they walked along in silence—not the silence of individual reflection, this time, but an alert silence, ready and wary of trouble.

'Perhaps a light...' she began to say to Tut-Gut, but she stopped when a light appeared immediately ahead of them. 'Thank you,' she said instead.

But Tut-Gut was shaking his head. 'Nowt to do wi' me, that,' he said softly. 'Don't ye know a will-o-the-wyke when ye see one?'

Sophy had already progressed from gladness to trepidation, for the ball of light did indeed resemble the wisps she had followed on her way to Aylfenhame before. But she knew well that these floating ghost-lights were not usually helpful, the way Balli's friends were. Those one encountered out in the wilds could be dangerous, and were best avoided.

She imagined this was even more likely when one was lost in the midst of the Outwoods of Aylfenhame.

'Be off with you!' said Tut-Gut. He sounded quite fearsome, and Sophy fully expected the wisp to do as he said.

It did not. Instead, it separated into two distinct wisps which hovered in the air for a few moments, bouncing against each other, and then began to float away in different directions.

The one nearest her began to change colour, from bright white to yellow to green, and blue, purple, red, pink... her attention was caught in spite of herself, and all her purpose drained away in the face of the wisp's beautiful, mesmerising colours.

She had gone some yards in pursuit of the creature before she was aware. A brief surge of alarm brought her back to herself, but only for a moment; then she was captivated again and drifting away after the wisp, feeling a vague but persistent dread that it would get away from her and she would never know what the next hue would be.

A voice drifted through the trees. It took Sophy several long moments to focus on it, and even then she received only the distant impression of a great show of temper. Someone was very angry about something, she realised vaguely.

'... *cap*, woman!'

That did not make sense. It was only part of a sentence, Sophy thought, feeling quite pleased with herself for this very clever realisation. But what could the rest of the sentence have been? She amused herself with a few foggy speculations, none of which entirely satisfied her, before another sentence pierced her reverie.

'...clothes or cap or somethin' of that kind. Hey! Old croaky! Yer wearin' stuff, now get it TURNED AROUND!'

Turn her clothes around? What a peculiar suggestion. She had not realised that Tut-Gut could be so very strange. Staring doubtfully down at herself, she attempted to find some way out of her heavy outer robe. This required a little effort, for her rags were not equipped with anything so sensible as a row of buttons or hooks. Instead they were tied on, with a set of torn lengths of fabric serving as fastenings.

Gracious, it was far too much work to untie them. They were so tight that she was hurting her damaged fingers in the attempt. A flash of rippling colours caught her attention again, and she was happy enough to give up her unpleasant labour and return to the contemplation of the wisp.

But then the voice sounded again, uncomfortably close this time. '...so intolerably FOOLISH! THRICE-CURSED HUMANS, ye don't deserve a single shred o' help from the likes o' me, an' why am I puttin' myself out fer a feeble-witted mushroom like yerself I should like t' know?'

Mushroom? Sophy thought vaguely. Now, that did not seem accurate at all. She was not a mushroom! Mushrooms did not wear rags and walk about the forests in the dead of unnatural night. She opened her mouth to say this, but some element of the angry speech she had just heard—perhaps the tone, or its *extremely* insulting nature—broke through the fog in her brain, and she stopped abruptly. Suddenly, the turning of her clothes began to seem *very important indeed,* and she fought anew with the clumsy ties to her robe. At last she managed to prise one of them open; she tore her way through the rest, and quickly stripped the revolting thing away. She almost dropped the garment in her haste, but she succeeded in turning it inside-out and slipped it back onto her shoulders.

All at once, the fog shrouding her thoughts and dulling her alertness slipped away altogether, leaving her in clear possession of her wits. What she saw next frightened her nearly out of her wits, for the wisp had drawn her to the edge of a precipice, and a few more steps would have carried her over it. She could not see how far she would have fallen, but she did not doubt that the distance was considerable.

She stood for a moment, breathing too quickly as she tried to calm her pounding heart and collect her thoughts. The wisp continued to hover before her, but its presence failed to affect her as it had a few moments ago. She observed its shifting colours with a mixture of distant interest and deep misgivings.

'Poxy Tut-Gut,' said a voice sharply, and she jumped. 'Ruined us a merry game, that you have.'

Tut-Gut came up and stood next to her. His own wisp bobbed at his shoulder in an oddly merry way, dancing about and flashing colours in the jauntiest style.

'Yes, Pinch?' said Tut-Gut. 'Was you sayin' somethin'?'

'No,' said the disembodied voice, a trifle sulkily.

'Are ye goin' to wear tha' shape all day?' Tut-Gut said sternly. 'An' ye might let a bit o' light back in, if it ain't too much trouble.'

Sophy heard something like a sigh, and then her wisp dissolved. Darkness enveloped her, and she could see nothing save Tut-Gut, illuminated by the weakening glow of the other wisp. Then the darkness began to recede, bit by bit, until the day seemed merely overcast and dull once more.

'I expect an apology,' said Tut-Gut. 'An' t' my companion here.'

The day lightened still more as the sun returned, and Sophy realised that somebody stood before her. He was a small somebody—smaller than Tut-Gut, even—and dressed in clothes as green as the fallen leaves he stood upon. He held a pipe in one hand, which he carried to his lips for a deep puff as he stood regarding Sophy.

Blowing out a stream of thick white smoke, he grinned at her and said: 'What's this? A witch?'

'I said sommat about an apology,' Tut-Gut said. 'I am almost *sure* I heard meself sayin' that.'

Pinch shrugged his tiny shoulders and pouted. 'For what? We did no harm.'

'Not for lack of trying!' Sophy said. 'You almost walked me over a cliff.'

Pinch chuckled and stepped back, waving an arm at the cliff in an inviting gesture. 'Go on, have a look,' he said.

Keeping a wary eye on Pinch, Sophy stepped forward and peeked over the edge. The "precipice" fell away a mere two feet, she guessed, ending in a puddle of muddy water. She would have had a shock, a bump and an unpleasant wetting, but that was all. Probably.

'I could have broken an ankle,' she said severely, staring down at Pinch from her full five-feet-and-nine-inches height. He looked very small indeed when she loomed over him like this.

'All right, sorry,' he said cheerfully. 'None of the doom-and-gloom came to pass, so why worry about it?'

'That will not do,' Sophy said.

Tut-Gut shook his head in agreement. 'No, indeed. Ye'll have t' make it up t'us, Pinch. You an' Pinket.' He nodded at the wisp still bobbing at his shoulder, and the wisp's colours grew dull and sulky in reply.

Pinch looked briefly consternated, but then he shrugged again. 'We have nothing much else to do.'

'Boredom, is it?' said Tut-Gut with strong disapproval. 'Ye merry folk ought t'get yerselves some manner o' respectable occupation.'

Pinch rolled his eyes. 'That is the very *definition* of boring, Gutty. What is it that you want from us?'

'Not sure yet,' said the hobgoblin. 'So ye'll come along with us for a time, an' make sure no more mischief afalls us.'

'Are you going a very *long* way?' said Pinch in dismay.

'All the way to Grenlowe.'

Pinch sighed and took another long drag of his pipe. 'Very well, off we go,' he said. 'But really, Gutty, you must tell me how you came to be off to Grenlowe—on foot!—with such *unusual* company.' He eyed Sophy as he spoke, then gave her a thoroughly insincere smile when he noticed the dark look on her face.

'If ye're good,' said Tut-Gut.

Pinch sighed again.

The next hour or so of Sophy's journey was not so peaceful as the first two or three. Silence was not to be had, for Pinch insisted on bickering with Tut-Gut and teasing herself, almost without interruption. When he had heard the tale of how Tut-Gut came to be her escort, he began to mock "Gutty" rather cruelly, because 'Anyone can see this one's no old croaky at all.' But nothing either Tut-Gut or Sophy said could convince him to explain what he meant by that, or how he came to see through the glamour she wore.

Further interruptions occurred, interludes which led to the augmenting of their little party. When a very brown little creature stepped out of a tree ahead of them, peeling itself away from the bark in a manner that made Sophy's skin crawl, they were obliged to stop again. The newcomer was nut-brown like Tut-Gut, with a head of tightly-curled hair the colour of chocolate, and a pair of twinkling black eyes. This proved to be Tara-Tat, a friend (of sorts) of Tut-Gut's, and Tara soon decided to come along with them.

Then along came a slender purple-gowned being with pale silver skin and hair. Her dress looked like an upturned flower, and she was utterly beautiful—until she smiled, revealing bright green teeth. Graen was a flower-fae, Pinch explained gravely, and she seemed to be in the grip of a wild admiration for him, for she insisted on trailing along behind him, wearing an expression of long-suffering adoration.

Their company thus increased to six altogether, with every sign that they might yet pick up further followers, it occurred to her to wonder how she had contrived to journey to Hidenory's cottage before without being interfered with. That had been a journey of many hours, but she had hardly seen or heard another soul—there had been only that glimpse of the tea-party beneath the trees, where no one had seen or acknowledged her. Was it Tut-Gut who attracted all this notice? Perhaps that was explanation enough; passing humans might excite little interest. But she remembered that she had not been quite alone, after all.

'Are any of you acquainted with Felebre?' she asked, as soon as she could make herself heard over the chattering conversation of her companions.

All conversation ceased abruptly. Everyone stopped, in fact, and stared up at Sophy with almost identical expressions of awe. 'Felebre?' said Pinch at last. 'Are *you* acquainted with her?'

Sophy's brows rose in surprise at this peculiar reaction. 'Not precisely acquainted,' she answered, 'but I have met her a time or two. She was my guide when I passed through the Outwoods before.'

'Your *guide*?' said Tara-Tat in disbelief. 'Felebre consented to guide *you*?'

Sophy blinked. 'Well; she did not say anything about it—or anything at all, in fact—but she appeared when I came through from England and brought me to Hidenory. Balligumph sent her.'

Nobody asked her who Balligumph was; she was growing used to the fact that his name seemed to be universally known in Aylfenhame. But there was a stirring of something like unease among her companions, and they all shook their heads.

'I doubt that very much,' said Tut-Gut. 'Felebre is not *sent* by anybody. Always goin' her own way, that one.'

Not sent by Balligumph? Then how had the cat come to be in Sophy's way when she arrived—and why did she take her to Hidenory? She was a little relieved to learn that her visit to Hidenory had not been planned by Balli after all, but then why had she been taken there at all?

'Felebre appears to do Hidenory's bidding,' she said.

That caused another stir. 'Hidenory the witch?' said Graen.

'Ye've fallen into dangerous company,' said Tut-Gut, eyeing her. 'Then ye're not an old croaky at all, just like Pinch said. No wonder ye tricked me! Fair play t' you.' He doffed his cap, but in spite of the jaunty tone of his voice, his face was grave.

'But then... who is Felebre?' Sophy said, confused.

Heads were shaken, shoulders were shrugged, and everyone made a show of knowing nothing. 'No one knows for sure,' Graen said at last. She crept closer to Sophy's leg and leaned in to speak in a low voice. 'Some say she is no cat at all, but something else. Under an enchantment, like you.' Her voice fell even lower. 'She is very powerful. Royalty is in her blood, some day. No one can keep her against her will, or persuade her to do anything she does not wish to do. No one would dare try.'

Sophy felt more and more confused. An image flashed across her thoughts: Aubranael as she had first seen him, tearing after Felebre down the streets of Grenlowe, laughing and merry with enjoyment of the game. And Felebre had given every appearance of enjoying it, too, darting this way and that to keep *just* out of Aubranael's reach before finally making her triumphant escape. How did this fit with Graen's description?

'So if she is helping Hidenory in some way, she does so of her own accord,' Sophy said thoughtfully.

'Oh, yes,' said Pinch. 'Hidenory is powerful, but she is no match for Felebre. Not at all.'

Sophy wondered whether Aubranael knew any of this. Then she wondered, yet again, where he might be. 'Another question,' she said.

'Do any of you know Aubranael?'

She hoped to observe another unanimous round of recognition—preferably a more positive one than before—but she was disappointed. The replies came back, all negative: no one had ever heard the name before.

'Very well; never mind it,' said Sophy, concealing her disappointment with an effort. It seemed she was not destined to enjoy a repeat of her time with Aubranael. Blind chance had thrown them in each other's way before; apparently only blind chance would bring them together again.

She sighed.

Everyone stared at Sophy, agog for some salacious story, but she did not feel inclined to satisfy their curiosity. An awkward moment passed before Tut-Gut said: 'Onward!' He marched off with a fine show of purpose, and Tara-Tat instantly stepped after him. Pinch and Graen followed, leaving Sophy to bring up the rear with Pinket. Curiously, the wisp drifted down to settle almost on her shoulder, its colours muted as if to avoid hurting her eyes. There was something oddly comforting in the gesture, as if the wisp sensed her sadness.

'Thank you,' she said, and the wisp bobbed an acknowledgement.

CHAPTER FIFTEEN

Well now, a fine mess was goin' on there! How long do ye think it took for word to spread in Tilby that sommat weren't right? Not long, no! Not long at all. An' they all came to find me, Mr. Balligumph. Expected me to have all the answers, they did. Course, I had no answers at all for 'em—not then, not yet. But we had a merry little band put together in a trice, an' then there was no stoppin' us!

The first thing we had to do was warn Mr. Aubranael. Good soul, he is— like him very much. Couldn't leave him labourin' under a misapprehension, like, could we?

Aubranael was in the midst of an argument with Grunewald when the note arrived.

'Just for a few days!' he was saying imploringly.

'Not even for five minutes!' Grunewald snapped in reply.

'Why not?'

'Because there has been quite enough masquerading going on already.'

Aubranael scorned that. 'I cannot believe that *you* would advise sense and caution instead of drama and adventure and chaos. Do not try to fool me!'

Grunewald gave a cat-like grin. 'Quite true; I cannot deny that I am *hugely* enjoying this mess we have made. It is thoroughly diverting. I have not felt bored for at least twenty-four hours.'

'So!' said Aubranael. 'By all means, help me to prolong the charade. With this face, I will soon be forced to give up the adventure and return to Aylfenhame, and everything will be over.'

Grunewald examined him with pursed lips and calculating eyes, but still shook his head. 'You do not realise, perhaps, that you have already enjoyed far more of my favour than I am in the habit of giving out. You are already a very long way in debt to me.' He smiled again.

That smile combined with the word "debt" worried Aubranael somewhat, especially if he was a being of considerable eminence. Abruptly the uncertainty about Grunewald's true nature and position began to irritate him enormously, and he could not help himself from saying:

'*Are* you then the Goblin King? I wish you would tell me the truth.'

'I am sure you do,' said Grunewald comfortably. 'But I do not see why you require repeated confirmation when your own eyes, ears and wits have given you plenty already.'

That was as close to a straight 'yes' as he was likely to receive, Aubranael thought with some sourness. But it was enough. His insides thrilled with a stab of fear: he was in debt to the *Goblin King*. Deeply in debt.

Somebody ought to have warned him! He had entered into this peculiar arrangement of theirs without any expectation of how deeply and dangerously he was involving himself. What might so eminent a personage as the Goblin King require of him in future?

'Nonetheless,' he said with an admirable attempt at calm, 'I must still entreat this one further boon of you.'

Grunewald's face hardened, all trace of friendliness disappearing. 'No. And it is not out of a mere contrary determination to be disobliging, as you may feel; nor do I speak out of any desire to shield you from further entanglement with me and my affairs. It is a matter of instinct.'

'Instinct?' Aubranael repeated faintly.

'Yes, and my instincts are without flaw. Naturally.'

'So your instincts direct you to deny my request?'

'Precisely.' Obviously growing bored with the conversation, Grunewald threw himself into the most comfortable chair in the room, lay back, and closed his eyes.

Aubranael sighed. He recognised a flat refusal when he saw one; he had no real illusions that he could persuade Grunewald around to his way of thinking. But he was desperate. How could he fulfil his promise to Sophy when he had lost the persona of Mr. Stanton? If he could not be restored to his borrowed face and name, then he could not marry her as he had promised.

At least, he could not do so in England. They could remove to

Grenlowe, perhaps, and enter into the equivalent arrangement in Aylfenhame; but would that suffice for an Englishwoman like Sophy? Would it be enough to dissolve the curse upon her? He would be far happier if he were able to wed her in both realms; just to make absolutely certain.

His only option besides Grunewald was to go in search of Hidenory once more, but he did not feel inspired by this idea. Her dwelling was excessively well hidden; without Felebre's guidance he doubted very much whether he would be able to find it again. And would Felebre consent to take him a second time? He did not know. He had seen nothing at all of Felebre since his last visit to the Witch of the Outwoods, and he had no idea where the mysterious cat could be found.

He had almost made up his mind to another round of remonstrating with Grunewald, out of pure desperation if nothing else, when a knock came at the library door.

'Come in!' called Grunewald in a cheery tone.

The door swung open to reveal a young footman—at least ostensibly. He was, of course, one of Grunewald's goblin entourage, under a glamour like the rest of the household.

The footman hesitated on the threshold, looking from Grunewald to Aubranael and back in some confusion. 'Er, Sire? A note for Mr. Stanton.'

Grunewald flicked his fingers in Aubranael's direction, and the footman's face cleared of confusion. He approached Aubranael, bowed and handed over a neatly folded paper note on a silver tray.

'Thank you,' Aubranael remembered to say. He snatched up the note and opened it with extreme haste; what if it was from Sophy?

A mere few seconds was sufficient to read it through. It was from Mr. Balligumph, and it was unmistakeably a summons.

Might be a fine idea to come by and see me, it said. *Quick as you can.*

It was signed with the troll's name and a jaunty sketch of a hat rendered with a few quick pen-strokes. Aubranael stared at it in confusion. What could possibly be on Balligumph's mind?

When he arrived at the Tilby Toll Bridge, his confusion deepened. He had expected a private audience, but a large group was gathered at the bridge, all talking animatedly with Balligumph. He recognised

Isabel Ellerby standing with her brother, and Anne Daverill. Thundigle was there, along with—to his surprise—the brownie who had been caught spying upon Grunewald. And Mary, Sophy's loyal servant, was also present.

He had got into the carriage to go to the bridge; not because it was very far to walk, but because he could not expect to wander through the village of Tilby with impunity while wearing his real face. But now he was obliged to reveal his true visage to a group of friends—people who had, previously, accepted him with alacrity and treated him with respect. Now they would learn how very unworthy of their regard he was.

It was a sore trial to him to open the carriage door and step down into the road, but he found that he had the courage if he just kept Miss Landon's beloved face in mind. If *she* had forgiven him, perhaps others would as well. And if they did not, he had Sophy's regard, and that was far more important.

'Ah! Mr. Stanton! How good of ye t' come.' Balligumph beckoned him over with one enormous hand. There was no trace of a smile on his face, but he did not look angry. If anything, he looked concerned. Even anxious.

Aubranael approached, trying to look confident. He felt the stares of his friends, their palpable puzzlement, and quailed inside.

But when he reached the group, Miss Ellerby put out her hand, smiled at him very kindly and said: 'Good morning, Mr. Stanton. We were very sorry to hear that you were gone from the neighbourhood, and very glad indeed to find that the truth is a little more complex.' She looked fully into his face without any trace of disgust. Probably she had been forewarned, so there was no shocked surprise; only compassion.

To his embarrassment, Aubranael's eyes filled with tears as he shook her hand. He had expected anger, disbelief, rejection and accusations; he had not expected kindness. He had certainly not expected to feel welcome. But each member of the little party shook his hand in turn and repeated Isabel's kind words, and by the end of it he felt more truly welcome than he ever had before.

'Well, well, very good,' said Balligumph. 'Capital. Now, to pressing matters. Mr. Aubranael, have you any notion at all where our Sophy is?'

Aubranael looked at him in confusion. 'At the parsonage, is she not?'

Balligumph shook his head grimly, and Aubranael felt a sudden surge of fear. Something had happened to Sophy?

'Thundigle,' said Balligumph. 'Tell all, if you please.'

The brownie drew himself up, straightened his waistcoat and stared up at Aubranael, his expression grave. 'Before I begin, Mr. Aubranael, allow me to apologise for my next words. It is not my intention to cause you any degree of disquiet.'

Aubranael stared, his alarm growing. What could Thundigle possibly have to tell him that required a formal apology first?

'Perhaps a seat,' Balligumph said kindly, and pulled Aubranael down to sit on the bridge behind him. The great troll nodded his head at Thundigle, and the brownie began his story.

He was not the speediest of narrators, and Aubranael soon began to long for him to adopt a more economical narrative style. But he got everything out in the end—a confusing tale involving a fair amount of hiding-in-drawers and accidentally-overhearing, and quite a lot of noticing-various-things and gradually-realising-the-truth.

And the truth, he eventually heard, was that the Sophy to whom he had just successfully proposed marriage was not Sophy at all. A flood of realisations came upon him all at once as he put together the various oddities about Sophy's behaviour in the last few days; the sudden revelation of the curse she lived under; her brief flashes of irritable temper. She had poured tea for him without spilling a drop.

And then there was the way she had kissed him.

It took him a while to realise that he was on his feet, making a great deal of noise. Balli's companions were gathered around him, trying with a variety of soothing gestures and well-meant words to calm him down. But Aubranael did not wish to calm down! He was engaged to an imposter, whose identity remained as mysterious as her (or his) intentions, and his Sophy was abroad somewhere in the world, possibly in danger, and quite alone! Nobody even knew for certain that she was in England. She could be in Aylfenhame. *Anywhere* in Aylfenhame.

At length he wore himself out and began to calm out of pure exhaustion. He had slept poorly ever since the loss of Hidenory's enchantment, and he could not remember the last time he had eaten. It must have been today... must it not?

'Now, now, have a seat again,' said Balli. He pressed Aubranael's shoulder surprisingly lightly for a creature of his size, but it was more than enough to send Aubranael spinning dizzily downwards to the ground. He sat for a few long moments, trying to breathe, his mind working furiously.

Whoever was wearing Sophy's face had been fairly well informed about her life—and had known all about Aubranael. Now that he thought about it, she had not seemed particularly surprised to learn that Mr. Stanton's face was not his own.

Who could possibly have known these things? He remembered Pharagora, and sighed. She had learned a fair few of his secrets, and Grunewald's, before she had been caught; and if she could do it, then others could too.

But then the supposed spy must have infiltrated Miss Landon's home as well, a thing very easily done, he was sure, but why? Someone must have felt an overpowering interest in his business and Miss Landon's in order to begin such a project, and why then interfere? And how? The art of glamour was not commonly known—certainly not in England, and not even in Aylfenhame. Not very many were sufficiently adept in the practice to mimic a real person with enough accuracy to fool even their closest friends.

His thoughts turned to Hidenory. She knew all about his masquerade, of course, and the reason behind it. And she certainly possessed the necessary talents. But he could imagine no reason at all why she might wish to take Sophy's place, and deceive him into marriage.

But that did not matter. He thought of the long, deep kiss Hidenory had given him before he had left her house; and he thought of the long, deep kiss he had shared with Miss Landon at the assembly. He was not a man of experience, so he could not say for sure; but he was *almost* certain that a kiss of that kind was somewhat out of character for a similarly inexperienced young woman like Miss Landon.

He had been kissing Hidenory both times, he was sure of it.

Aubranael stood up. 'Why are you all here?' he said, aware that the question sounded abrupt but unwilling to waste any more time.

Miss Daverill spoke up first. 'I went into the parsonage this morning, and if it *is* rude to walk in without a direct invitation, well, I make no apology for it! Sophy has never given two straws about it. But it was *not* Sophy I saw in the parlour! Quite another woman entirely! I suppose she must be something to do with the new parson—his mother, or something—but as I had heard nothing at all about a new arrival, I went to see Isabel.'

Miss Ellerby nodded and took up the tale. 'I was concerned as well, for I have three times attempted to visit Sophy these last two days, and every time she has denied me! And I received no reply at all to my notes, either.'

Mr. Ellerby said: 'My sister and Miss Daverill were determined on consulting Mr. Balligumph. If a new parson had arrived in Tilby, he would certainly know about it; and being a close friend of Miss Landon's, he might be supposed to know what had become of her as well.'

'And Mary and I accompanied them, of course,' said Thundigle. 'Once we had compared our separate information, we were highly concerned.'

Aubranael looked at Pharagora, but she merely gave him a small smile and said nothing.

'So we are all here to help Sophy?'

A chorus of assent and emphatic nods answered him, and he felt relieved. It was good to have help.

'Very well, then,' he said. 'I believe I may know who has taken her place.'

'I do, too,' said Pharagora, and everyone stared at her.

Half an hour later, Aubranael knocked at the door of the parsonage, feeling tense and curiously exposed. He was alone, at least ostensibly: the Ellerbys, Thundigle, Mary and Miss Daverill were sitting in his carriage just around a turn in the road, out of sight of the parsonage but close enough to come to his aid. Mr. Balligumph had stayed at the bridge; he was calling in his many "associates", he said, gathering every scrap of information he could about Miss Landon's actions over the past few days (either one of the Miss Landons, that is). Pharagora was assisting him in some unspecified way.

Aubranael's task was to confront the version of Miss Landon who was currently staying at the parsonage. He was not surprised when no immediate answer came in response to his knock; she must first establish that it was *him*, and not one of Sophy's friends coming to complicate her masquerade. Once she had established that to her satisfaction, she would come to the door.

And the door opened, revealing the old woman he had met the last time. It occurred to him—rather belatedly—to feel some relief at the morning's revelations, for it meant that that the curse afflicting the person before him had nothing to do with *his* Sophy.

'Miss Landon,' he said with what he hoped was his usual smile.

'Ah! Mr. Stanton!' she said winningly, beckoning him inside. 'I was hoping *very* much to see you this morning.'

He followed her through to the parlour, trying his best to appear at ease. 'You are looking well,' he said. 'I trust you are in good health?'

She sat down with curious grace, given her appearance, and chuckled. 'I look in the very best of health, do I not? I believe these rags are very becoming.'

'Why do you wear the rags?' he asked, with real curiosity. 'I presume it is merely the appearance of age that is beyond your control; not the attire as well.'

She shrugged one shoulder, her expression suddenly bleak. 'But why would I bother? I will be ugly however I choose to garb myself.'

Aubranael could think of no sensible response to such a statement, especially in the face of the violent bitterness she evidently felt at her condition. Instead he said, 'And how is Felebre? I have not seen her since my visit to your abode. Why, that must be a full month at least.'

'She is, as usual, an enigma,' came the reply. 'I do not see her for weeks, and then all at once she will arrive with some—' Abruptly she broke off, and stared at Aubranael with such obvious consternation that he could not help smiling.

'Hello, Hidenory,' he said.

The silence stretched as Hidenory visibly attempted to find a way to prolong the masquerade. But then she sighed gustily, and slumped in her chair. 'And it was all going so *well*,' she said peevishly. 'A curse upon all clever gentlemen! The stupid ones are, after all, so much more worth knowing.'

'A curse?' Aubranael repeated. 'Truly?'

'No, of course not,' she snapped. 'I am not a *complete* monster.'

'That remains to be seen,' said Aubranael coldly. 'Your behaviour does require some explanation.'

'It is true about the curse.'

'So you *did* just curse me!'

Hidenory smiled maliciously at him. 'Perhaps he *is* just a little bit stupid, after all,' she said, apparently to herself. 'No, foolish boy, the curse upon *me*. Only it is not so very obliging as to afflict me for only a few days every month. I must spend each and every day in this abominable guise! Every daylight minute! Only at night may I return to a more... pleasing shape.'

'And you were attempting to use *me* to break the curse,' Aubranael said. He spoke as angrily as he could, in order to smother the stirrings of sympathy he was beginning to feel. He of all people understood her pain.

'I thought you would understand me,' she said, unconsciously echoing his thoughts. 'I was going to tell you the truth in time!'

'After we had been bound together for eternity?' he said acidly.

'I would have made you happy,' she said, with a salacious smile he found thoroughly unnerving.

'I doubt that. And what of Miss Landon? What have you done with her?'

'Nothing too terrible, if that is what is worrying you.'

'Of *course* it is worrying me! Do you feel nothing at all?'

'Not often, no,' said Hidenory with perfect unconcern. 'Not anymore.'

'Where is Sophy?'

'She went through the door.'

'Which door?'

'The same door you went through.'

'So she is at Grunewald's house?'

Hidenory rolled her eyes. 'No, of course not. What use is a door that always opens in the same place?'

'Quite useful, as a rule,' said Aubranael. He stood up and crossed to her chair, allowing every shred of anger he could muster to show upon his face. He was able to loom over her quite satisfactorily from this position. '*Where is Sophy?*' he repeated.

Hidenory smiled up at him. 'Truthfully, I have very little idea.'

For a moment Aubranael was sorely tempted to hit her. That smirking smile of hers...! The brazen way she admitted to him that she had *lost* his love! But she was a lady, even if she was evil, and besides, he did not hit people who were at a disadvantage.

He did not hit people at all, come to think of it.

He took a deep breath and said, with as much calm as he could manage: 'Tell me what happened.'

Hidenory's recitation was brief, and within a very few minutes he had the whole story. Sophy had gone through the door, expecting to find help on the other side. But she had been knowingly sent into a trap. Tut-Gut had a reputation in Aylfenhame: he was not among the most evil of the fae, but he had a vicious side, and he was very willing to put to use any lost souls who wandered into his cottage.

Aubranael began to lose the little concern he had felt for Hidenory's safety. Unceremoniously he grabbed a handful of her robes in one hand and her arm in the other, and hauled her to her feet.

'We are going to find Miss Landon,' he hissed at her. 'You are going to help us, or I will personally ensure that your personal curse becomes the *least* of your worries.'

Hauling Hidenory behind him, he opened the front door of the parsonage to find Mr. Ellerby standing on the other side.

'Ah,' said the other young man. 'The ladies were beginning to feel concerned.'

'We will be taking this *lady* to see Mr. Balligumph,' said Aubranael, shoving Hidenory forward. 'And then we are going to the Outwoods of Aylfenhame to find Miss Landon.'

'Oh,' said Mr. Ellerby. 'Very well.'

Aubranael was surprised—nay, *astonished*—to find Grunewald awaiting them at the bridge. He was sitting with Mr. Balligumph, sipping a cup of tea and looking thoroughly comfortable. The Goblin King smiled pleasantly at Aubranael and Mr. Ellerby, and then smiled upon Hidenory with *very* warm approval.

Aubranael turned Hidenory over to Balligumph, with a quick recital of everything he had learned, and then turned his attention to Grunewald with a quizzical smile.

'I was asked to come,' said Grunewald in answer to his unspoken question.

'Are you here to help us?' said Aubranael. He found that difficult to believe: Grunewald had made it very clear that he had no desire to help Aubranael any further at all.

But Grunewald nodded once, and smiled. 'To be precise, I intend to *begin* by paying my very particular compliments to the lady.' He rose and did so, bowing over Hidenory's withered hands and murmuring something about *excellent scheme* and *admirable wits* and *congratulate you most sincerely*.

Hidenory smiled in triumph. 'I knew *you* would appreciate the scheme,' she said proudly.

But Grunewald's tone turned gently chiding as he said: 'But it is a *trifle* outrageous, do not you think? I cannot help being mildly discontented with you, my dear. This young man is quite a delicate flower, you understand. He could never keep up with you.'

Aubranael bridled at that, but he stopped himself from raising any objection. Grunewald's observation was not entirely unfair, and besides, he appeared to be working his way around to declaring himself on Miss Landon's side.

Hidenory realised the same thing, for she glared at Grunewald and snatched back her hands. 'You admire my cunning but you will devote your own to undoing all my fine work? Ah! Treacherous indeed.'

'You will have heard the adage,' Grunewald said smoothly. 'Never trust the Goblin King, eh? But no matter. This is how the game proceeds, is it not? It is all a matter of wit and counter-wit. You have played your very best pieces, and now we will play ours. And may the best goblin win.'

'Much as I appreciate the prospect of receiving your help,' Aubranael said, 'I cannot understand you. Yesterday you swore you'd had done with me.'

Grunewald turned his glittering green gaze upon Aubranael. 'Not at all, my dear fellow. I merely refused to give you the specific *type* of help you were requesting.'

'And you warned me not to place myself too far in your debt,' Aubranael reminded him. 'Does that no longer stand?'

'Oh, it does. But,' he said gently, 'has it not occurred to you, dear Aubranael, that this matter is somewhat larger than you and your romantic affairs?'

Aubranael blinked. 'I do not understand you,' he repeated.

'That is very evident. But do not let it concern you. I am here on Mr. Balligumph's request, and so it has nothing at all to do with you.'

Silenced, Aubranael felt a little injured by this cold statement. Then he realised that he would benefit from Grunewald's help in finding Sophy, but without being considered to be any further in debt to the Goblin King himself. He swallowed his feelings of affront—if he had come to think of the Goblin King as a friend, he was indeed a fool—and nodded.

'But,' he said, frowning, 'how do you know what any of this is about?'

'I do not know, for certain,' Grunewald said, with a sideways glance at Hidenory. 'But the common thread to all your various little tales is the cat. Felebre. And that may be far more significant than you know.'

That silenced Aubranael altogether. Felebre? His friend and companion? The cat had always been enigmatic, but Aubranael had never doubted that she was much as she appeared to be. A cat. One who enjoyed the hunt and the chase, and who did not shun him because his face was unsightly.

But it had been Felebre who had guided him to Hidenory, he remembered. How else had the cat been involved, and what did it mean?

'Very well, now,' said Balligumph, interrupting his train of thought. The troll had hitherto watched the proceedings with great interest but without making any attempt to intervene. Now he stood up and clapped his hands together, instantly focusing everyone's attention upon him. 'Who is to come along to the Outwoods?'

Everybody volunteered without hesitation, excepting Hidenory and Grunewald.

'Ye'll come along too, miss,' said Balligumph, eyeing Hidenory with a glimmer of fury in his bright blue eyes.

Hidenory waved a hand dismissively.

'An' what of His Majesty?' said Balligumph, looking at Grunewald.

'I can do a little better than that, I believe.' Grunewald produced a gleaming silver horn from somewhere, put it to his lips, and blew a long note. The sound was so loud Aubranael was forced to cover his ears; even then the noise beat down upon him, a riotous racket comprising the mingled notes of thousands of horns blown at once. Finally the notes died away, leaving silence.

Balligumph nodded approvingly, and Hidenory began to look afraid. Miss Daverill and Miss Ellerby were standing as far from the troll as they could, Aubranael noticed, and now they began to back away from Grunewald as well. Poor Mary looked terrified but grimly resolved; she had Thundigle at her knee, patting her leg to comfort her. Mr. Ellerby was keeping up a protective stance over the entire group.

Would this curious mix of company be enough to find Sophy, he wondered, and to rescue her from any dangerous predicament she might be in? He could only hope so.

Then the wind began to blow. It was a harsh, cold wind, utterly unsuited to the warmth of an afternoon in June, and it brought with it the distant howling of hounds.

Aubranael stared at Grunewald, awed and afraid. Could it be... had he just...?

He did not have time to complete these fragmented thoughts, for a terrific gust of wind threatened to knock him off his feet. He saw it then, approaching from across the fields: the Goblin Hunt. Borne by the wind, they came: a sea of hounds, ghostly and insubstantial, galloping through the air at full tilt and baying for blood. Suddenly he was surrounded by the dizzying whirlwind of the Hunt; ghostly shapes swirled and danced around him with appalling speed, bringing a wind cold enough to chill him to the bone. Each hound bore an insubstantial goblin upon its back, and each rider bore a raised spear or a knife or a garden rake—anything at all, it seemed, so long as it could be enthusiastically brandished.

Grunewald shouted something over the wind. It was in a language Aubranael could not understand, but it brought the Hunt into a knot gathered tightly around the Goblin King and Hidenory. Grunewald shouted something else, and abruptly the Hunt wheeled and galloped away.

'Follow them, then!' hollered Balligumph. 'An' be quick, now, or ye'll be left behind!'

A flood of energy rushed through Aubranael, strengthening his tired limbs and clearing his mind. He remembered the day he had met Miss Landon: he had been running through Grenlowe in pursuit of Felebre, and he had almost knocked Sophy down.

Well: to run swift and sure was something that he knew how to do. He would do it again, and if he was lucky, he would find Miss Landon once again.

CHAPTER SIXTEEN

After another hour or two of walking—or perhaps it was ten or twenty or more—Sophy was no longer feeling grateful for her guides. She felt like a long-suffering nurse escorting a party of young children. Pinch *would* insist on teasing Tut-Gut, and he would not leave off, no matter how earnest her entreaties; and then Tara-Tat began needling Graen, and before long the two were squabbling mightily in their high, piping voices. Pinket alone proved a restful companion, but perhaps that was merely because he lacked the means to make any noise. She had no notion what might be passing through the wisp's thoughts—if anything at all.

But after a long time—two hours or ten?—the combatants appeared to exhaust themselves, and a heavy silence descended on the company. It possessed a decided air of sulkiness and more than a hint of petulance, but Sophy cared not a whit for that. She took full advantage of the reprieve: collecting her scattered thoughts, calming her shredded nerves and reassembling what was left of her patience.

When the voices began again, her heart sank with dismay and she stared hopelessly at her troublesome companions. 'Please,' she sighed. 'Please, just a little more peace!'

The company halted as one, and four small faces stared up at her in blank incomprehension. The murmur of voices continued, but she could plainly see that the mutterings were not coming from any of her companions.

'But who is speaking?' she said, staring all around herself in puzzlement. 'I see no one.'

A shriek of laughter split the air, muffled as if reaching her ears from some distance away. The sound resonated in her memory: she had heard it before, and not very long since. When she had journeyed through the Outwoods before, on her way to see Hidenory, she had heard just the same style of conversation: low mutterings, a babble of voices all talking at once, and an occasional cackling laugh that raised the hairs on her arms.

'Where is that coming from?' she said, frowning.

Her companions began to hear it, too, for their faces echoed her confusion—and curiosity. They rambled through the trees in a scattered way, Tara-Tat with Tut-Gut, Pinket with Pinch, and Graen following Sophy herself, all searching for the source of the noise.

At length a shout went up. 'Here!' carolled Pinch, and Sophy heard the rustling crash of a small person hurling himself into the undergrowth. He kept up the shout, like a rider leading the hunt as he barrelled away through the trees. Sophy followed.

She soon saw what had attracted Pinch's attention. As she covered the ground with her long strides—never quite catching up with Pinch in spite of her much superior height—she glimpsed a long table through the trees, with a gaggle of fae seated around it. The table was *very* long indeed, she realised: it stretched on and on through the forest, and while she could see the head of the table she could not see the other end.

It was undoubtedly the same table she had seen before.

A tall, velvet-upholstered chair stood at the head of the peculiar table, and in it sat an Ayliri girl, her skin and hair as dark as Aubranael's, her build lithe and youthful. Sophy could make out very little else, for the lady was slumped over onto the tablecloth, her face resting on her folded arms. She appeared to be asleep.

Some manner of party was in merry progress around her, none of the guests seeming to notice their slumbering hostess. Sophy saw brownies like Thundigle, hobgoblins like Tut-Gut, elves and flower-fae like Pinch and Graen, knobbly-kneed goblins, a troll almost as large as Balligumph taking up three places all by himself, and even an assortment of hatted-and-coated woodland creatures sitting up at the table. They were all drinking tea, but not in the refined way Sophy was used to. Each guest had an enormous tea cup set before them and they were guzzling tea at a mighty rate, pausing frequently in the midst of their chatter to refill their giant cups from one of the teapots that were clustered atop the table.

And there were a great many of these, all in different sizes and decorated in riotous colours. As far as Sophy could see, they were never empty, no matter how many times the tea cups were refilled.

Pinch drew up and stopped near the sleeping hostess, his whole body registering a mixture of surprise and glee. He began to bounce on his toes, and as Sophy came up behind him she heard him say: 'The Teapot Society! What felicity!'

'But what is that?' Sophy asked, gasping for breath after her headlong dash through the trees. As she stood taking in the strange sight, Tut-Gut and Tara-Tat and Graen and Pinket appeared beside her and stared too.

'A tea party that never ends!' Pinch said, beaming up at her. 'Each pot contains a different kind of tea, and they will pour forever. Imagine it! Lavender and honey! Jasmine and cream! Thyme, moonflower, honeysuckle, white ginger, sunblossom, sweet and sour apple, lemon and sage!'

Sophy noticed that, in between bouts of tea-drinking, the guests were also eating. There were little coloured boxes nestling between the teapots, though she could not see what they contained. 'What are they eating?' she asked Pinch.

His eyes rolled up in an expression of acute ecstasy. 'Only the very *best* cakes in Aylfenhame!'

'And I suppose the cakes never run out, either,' Sophy surmised.

Pinch shook his head gleefully. 'An empty chair!' he shouted in delight, and ran towards it. The chair in question looked placed especially for him, Sophy realised, for it was tall enough to allow him to reach the table, just wide enough to accommodate his tiny frame, and three tiny teapots with matching cake-boxes were set out ready.

Sophy began to wonder whether there might be a chair for her, too, but she had barely begun her search when something very strange happened.

Just as Pinch swung himself up over the arm of his chosen chair, the sleeping hostess awoke. She sat up abruptly, stared in horror at Pinch and screamed: 'NO! You must not sit down!'

It was too late, for Pinch was already comfortably ensconced in the chair and reaching for the first cake-box. Sophy realised that Graen had also found a seat, and Tut-Gut and Tara-Tat were sharing one further down the table. Only she and Pinket remained aloof.

The babble of conversation had stopped instantly at the hostess's shout, and all of the tea-drinkers were staring at her.

'Why must they not be seated?' Sophy said into the silence.

The Ayliri woman fixed her enormous eyes on Sophy. They were dark gold in colour, like antique bronze, and filled with a vast sadness. 'It is too late,' she said softly, and three fat tears rolled down her cheeks.

Sophy could not even begin to guess what the girl's behaviour meant, but it was alarming her. She was tired of feeling alarmed, tired of trouble and danger, and that tiredness made her short of patience. 'What is it?' she repeated. 'Explain yourself, if you please!'

But the girl closed her eyes and slowly sank back down onto the table. 'I am so very sorry,' she whispered before, apparently, falling asleep once more. The guests appeared to take this as the signal to resume their merriment, for the low roar of mingled voices picked up immediately.

Sophy sighed. 'Pinch,' she called. 'Tut-Gut? Tara? I believe we had better depart at once.'

Pinch did not appear to hear her, and neither did the hobs. She called their names and Graen's once more, quite loudly, but to no effect. Even when she stood at Pinch's elbow and spoke directly into his ear, he made no sign of having heard but continued guzzling tea and stuffing cakes into his mouth. He was talking all the while to the guests on either side of him, laughing frequently as if he was having the very best time of his life.

Tut-Gut and Tara-Tut and Graen were behaving in exactly the same way, and were equally oblivious to her attempts to communicate with them. It was as though they had slipped sideways into a different world, and though Sophy could see and hear *them*, they could not see or hear her.

Sophy's alarm blossomed into fear and dismay. She stared for a long moment at her lost friends, then at Pinket who still bobbed at her shoulder.

'I do not like the look of this at all,' she told him. 'What do you think?'

Pinket began weaving about in the air and spinning around her head. Taking this as a sign of disquiet, she nodded. 'Something must be done,' she said firmly.

Marching up to the head of the table, she addressed the hostess once more. After all, the sleeping lady appeared to be the only one who could hear her. 'Please wake up,' Sophy begged. 'My friends cannot hear me; something appears to be terribly amiss.'

The lady turned her head to face Sophy, though she neither opened her eyes nor sat up. 'They will never hear you again,' she said in a low voice. 'I am very sorry.'

'What do you mean?' Sophy said, frightened. She stared down the long, long length of the table, at the many, many creatures merrily stuffing themselves, and felt a deep sense of foreboding. What were they all doing here? Had they all happened upon the tea-table, like Pinch, and cheerfully joined in? Where *was* the end of the table? How many creatures were sitting here, talking and laughing and eating cake, and how long had they been at the party?

'So many years…' whispered the lady. 'You had better leave them. There is nothing to be done for them.' At last she pushed herself upright, her arms shaking with the effort, and propped her chin on her hands. Staring hopelessly down the length of the table, she sighed and said: 'But they are enjoying themselves so much, are they not? That is something.'

Sophy quickly grew tired of these mysterious pronouncements and began to feel like shaking the girl until she spoke a little more clearly. 'What is the Teapot Society?' she said, employing a firm tone to show that she expected a clear answer. 'Why are you all here? What is this about?'

'You had better leave them,' the young lady repeated, with the faintest of smiles at Sophy. 'I know it is hard, but you must be grateful that *you* were spared. Go at once! And whatever you do, do not take a chair!'

'I am not leaving without my companions,' Sophy said, fixing the maddening Ayliri with a cool stare.

'Then you are not leaving at all,' came the reply, 'and you may as well take a chair after all. There, I see a comfortable one near to me. It is perfect for you. You will find your favourite tea in the first teapot, your true love's favourite in the next, and in the third, something entirely new.'

'I will wait until I reach home for a cup of my favourite tea, thank you, and I do not have a true love.'

'Why, of course you do,' said the lady, staring at her in surprise. 'For there is the teapot, as sure as my name is Lihyaen.'

Sophy began to think that the woman was soft in her wits. And no wonder, if she had been sitting here for years as she had implied. 'Are you keeping the guests here?' she demanded. 'Have you some form of enchantment upon them?'

'Yes, of course,' said the girl faintly. She was beginning to sway with weariness, wilting slowly but inexorably back onto the table.

'Then you must remove it!' Sophy cried, aghast. 'Why would you do such a thing?'

'It is not of my making,' whispered the girl. And then she began to snore.

Sophy stared at her helplessly. Then she stared down the table at Pinch, Tut-Gut, Tara-Tat and Graen, who were still laughing uproariously and quaffing tea. What could she possibly do for them? She was hopelessly out of her depth; her knowledge of curses and enchantments was limited indeed, for they were rare in England.

She stood for several long minutes, paralysed with indecision, her thoughts racing but her mind blank of inspiration. She tried shaking the sleeping lady again, but this time she did not wake up, and nothing Sophy did could distract Pinch and the others from their repast.

Then several things happened at once.

The first thing was the appearance of Felebre. The great purple cat came galloping into the tea-party clearing, leapt up onto the table with extraordinary grace and raced up to the head of it. There she sat, and proceeded to lick the sleeping girl's face all over. Nor did she ignore Sophy, for she rubbed her long body against Sophy's hip on her way past.

'Felebre!' Sophy cried in relief. Then she questioned her own feelings, for had not Felebre been responsible for leading her to Hidenory? The cat was in some measure responsible for Sophy's current predicament, so she ought not be pleased to see her. But the cat's behaviour towards the sleeping girl—and Sophy herself—was strange: gone was her quiet dignity, and in its place she displayed a kind of bounding joyousness, like a gambolling kitten. Sophy noticed, with faint unease, that Felebre's eyes and Lihyaen's were almost the same colour.

She was not given a great deal of time to consider these points, for a great howling reached her ears, distant but growing rapidly closer. It sounded as though a pack of hunting dogs was approaching through the trees; and why not? Plenty of stranger things had happened. But they were moving impossibly fast; barely had she had time to register the sound before the dogs swept through the trees and crashed over the table.

They were incorporeal, mere hound-shapes sketched in the air, but they made enough noise for five hunting-packs together. Goblins crouched low over their backs—solid creatures, these, with ferocious grins wreathing their pointed faces. They came at her at a dead run and swarmed over her, howling and yipping and bellowing as they rode victorious circles around her.

Sophy barely had time to feel afraid—yet again—before another thing happened. A tall figure appeared in the wake of the goblin hunters; tall and lithe and brown-skinned, with long dark hair flying everywhere in the wind. She caught the briefest glimpse of his disfigured face before she found herself swept up in a fierce embrace and held very closely indeed against a hard male body.

'Miss Landon, I am so relieved...' he was saying into her ear. 'I have never been so afraid in all my life!'

'Aubranael?' she said in confusion. 'How came you to be here?' And how came he to recognise her in her hag-form? But when she glanced down at her own hands, they were smooth and young once more. Hidenory's enchantment had worn off, she supposed, or it had retreated in the face of some greater power. She did not much care which; she was only relieved to be restored to herself.

But... Aubranael. His embrace confused and embarrassed her— and prompted some other feelings as well, to which she could not precisely put a name. But she was so relieved to see him, too, that for one *very* shocking instant she melted against him and allowed herself to be held, and hang the impropriety.

Aubranael smiled into her face and made as if to kiss her. Shocked, Sophy pulled away.

'I forgot,' he said, his face registering some manner of sudden realisation. 'I apologise. There is much to explain.'

But Sophy had not time for his explanations just at that moment, for her attention was distracted by the sight of Mr. Balligumph stamping mightily through the trees and bearing down upon the tea-table at great speed. '*Balligumph?*' she said incredulously. Behind the troll came Isabel Ellerby carrying Thundigle, and Charles Ellerby carrying another brownie. Behind *them* came poor Mary, staggering as though her feet pained her very much. They caught sight of Sophy, and their faces lit up with delight and relief. Sophy's own heart thumped weirdly with a mixture of emotions she could not immediately put a name to. Had all of these people come here—into the heart of Aylfenhame—in order to find *her?* For a moment she was so overcome with love and gratitude and relief that she could not speak.

Then she saw Anne. Her young friend had found a seat at the table and was already in the thick of the party, with three teapots set before her and three matching cake-boxes. 'Oh, no,' Sophy groaned. 'Anne *would* be the first to sit down!'

The next half-hour was a mess of pure chaos. Her attempts to extricate Anne from the never-ending tea party were as unsuccessful as her attempts to free Pinch, Graen and the others, but that did not keep her from trying. But then the gathering was greatly augmented when fully half of the goblin hunt-riders found seats and began to gorge themselves; the rest might have followed suit, but a barked command from—inexplicably—Mr. Green recalled them before they could commit themselves. How came Mr. Green to be here? And how was it that he commanded such unthinking obedience from a small army of goblins? Sophy wanted to ask, but she could find no opportunity amidst the chaos.

When Isabel and Charles Ellerby began to drift towards the table, Sophy did her best to intercept them, but she was too late. Soon they, too, were honoured guests at the sleeping girl's party, sitting either side of Anne and joining with her in every gaiety. Felebre took up a position near the strange hostess's head and lay there, watching the festivities with an unreadable expression, her tail twitching at the tip. Balligumph attempted to reach Sophy with some manner of message for her, if she was reading his gestures correctly; but his bulk was against him, and he could not find a path between the trees and the table, and past the remnants of Mr. Green's goblins.

And then there was Hidenory, of whom Sophy was powerfully aware. The witch kept to one side, watching the proceedings with an inscrutable expression on her face. Twilight was rapidly approaching; she would soon be restored to her youth and beauty, and then what would she do? For Sophy read a degree of resolve in her pose and in the set of her withered old lips. But she could not guess what the witch might be planning; she could only keep a part of her attention fixed upon her, in the hopes that she might be able to protect herself—and if necessary, her friends—from any further interference.

Aubranael left her side; for a moment she panicked that he had succumbed to the lure of the table, but she spotted him bending solicitously over the sleeping girl. He began talking to her, words which were lost amidst the roar of merriment. Sophy considered following him, but quickly changed her mind. She wanted to speak to Balligumph; he was always the voice of reason, the source of exactly the piece of information one needed. If anybody knew how to resolve the problem of the Teapot Society, it would be he.

She began to force her way through the hound-riders, past the haphazardly-placed chairs at the tea-table and between the slender trees that arched over the tea-drinkers. Balligumph saw her intent and planted himself firmly, looking as immoveable as a small tree, or perhaps a very large rock. She had almost reached him when Mary bustled past her, making her way towards the table. Sophy saw an empty chair nearby.

'No!' she cried, catching at Mary's wrist. 'Mary, you must not! You see the consequences before you.'

Mary clucked her disapproval, and gently—but firmly—withdrew her arm from Sophy's grip. 'What a thing to say! I would think my Sophy would remember that I was *never* a tea-drinker. I had far rather drink washing-up water.' She picked up one of the discarded tea cups and, to Sophy's mild amazement, began to tidy up. 'Such a shocking mess,' she was muttering. 'I cannot think too well of any lady who permits such a ruckus as *this* at her own table.'

Sophy's astonishment grew when the red-capped hob who had previously owned the tea cup in question looked directly at Mary, his face a picture of horror. He swiped at the cups she was holding, but Mary was too fast for him. 'Fear not, little master! I will bring them back, fresh and new, in a trice.'

She continued to tidy with the efficiency of long years of practice: polishing soiled teapots, collecting tea-stained cups and wiping up cake crumbs. While they had ignored—or been oblivious to—Sophy's presence entirely, the tea-drinkers watched Mary's progress with full comprehension, and no small amount of anger.

'Mary, I think perhaps you had better take care,' Sophy said, darting after her old friend. When a teacup fell from Mary's overloaded arms and smashed upon the floor, a tide of angry muttering swept over the table and Sophy's fear for Mary grew.

But then she noticed something else. The owner of the broken cup—a little flower-fae who resembled Graen—began to blink and yawn, as though waking up from a long sleep. She stared around herself with confusion, her face registering complete surprise at her situation. The effect lasted for only a few moments, but to Sophy it was highly significant.

Experimentally, she picked up one of Pinch's tea-cups and began to ostentatiously polish the tea-stained exterior. It was not long before the cup fell through her fingers and fell upon the table. It broke into four pieces.

'Oh, gracious,' she murmured. 'How very clumsy of me.'

Pinch blinked at her in complete astonishment, his expression dazed.

'Ha!' Sophy cried, delighted. 'Very well: breaking things is, after all, one of my *particular* talents.'

She began to smash tea cups with enthusiasm, even sending a few of the precious teapots onto the floor. Mary quickly caught on to her plan and began to follow suit: it evidently pained her immensely to destroy such beautiful tableware, but she did not hesitate. They worked their way down the table, smashing everything they could reach, and behind them they left a trail of dazed and blinking party guests.

Then Sophy heard Balli's heavy tread behind her. She turned just in time to see him forcing his way through to the table; once he reached it he swept out his great arms and sent at least twenty tea-things crashing to the floor. 'Sometimes,' he winked, 'size is a great boon.'

Sophy grinned at him. She turned back to her work, making her way rapidly towards the head of the table and Aubranael. He had left off speaking to the girl and was now hurling crockery into the trees with quick, efficient movements. Most of the items he threw collided directly with the slender trunks and broke on impact.

All at once, the tea-drinkers seemed to awaken en masse from the weird enchantment that had held them in thrall. Observing the destruction in progress, they immediately began to participate, and for a full minute the clearing resounded with a terrific din of splintering porcelain, and the cackling laughter of the erstwhile cake-eaters.

At last, every single item of crockery lay in pieces along the table or the floor or between the trees, and a heavy silence descended. There must be hundreds of creatures gathered around the table, Sophy thought, and for a long, heavy moment not one of them spoke.

Then they all began to talk at once.

There was much angry gesticulating and excitable waving-of-arms, a great many scowling faces, almost as many highly confused ones, and so many opinions expressed altogether that Sophy could distinguish nothing sensible at all. After a few minutes of this, a few of the tea-drinkers retreated from the table and disappeared into the trees. Many others followed, and the throng quickly depleted itself.

As soon as Sophy had room to move and breathe, she hastened to find Anne, Isabel and Charles and ensure that they were restored to themselves.

'I am so sorry,' she said breathlessly, pressing each of their hands in turn and staring anxiously into their faces. The confusion was clearing from their eyes and they began to look much more like their usual selves.

'That was the oddest thing,' Isabel said thoughtfully. 'I can hardly remember what I was thinking, but it was absolutely imperative to drink as much tea as possible. I had an intense fear that it would run out before I had drunk my fill, and then something terrible would happen.' She paused, and then said in a low voice, 'Though it is awfully shocking to mention such things before company, I cannot help asking... do you imagine there is a commode somewhere here abouts?'

Sophy laughed with relief to find such a commonplace concern on Isabel's mind, but before she had chance to reply she noticed something odd.

Pieces of broken porcelain were creeping across the table-cloth and pressing their edges together. As she watched, several splintered chunks reformed themselves into a perfect tea cup, which wobbled upright and then sat there with—she could have sworn—an air of smugness.

All across the table and the floor, the same thing was happening. The Teapot Society was reforming itself before Sophy's eyes, and it was all coming together *very* quickly indeed.

'Back from the table!' roared Balligumph. His great, deep voice easily carried across the clearing, and no doubt far beyond. As one, all of the remaining goblins and tea-drinkers jumped backwards. Sophy and her friends backed away, too, eyeing the inexplicable crockery warily.

Sophy noticed that Hidenory had given up her silent vigil and was now making her way towards the head of the table, where Aubranael still sat. A nameless fear seized her heart and she began to push her way towards him. If Hidenory intended him some form of harm, she had little idea how she would intervene; but she knew she must at least *try*.

'All right, that's quite enough!' roared Balligumph. 'I will be makin' an end t' this unnatural business an' no mistake. Who among the lot of ye can tell me what this nonsense is about?'

His gaze was fixed on the sleeping girl who, Sophy now saw, was no longer sleeping at all. She was sitting up, her thin body trembling with the effort and her eyes fixed on Aubranael's face. He was sitting with one arm around her shoulders and his free hand at her waist, lending her his strength.

Their faces wore identical expressions of stricken horror and wonder, and they were so lost in the contemplation of each other that they patently did not hear Balligumph's shout.

Sophy felt a small, unpleasant sensation growing somewhere inside of her as she watched this display. Aubranael's every gesture, every movement, was full of a heart-breaking tenderness, and he stared at her as though he never wished to release her ever again.

'OI!' roared Balligumph, so loudly that Sophy could feel the trees shake. 'AUBRANAEL! CRAZY LADY! I'M WANTIN' AN ANSWER HERE!'

Aubranael and the lady both turned to stare unseeingly at Balligumph, incomprehension written on both their faces. 'I beg your pardon?' said Aubranael.

Balligumph glowered at him, and took a deep breath. 'I said,' he repeated in a more reasonable tone, 'does one of ye two crazies have any notion at all what in the blazes is goin' on here?'

Aubranael stared down the long, long table: at the tea-cups and teapots still gluing themselves back together; at the crowd of goblins and elves and flower-fae and hobs and brownies and humans staying as close to the trees as possible; and finally at Sophy herself.

'Yes,' he said in a heartbroken voice. 'I—that is—some of it.'

'Yes,' said Balligumph in a knowing way. 'I had a feelin' ye might. Would ye be plannin' t' explain? Or shall we ask the lady Lihyaen?'

CHAPTER SEVENTEEN

Aubranael was a child again.

He had gone to the aid of the sleeping girl because something in her hopeless, helpless posture had touched him deeply. As he approached he had noticed something odd about the thin brown arms that lay splayed across the table top: the sleeves of her dress barely extended past her elbows, and their cuffs were frayed to ribbons. The dress itself had once been white, he judged, with roses or some other bloom printed across it; now it was grey with age and dirt. In places, the fabric appeared to be rotting away.

As he had helped her to sit—instinctively lending her an arm of support when she wavered—he had found himself looking into large, sad golden eyes.

He had seen those eyes before.

At once, a flood of memory bore him away from the scene of the mad tea-party and back more than twenty years. He saw the soaring white walls of the Royal Palace once more in his mind's eye, and the heavily fragranced gardens he had run through as a boy. He had been no one of any eminence, merely the son of one of the many gardeners; but the little princess, Lihyaen, was similar in age and temperament and they had long been the greatest of friends.

Until the day she had vanished during a game of hide-and-seek. He had spent hours searching the gardens for her, running through the low-hanging trees and fragrant bushes until he was tired and footsore—and increasingly frightened. At last he had gone indoors and crept up the long, long flights of stairs to her nursery—a room he was never allowed to go into. But he found no guards at the door to prevent him, and none of her nurses waited there to shoo him away. Lihyaen's pretty chamber was silent and empty, and something about the circumstance felt mightily *wrong* to him in a way he would have been hard-put to describe.

Heart pounding, he had crept into every corner of her room, searching through cupboards and chests and under chairs in case she had hidden herself away in any one of them.

She had not; but the door to her bedchamber stood ajar...

The little princess lay in her bed, her dark hair strewn across her pale silken pillows and her face turned towards the window. Had she grown tired, and returned to rest without informing him? But a glance at her face had told him that she was not resting. Her eyes—large and golden like her mother's—were wide open, staring sightlessly at the failing daylight beyond the cool glass panes. She made no movement of any kind; not even when, sobbing with fright, he had shaken her arms and touched her face and put his cheek against hers.

So absorbed was he that he failed to notice the other person in the room. A soft footstep alerted him, and a faint *swish* of fabric. He looked up to see a tall, white-cloaked figure disappearing through the open door into Lihyaen's nursery.

He had felt rage for the first time in his young life. Shaking with it, he had torn through the doorway in pursuit, with no clear idea in mind as to what he intended to do with the mysterious intruder should be succeed in catching them. His young brain only wished to *rend* and *claw* and *howl his fury* until the cloaked one reversed whatever he had done to Lihyaen.

He did not receive the opportunity, of course. He had hurled himself, howling, at the intruder's legs—and received a face-full of something that *burned* as his reward. The memory of that blinding agony could still make him shudder, more than twenty years later.

His face had never been the same, and of course Lihyaen had never come back. The princess was given a ceremonious burial; a mere few months later her mother, Queen Anthelaena, had died—of grief for her daughter, many said.

And then King Edironal had disappeared; walked out of his palace one day, and never returned. So the kingdom of Aylfenhame had drifted on, year after year, with no liege lords and no one with a clear claim to the throne.

Except, perhaps, his daughter. And as Aubranael stared into the strange girl's face, a wild hope built in his heart. She looked young; too young. But perhaps—perhaps she had *not* died. Perhaps the dearest friend of his youth and heart had survived after all...

'Lihyaen?' he whispered.

And her dreamy, vacant eyes had sharpened and fixed full upon his face, her own full of wonder. 'How is it that you know my name?' she said.

He could have wept. He *was* weeping, he realised, as a warm tear ran down his cheek. 'Because I am Aubranael,' he said softly.

At first, she could not see it. Her eyes tracked over his face, pull of puzzlement and doubt. 'But you... your face?'

He smiled sadly. 'Since the night you died,' he said.

She lifted one spindly arm, shaky with the effort, and touched the soft skin beneath his left eye. She stared into his eyes for a long time, and at length a dawning recognition swept over her face.

'It *is* you,' she whispered.

Then she began to cry. He held her while she wept, aghast at her skeletal frame, the way her thin, weak body shook with the effort.

'But how...?' he said at last, when the storm of weeping had abated a little.

'A changeling,' she sobbed. 'Fairy stock. It was not *me* that you saw.'

Aubranael began, inwardly, to curse himself. There had been rumours at the time; some had whispered that the princess was *not* dead, that the corpse left behind was a mere seeming fabricated from ill wishes and nightmares. But mere common wisdom told him that no stock could be so perfect; there was always some little detail amiss, something to tell the observant onlooker that this seeming was *not* their loved one.

Lihyaen's had been perfect.

He did not realise he was whispering broken apologies, over and over, until Lihyaen silenced him with a hand to his lips. 'It is not of your doing,' she said wearily.

'But how came you to be here?' he asked, his awareness returning at last to the peculiar tea-party going on around them.

'This was my *reward*,' she said, her weariness giving way to a momentary bitterness. 'Because I had been such a good girl, I was to receive a party all of my own.'

Aubranael stared, aghast, at the rotting dress she wore; at her too-thin frame, her lack of strength even to hold herself upright. 'Have you been here *ever since*?' he cried.

'It is such a lovely party,' she said expressionlessly. ''Twould be such a pity to break it up, do you not think?'

She spoke in a wooden tone, and he realised she was quoting somebody. 'Who did this?' he hissed. 'They will pay for it!'

She shook her head, swaying slightly in her seat. 'I do not know who it is, so you cannot make him pay.'

He became aware of a tumultuous crashing sound. It bore in upon his rage-filled reflections with inexorable determination, and he looked down the length of the table for the first time in some half-an-hour.

All the tea-party guests—and Sophy, and Mary, and Thundigle and even Balligumph—were smashing crockery. They were doing so with gusto and every appearance of high enjoyment.

Smashing things did seem like a wonderful idea to him at that moment. It did not occur to him to question *why* his friends were destroying the tea-things; he merely gathered an armful of his own and began flinging them into the trees. They made such a satisfying, splintering noise as they hit the trunks and exploded into shards. He continued throwing things until there was nothing left to throw.

Silence descended, a brief one; then a roar of noise erupted as every member of the assembled company began talking at once. They were saying nothing of any import and Aubranael quickly lost interest in the proceedings. He turned his attention back to Lihyaen, who had slid forward onto her elbows in the absence of his aid.

There followed a painful conversation. She began to question him in turn, and he was obliged to relate to her the pattern of his life since her apparent death. Her eyes kept returning to the twisted mess of his face, and he read guilt as well as horror in her stricken expression. Heartsick, he did his utmost to soften the misery of the past twenty years as he spoke, and represent a balanced picture of his life. But she was not fooled. She read his every look and gesture, and her eyes told him that she understood perfectly.

Now it was her turn to make apologies, and his to dismiss them. In the midst of this ritual, an insistent noise began to intrude itself upon Aubranael's inner world, and he frowned.

'AUBRANAEL! CRAZY LADY! I'M WANTIN' AN ANSWER HERE!'

He looked up, noticing absently that night had fallen. Balligumph stood some way down the table, waving his arms and roaring in his direction.

'I beg your pardon?' he said.

'I said,' the troll repeated in a more reasonable tone, 'does one of ye two crazies have any notion at all what in the blazes is goin' on here?'

It fell to Aubranael to repeat Lihyaen's story, and his own; Lihyaen was patently exhausted by the unaccustomed exertions of the afternoon, and lay motionless against his chest. He kept his eyes averted from those of his audience as he spoke: he could not bear the shock, horror, revulsion and pity he knew he would see there.

At length he reached the end of his tale. Nobody spoke; silence stretched on, broken only by the rustling of the leaves in the night breeze.

Aubranael noticed two things.

Firstly, Felebre sat beside Lihyaen, leaning against the princess's legs.

Secondly, Hidenory—restored to her youth and beauty now that night had fallen—had approached during his tale, and now stood only a few feet away. She was staring at Lihyaen, her beautiful face twisted with a horror far beyond that of her companions. And Aubranael would have sworn that he saw remorse somewhere in her eyes.

His own narrowed as he watched her. 'Hidenory,' he said softly, 'is something amiss?' His arms tightened around Lihyaen in a protective gesture: he did *not* trust Hidenory anywhere near his princess.

But Lihyaen straightened in his arms, her thin body turning rigid. '*Hidenory?*' she repeated, her eyes searching the witch's face. 'Nurse Hidey?'

Hidenory said nothing, only stared impassively down at Lihyaen.

'No, no,' said Lihyaen, slumping down over the table once more. 'You cannot be: you are nothing like her.'

Hidenory smiled sadly, and as Aubranael watched her pale, blonde beauty slowly vanished. Her skin darkened until it was similar in shade to his own; her hair darkened to almost black; and though her eyes remained blue, her features began to change. At length the slow transformation was complete, and Aubranael saw before him an Ayliri woman of middle years, her face and figure pleasing but by no means so stunning as the enchantment she usually wore.

'Hidey,' said Lihyaen in wonder. 'How…?'

At the same time, Aubranael said: '*Hidey?* What is your

involvement with this tale?'

Hidenory groaned and covered her face with her hands. 'I was in charge of Lihyaen that day,' she said in a muffled voice. 'And I... I agreed to be absent, if—if he would—' She sighed and removed her hands, her fingernails leaving red marks on her skin as she drew them away. 'I made a bargain,' she said, straightening her spine and lifting her chin. 'For Glamour! I wanted it so badly! And he gave it to me, in exchange for a half hour's absence—no more. I swear,' she said sadly, 'I had no idea of the extent of his plans... though it can be no defence. I knew he could have no good purpose in seeking the bargain.'

Lihyaen was staring at her former nurse, her face a mixture of stricken dismay and confusion. She made to speak, but Hidenory held up a hand and said: 'It can be of no use to apologise: I can never express to you the extent of my regret, nor will I ever be able to repay the debt I owe you.

'Besides,' she added quietly, 'I have been punished in my turn.' She passed a hand over her face, and in its wake her hag-like visage was restored.

Aubranael struggled with himself. His rage was building again, and he suffered a strong desire to lay all of his sufferings and Lihyaen's at her door, and take his revenge accordingly. But to do so would serve no purpose at all; and in spite of his attempts to harden his heart, the pain and remorse in Nurse Hidey's face touched his soul and dampened the flow of his anger.

He forced himself to focus instead on unravelling the remains of Lihyaen's story. In a voice of studied calmness he said: 'But who was it? Who did you bargain with? *Who took Lihyaen?*'

Hidenory stared at him and slowly shook her head. 'I know nothing of him. I am sorry.'

Aubranael stared hard at her, but he could discern nothing but sincere regret in Hidenory's expression. Perhaps that meant nothing; she was, after all, the very mistress of pretence. But for the present he must satisfy himself with this unhelpful answer.

Lihyaen shook her frail head, growing agitated in the circle of Aubranael's arms. 'But I do not understand,' she said fretfully. 'How came you all to be here, all of a sudden, on this day? Aubranael and Nurse Hidey together? It is the most improbable of coincidences.'

No one had any ready answer to this—until Sophy spoke up. 'I do not believe it is any coincidence at all,' she said calmly. 'Such a thing is very unlikely, is it not?'

A brief smile touched Aubranael's face. That was so very like Sophy: a voice of cool reason in the midst of chaos. It took him a moment to realise that her gaze was settled meaningfully upon Felebre, who had jumped up onto the table.

'Felebre?' he said in confusion. 'What do you mean?'

'Felebre has been very busy, has she not?' said Sophy. 'She has been keeping company with Aubranael for years, so I understand, and also with Hidenory.'

Hidenory nodded her assent.

'I do not know what her intentions have been throughout all this, but that she is the means of bringing us together there can be no doubt.' Sophy regarded Felebre in silence for a moment, and then added: 'And she has shown far more affection for Lihyaen in the past half-hour than I have ever seen her show to anyone.'

Aubranael stared at Felebre: her unusually large frame; her sleek, purple fur; and her enormous golden eyes. Not for the first time, it struck him that there was a hint of royal majesty about her posture and bearing.

But Lihyaen was trembling in his arms, and he sensed that her exhaustion had reached a crisis. She simply had not the strength for the demands of the evening.

'All further reflection must now wait,' he said hastily. 'Lihyaen is in sore need of rest.' He stood up and made to draw her with him, but she stared up at him in despair.

'Do you imagine it can be as simple as that?' she said sadly. 'If I could simply rise to my feet and go, would I not have done so many years since?'

Aubranael stared at her in dismay. 'But—but how can you be liberated?'

'It is the easiest thing in the world,' she said promptly. 'When another willingly takes my place at the head of the table, then I may go.' She blinked up at Aubranael and said: 'You may imagine the eagerness of my guests to volunteer themselves.'

A clamour went up as—to Aubranael's astonishment—at least half of the assembled guests spoke up at once, and a chorus of 'I will!' and 'I pledge myself!' scattered across the clearing like birds.

But no one stepped forward, and nothing happened: Lihyaen did not appear, by any miraculous chance, to be liberated from her servitude.

Grunewald's acid tones broke the silence. 'You have to *mean it*,' he said dryly. 'When has an empty promise ever broken the chains of a curse?'

Aubranael looked at Lihyaen. He had failed to protect her years ago; he had nothing at all to offer her now. But here was the means to make amends for his various failures.

He opened his mouth to commit himself—and hesitated. His eyes strayed to Sophy's face. She looked steadily back at him, her face calm, her expression grave. She *knew* what was passing through his thoughts, he felt sure of it, and she neither condemned nor encouraged it.

To serve one, he would have to abandon and neglect the other. He looked from Sophy's dear face, devoid at present of the sunny smile he loved, to Lihyaen's exhausted countenance as she leaned against him, her eyes shut. How could he possibly choose?

'I will take the chair.'

The words were spoken loudly and firmly, sent forth into the still air with all the resolution of a bold character and a wilful mind. The voice was Hidenory's.

She stood nearby, looking down at Lihyaen with an indescribable expression on her beautiful face. Holding out one slim, youthful hand to the princess, she said: 'Shake hands with me.'

Doubtfully, the princess extended her own thin fingers and grasped Hidenory's. In a flash the two changed places: Hidenory sat in Lihyaen's chair, her back straight and her chin proudly lifted; Lihyaen stood swooning by the table. Hastily he jumped up and ran to support her, catching her before she fell into an undignified heap among the trees.

'Why?' Aubranael asked the witch.

She smiled sardonically. 'I already bear the burden of one curse; why not two?'

Aubranael merely stared at her.

'Somewhere there is the means to destroy this cruel enchantment,' she said more seriously. 'Someday, somebody will discover it. And I shall, in all probability, be much asleep until that time comes. And I am very tired.'

A small, brown face popped up at the table next to Hidenory's chair: Pharagora. The brownie had taken the chair at the witch's right hand, and now she sat smiling at her. 'I am tired too,' the brownie announced. 'And thirsty. I will keep you company awhile.'

Several others followed the brownie's lead, though Aubranael did not recognise any of the hobs and goblins and other fae who were taking their seats at the table. But with the change of hostess and the arrival of new guests, the Teapot Society began to regain its strength: Aubranael could feel the curious pull of the well-laid table exert itself once more, and he had to fight the temptation to claim a seat and a teapot himself. He had not the time at present to think through all the implications of Hidenory's uncharacteristic self-sacrifice: his first duty was to Lihyaen and Miss Landon, and all their friends.

'It is perhaps time to leave,' he said, looking at Sophy and then at Balligumph.

'Yes,' Sophy murmured, and began at once to collect all of her particular friends and associates together. Grunewald gathered his scattered goblins with a sharp whistle and a bellowed command; Balligumph organised the retreat. 'All right, now, off ye go! Ahead o' me, every one o' ye. I'll keep the wily table from swallowin' ye on yer way past.' He gave a low, rumbling chuckle, his bright eyes sharp as he shepherded every erstwhile table guest safely past him. At last only Aubranael and Lihyaen remained—and Sophy, who had turned at the last and now stood watching him.

'Ye'll take care o' the lady?' Balligumph asked him.

Aubranael nodded. 'Will you take care of Miss Landon?'

The troll nodded gravely. 'That I will.' He tipped his hat, one great blue eye closing briefly in a knowing wink. 'Be careful wi' yerself as well as wi' the lady, now. We'll meet again, of that I have no doubt.'

Aubranael nodded his thanks in distracted fashion, his eyes already searching out Miss Landon's face. She was staring at him with the same solemnity as before, and he could read none of the things that must be taking place behind her eyes. He opened his mouth, searching desperately for some parting sentiment that would express everything he felt: his regrets, hopes, apologies, desires and, above all, his affection. Would he meet *her* again? Could he truly allow her to leave without being assured of it?

But no merciful ray of inspiration graced his weary and befuddled mind. 'Farewell, Miss Landon,' was all that he managed to say.

She made him the slightest of curtsies and turned away. Torn,

Aubranael watched her go.

Balligumph nudged him, almost hard enough to knock both he and Lihyaen over. He looked all the way up into the troll's kindly face, uttering a long, long sigh as he did so.

The troll winked again. 'Up wi' yer chin, now. All will yet be well.'

Then Balligumph, too, turned and left, his footsteps sending tremors through the clearing.

'Well then, my dearest,' Aubranael murmured to Lihyaen. 'Let us go.'

* * *

Mr. Balligumph and Mr. Green shepherded Sophy and her friends back to Lincolnshire. Balli led the way, warding off interference by virtue of his sheer size, if nothing else; though Sophy had come to realise that the name of Balligumph inspired respect in Aylfenhame, and she doubted many would dare to challenge him.

Mr. Green's behaviour was oddly solicitous. Sophy felt excessively confused by him, and wary: that he was not as she had believed him to be was clear enough, and that raised uncomfortable questions about his friend, Mr. Stanton. As Mr. Green she had found him satirical, sardonic, careless and sometimes mocking; but on the return journey from the Outwoods he was sensitive to everybody's comfort, and frequently circled back through the party to assist the ladies over obstructions, to pick Mary up when she tumbled, and to find room atop the goblins' ghostly mounts for the smaller folk when they grew tired.

His goblins, however, continued to alarm her. There were so many of them: they surrounded Sophy's little company on all sides, ringing the weary party around in a surging wall of noisy activity. The hounds howled in ghostly voices, thin and chilling like the distant calling of dogs carried on a strong wind; the goblins yipped and spurred their steeds faster and faster, riding wildly around and around the slowly-moving company. The display was dizzying, but Sophy supposed she should be grateful for it: between Balligumph and Mr. Green's inexplicable goblin escort, nothing wicked could hope to gain access to the knot of humans and fae sheltered within.

She tried to refrain from thinking too much on that strange journey, but without much success, for her thoughts spun around and around and she could not call them to order. She had too many questions, and they were so important that she could not lay them to rest. Who *was* Mr. Green? Here in Aylfenhame she wondered that she could ever have thought him human: there was a wildness to his leaf-green eyes that startled her every time his gaze met hers; he was quick and lithe and fleet of foot, far more so than any human could ever hope to be; and the control he exerted over the goblins and their steeds was truly remarkable.

And if Mr. Green was, in truth, a being of Aylfenhame—and a powerful one—who was Mr. Stanton? Was he an Englishman after all? He could be; perhaps he had simply fallen in with the mysterious Mr. Green and formed an unlikely friendship.

Or perhaps not. This possibility depressed her: if he, too, was a powerful denizen of Aylfenhame, what could he really want with her?

When at last they had all stepped back through the veil into England and gathered at Balligumph's bridge, a degree of quiet descended and Sophy's frayed nerves began to calm. The goblins and their chilling steeds did not accompany them as far as Tilby, and Sophy was relieved to leave that whirlwind of baying and leaping and circling behind. Mr. Green, however, did follow; and she found that she was the focus of his attention and Mr. Balligumph's.

'Now, Miss Sophy,' said Balli kindly. 'Come up an' lean on me. We've a deal o' news to share, an' ye may find some of it a trifle surprisin'. There, very good.' He seated Sophy on the wall beside him and bade her lean against his tree-trunk of a side; she did so gratefully, suddenly conscious of great physical exhaustion. And no wonder, for she must have walked the length and breadth of the Outwoods over the past two days.

Then followed an extraordinary tale, narrated largely by Balligumph, with interjections from Mr. Green—or Grunewald, as she learned he was really called—and occasional assistance from Thundigle, Mary, Anne, Isabel and Mr. Ellerby. She was not obliged to exert herself very much, for her side of the tale was told by Tut-Gut, Pinch and Graen; she had only to master herself long enough to recount the involvement of Felebre and the actions of Hidenory.

This was fortunate, for the news from Balligumph sent her already overtaxed mind spiralling beyond her control.

Mr. Stanton was Aubranael. Aubranael and Mr. Stanton were one and the same.

She had much to reimagine and reinterpret; every meeting with Mr. Stanton must be gone over again; every aspect of Aubranael's behaviour at the tea-party revisited; every thought she had ever had about him must be edited in light of the revelations she was now receiving.

And she did not know precisely how to react. Her heart ached for the insecurity that had led him to practice such a charade; but she could not help feeling offended—nay, *hurt*—that he had felt such a masquerade to be necessary for *her* sake. Did he think her so shallow? And whatever the reasons behind it, it had still been a long-practiced, carefully planned deception of the most cold-blooded kind. Had he ever planned to tell her the truth?

Perhaps it did not matter. He had Lihyaen to attend to now; she might never see him again. The manner of his farewell had certainly suggested as much to her own heart. But insecurity was something she could always forgive, for she was so intimately acquainted with it herself.

'All's well, Miss Sophy?' Balligumph was saying, peering down into her face with concern. She had been staring sightlessly at the darkening sky for some time, she realised, and a silence had fallen upon her companions as they awaited some manner of reaction from her.

It cost her a considerable effort, but Sophy managed to push away the painful thoughts that crowded her heart and muster a smile for Balligumph. He was such a dear friend, and he had always taken such very good care of her. 'All shall be well, I promise it,' she said firmly. 'I am only tired.'

'Aye, an' I shouldn't wonder! Best be off home soon, eh, and get some shut-eye?'

'Indeed.' Sophy recognised her cue to stand, but for the moment she could not muster the energy to pull herself to her feet. Her eyes drifted shut for an instant, and she hurriedly opened them wide again.

Grunewald stood in front of her, peering down into her face. When she opened her eyes, he smiled widely and tipped his hat to her.

'Our friend Aubranael has exceptionally good taste, I do believe,' he said. 'I can read your thoughts, I think, and so you may take it from me: you have not seen the last of him.' He winked, and Sophy could not help smiling in return. His certainty cheered her, for he knew Aubranael better even than she did: had he not spent these past few weeks living with him entirely? Perhaps he was right.

Isabel took a seat beside Sophy and took her hand, pressing it in the friendliest manner imaginable. Anne did the same on her other side, and Sophy's smile grew. 'I cannot tell you how grateful I am,' she said. 'That you should all take such risks on my behalf! It is very humbling.'

She was treated to a chorus of affectionate denials in response, and much in the way of caresses and kisses from Anne, Isabel and Mary. Even Thundigle squeezed her thumb, his eyes shining with emotion, his lip quivering as he attempted to express his fears on her account. Sophy's heart was so full she could barely contain her own emotion, and she felt considerable relief when a great clattering of approaching carriage-wheels interrupted them.

Within moments, three carriages drew up on or near the bridge. Anne's sisters spilled forth from the first; Mr. and Mrs. Ellerby all but fell out of the second; and the third stood quietly waiting, Mr. Green's coachman visible holding the reins.

'Anne!' shrieked a chorus of female voices, and Anne's sisters descended upon her. Their mother was close behind, and the four of them swiftly bore Anne away. Then Mr. and Mrs. Ellerby swept over the bridge and fell upon their children, with much high-pitched protestations of alarm on Mrs. Ellerby's part and a number of rather thunderous questions posed by Mr. Ellerby. Drowsily, Sophy realised that her friends had been absent for some time, quite long enough to alarm their families. A twinge of guilt smote her, for it must be her fault: but she was too tired to give it very much room in her heart. She merely watched sleepily as her friends disappeared into their carriages and were driven away.

'How curious that they should all appear at the bridge, and at the very same time,' she murmured, her eye on Thundigle.

The brownie adjusted the angle of his tall top-hat and flashed one of his rare smiles. 'It does not take so very long to send a message from one side of Tilby to the other,' he informed her gravely. 'Not when one enjoys the friendship and regard of Mr. Thundigle of the Brownies.'

The third carriage drew all the way up to the bridge and stopped. Grunewald bowed before her, held out his hand and said: 'Miss Landon? My carriage is at your disposal.'

Sophy gave him the sunniest smile she had at her disposal, and allowed him to help her to her feet. She was truly touched by the gesture, and swiftly revised her opinion of the erstwhile Mr. Green. 'I am much obliged to you,' she told him. But before she stepped inside, she turned to Tut-Gut, Tara-Tat, Pinch, Pinket and Graen who stood, a little forlornly, with Balligumph.

Tut-Gut cleared his throat. 'In spite of yer tricks, I must say it has been a pleasure,' he said gruffly. 'Ye're a tricksy sort, in the best kind o' way.'

Balli chuckled at that, and Grunewald smiled in his sardonic way. 'Thank you,' Sophy said gravely. 'But I do not think our friendship is over, just yet.' She surveyed the small faces before her sternly, and put her hands upon her hips. 'Who was it who saved you—Pinket excepted—from the Teapot Society?'

'Mary and Sophy!' carolled Graen and Pinch together, and Tut-Gut and Tara-Tat nodded. Pinket bobbed beside her head, flashing with a blinding white light.

'That puts you all in our debt, do you not think?' Sophy said with a smile.

Mary drew herself up to her full height and looked down her nose at the assembled fae, a smile twitching at the corners of her mouth. 'So it does! And a good thing too, for we are in sore need at present.'

'In that case,' said Tut-Gut, and grinned. 'What is it yer needin'?'

'Sleep,' Sophy said promptly. 'We shall be delighted to receive you at the parsonage for tonight; and in the morning, we will discuss our options.'

Tut-Gut bowed, and Tara-Tat, Pinch and Graen hurriedly followed suit. They all piled into the coach, and Sophy saw Mary and Thundigle safely inside. She turned back to Balli and stretched up on her tiptoes; he put down his head to receive her kiss on his broad cheek, and grinned at her. 'Ye're a good girl,' he said fondly. 'Get yerself some shut-eye, Miss, and see me again in the mornin'.'

Sophy promised, and allowed Grunewald to hand her into the coach. His bright green eyes twinkled at her with amusement and respect, and the last thing she heard before the door closed behind him was: 'Tricksy indeed! He has the right of it.'

EPILOGUE

Well, now, an' how was that fer a wild tale? Ye wouldn't think so much could happen in a place like Tilby, but every word is true—that I swear.

Matters quietened a great deal afterwards, an' a good thing too. The fine people o' Tilby are much like the rest o' their kind: they like their peace an' quiet. An' who can blame them? I like a little quiet meself.

Miss Sophy left Tilby, as you might ha' guessed. Took herself an' Mary an' Thundigle off t' Grenlowe. Oh, they are fine an' thrivin' an' happy indeed— thanks fer askin'! Ye may be able to find them there, if ye would like to visit: just ask fer Silverling—thas the name o' Miss Sophy's shop.

Tilby got theirselves a new parson. His name is Mr. Reed, an' I can't say as I've taken to him all that much. Oh, he's popular in these parts: a young gentleman, and unmarried. Richer than poor Mr. Landon, too; they say he has other income o' some kind. Ye may imagine the delight felt by some o' the young ladies. He courted Miss Adair fer a time, an' when she proved too high-an'-mighty fer him he transferred his affections, as he is pleased to term them, t' Miss Ellerby. I hope she'll have better taste. He is a fine, pompous chap, everso pleased wi' himself and none too pleased wi' the rest o' mankind—or fae-kind neither. He won't have a brownie anywhere near his house! He needn't ha' worried, for they dislikes him every bit as much.

Grunewald is still about. He likes tha' Hyde Place, I suppose, or perhaps there's somethin' else as keeps him by. He has yet to delight the Tilby folk by marryin' any one o' their daughters. Nothin' has ever been seen o' Mr. Stanton, of course, nor Aubranael; not in Tilby, anyhow. Miss Adair is said to be inconsolable; but her Mama is takin' her to London soon enough, an' there she will find many a rich gentleman to mend her wounded heart.

Oh, ye'll no doubt be pleased t' hear that Miss Daverill is married. Yes! She is an odd little thing, an' can be a tiny bit tirin', I'll not deny; but still I was pleased as punch when she became Mrs. Ash. They's said to be quite the happy couple.

Well, but I'm ramblin' on, an' all ye really want to hear about is Miss Sophy

225

and Aubranael! So hearken t' me just a few minutes more, an' I'll tell all…

Sophy sat in her favourite rocking-chair in the front parlour of her shop, a pile of sewing in her lap and a cup of steaming tea at her elbow. The late summer sun shone through the open window, bathing her in golden light; she could not help smiling. Not since the death of her father had she felt such blissful contentment.

There was a kitchen in the back of the building, and Mary was hard at work within it; Sophy could hear her singing. Thundigle was helping her, whistling along with her song as he did so. They were making delicate pastry tarts, filling them with a jam made from the strange and delicious fruits that grew among the orchards of Grenlowe. Later they would pack them into a basket and wander the streets of the town, selling the contents. The basket would be empty within half-an-hour, in all likelihood, for Mary and Thundigle's confections were becoming legendary.

Almost as legendary as Sophy's wares. She had taken possession of this shop six weeks ago, with Grunewald's help, and the assistance of her friends from the Outwoods had been invaluable. Graen had brought her fabrics so delicate and light they could have been wrought from flower petals; they smelt deliciously of nectar and honey and roses and many other fragrances Sophy could not put a name to. Pinch had brought her ornaments: tinkling bells and twinkling gems; coloured stones and beads of blown glass; delicate pearlescent shells and spun cobwebs; even some of the ribbons she had seen and coveted so many weeks ago at the Grenlowe market. Pinket had infused some of the gems with his wisp-light, until they shone like stars. Tara-Tat had brought her tools: the sharpest, strongest needles Sophy had ever seen; scissors that cut any material with ease, and never grew dull; bobbins of fine thread that never ran out. And Tut-Gut had worked long hours to help her sew her first wares: fine, beautiful gowns of all shapes and sizes, with gloves and boots and reticules to match.

Her fame had spread very quickly, for the creations she produced had never been seen before in Grenlowe. She was never idle, and her increased prosperity allowed her to pay Mary and Thundigle very handsomely for their work in keeping house and shop—much higher wages than her poor father had ever been able to muster. And with

their burgeoning bakery business in progress, she felt that her two dear friends had never been happier either.

She saw Balligumph frequently, for she made the crossing to Tilby as often as she could. She visited Isabel and Anne, too, and sometimes received them at Silverling in return. Even Grunewald periodically paid her a call: so often, in fact, that she began to suspect him of some ulterior motive, though he would never confirm her suspicions. She was interested to note that Grunewald's visits often coincided with Isabel's, though he always seemed sincerely surprised to see her there.

But there were clouds in her sky. The first related to Hidenory, and the events of a few weeks previously. The Witch of the Outwoods had provided a perfectly plausible story about her past, at least on the surface; but something about it rang false to Sophy. Perhaps it was because she struggled to see Hidenory—strong, powerful, proud, predatory—as Lihyaen's 'Nurse Hidey', an ordinary woman committed to the care of a little girl. It did not *fit*. Besides, was it possible for the powers of Glamour to be bestowed in the fashion Hidenory had claimed? Sophy did not know, but she doubted.

And nothing that she knew about Hidenory, or that Hidenory had claimed about herself, seemed to allow the possibility of her freely making so considerable a sacrifice as to take Lihyaen's place at the never-ending tea party. Sophy felt sure that some other motive had been at work, one that Hidenory kept to herself; and she was, at times, troubled.

But the greater sadness that she felt related to Aubranael. Surrounded with friends and well-wishers as she was, she had yet to hear from *him*. She had no notion at all what had become of her dear Ayliri friend and the princess Lihyaen, nor of Felebre (who, she presumed, had gone with them). She was often tempted to make her enquiries of Grunewald, but her pride revolted at the idea; and he never mentioned them.

Time and reflection and happiness had dulled the hurt and resentment she had felt towards him. His masquerade had not truly injured her, nor anybody else worth caring for; she suspected that the only real damage he had caused had been inflicted upon himself.

And she could imagine his feelings, to some degree. How often had she been dismissed from consideration—rejected and neglected—merely because she was not *beautiful!* How much worse must it have been for him; not only lacking in beauty but actually disfigured, cursed with a truly repellent aspect? She had sensed his loneliness from their first meeting: it had echoed her own, only his was so much deeper.

She regretted his absence, for all these reasons and more. She began to feel that, given sufficient time, she could indeed have loved him: his behaviour to her in both guises had always been so considerate, so gentle, so truly caring, and his tastes, his interests, his ideas had matched her own so well.

Her heart ached to think of him, adrift somewhere in Aylfenhame without, perhaps, the comfort of friendship to assist his labours. But that was absurd of her: he had Lihyaen, and though the princess had suffered much and would require a great deal of tender care during her recovery, he was no doubt delighted with her company. She had seen his love for her so clearly at the tea-party. It had simultaneously warmed her and broken her heart; for Lihyaen was beautiful, or she would be once the glow of health and happiness returned to her face and form. Insecurity often gnawed at Sophy's heart, though she tried her best to chase it away: did she feel that Lihyaen did not deserve Aubranael's regard? Did she truly wish to deprive her of it, and secure it to herself instead? No; the princess was in far greater need of love than Sophy herself, and it was selfish to wish for a change in Aubranael's heart.

But such reflections did her no service. They dimmed the sunshine of her days, and sapped the warmth in her heart. She sat up in the chair, picked up the folds of fabric in her lap and recommenced her sewing. The best cure for sadness was labour, she had often found, and she had plenty of *that* to sustain her.

Barely had she begun anew when the bell over her front-door sang out and a great, sleek purple cat stalked into the shop and circled, nose lifted and tail twitching as she tested the air.

'Felebre!' Sophy cried in surprise.

The door remained open and in another moment somebody else came into the room: a tall, slender Ayliri woman, her dark hair neatly braided, her clothes simple. When she turned her face towards the rocking-chair, Sophy saw large golden eyes containing an expression of high discomfort—even fear.

Close behind her came Aubranael.

He was dressed as Sophy had first seen him, in a simple tunic and trousers, tall boots and his enormous wide-brimmed hat; his hair flowed unchecked down his back. He hovered solicitously behind Lihyaen, but his eyes sought out Sophy's. He held her gaze, his face grave; no hint of a smile had he to offer, and the delight that had always graced his face when he saw Sophy was absent as well.

Sophy's heart began to pound and—to her acute embarrassment—her face flushed up with colour. She tried very hard to appear composed as she folded up her sewing and laid it upon the table beside her.

'Princess Lihyaen,' she said in a voice of practiced calm. 'And Aubranael. How kind of you to visit us here.'

The words emerged too cool, too grave; Sophy's heart sank as she realised they must sound sarcastic to Aubranael. Would he take her words as a veiled reproach?

She could not tell, for he still said nothing: only swallowed visibly, and dropped his gaze to the floor. It was Lihyaen who stepped forward and shook Sophy's hand, a hesitant smile lighting her face.

'Oh—but should I have curtsied?' said the princess in momentary confusion. 'Aubranael *did* tell me all about the manners of England, but I fear I have forgotten. I am so pleased to meet you, Miss Landon.'

Sophy gazed at her, mute and nonplussed. She did not know how to interpret this show of friendliness, offered by somebody who remained a complete stranger to her. Not only that but, by slow degrees, her treacherous heart had been painting poor Lihyaen in the colours of an enemy: the one who had taken Aubranael away, perhaps forever. In light of the young woman's sincere friendliness, Sophy could only feel deeply ashamed of her own thoughts.

'I will shake your hand, and very gladly,' Sophy said, mustering a smile. 'Never mind the manners of England: we are in Grenlowe and will do as the Ayliri do. It is I who should be curtseying to *you*.' And Sophy did so, curtseying as deeply as she would have to English royalty.

Lihyaen merely looked confused, and glanced uncertainly at Aubranael. Sophy looked at him, too, and waited: it was time he explained himself.

Poor Aubranael flushed under the weight of their combined gaze, and began to stutter. Then he sighed, pulled off the concealing hat and dropped it carelessly onto the floor.

'Miss Landon,' he said. 'I cannot even begin to apologise to you for—'

'Indeed you cannot,' Sophy interrupted hastily, 'and I beg you will not try, for it is not at all necessary.' She could not bear to see him looking so downtrodden, so dejected and so unsure of himself: better to sweep his apologies away than hear him stutter and stumble his way through them on her account.

Aubranael blinked at her, nodded, and said nothing for a moment. 'I… it is intolerable cheek on my part, but I have come here seeking your aid.'

Sophy's brows went up in surprise. She had struggled to guess at his reasons for coming to her shop, but that he might be in need of something from *her* had not crossed her mind. 'By all means, you need only ask,' she said.

Aubranael's expression softened, and he looked at her with a glow of approval which brought the colour back into her face. 'Ah, I should have known that you would be everything that is generous!' he said. 'Even in spite of my—' he stopped. 'But you have forbidden that topic, and so away with it! The favour I seek is on behalf of Lihyaen.' He smiled affectionately at the princess, who stood stroking Felebre's soft-furred head and looking around the shop with great curiosity.

'It is… not possible to return her to the palace. You may imagine the difficulties—the dangers. At present we have agreed that it is not advisable, and not what she needs.' He looked back at Sophy, his smile fading. 'She has suffered much, and I believe that she is most in need of… security. A quiet, ordinary life, full of simple pleasures and the company of friends. To my infinite regret, I cannot provide her with any of this.

'But Grunewald has kept me apprised of your accomplishments, and the success of Silverling. I had wondered—hoped—that you might—'

'I shall be very happy to take care of Lihyaen,' Sophy said. And she meant it. Something about Lihyaen's honest curiosity about the shop, her unalloyed warmth, and her affectionate treatment of both Felebre and Aubranael had won over Sophy's heart almost instantly. She could see Aubranael's protectiveness towards Lihyaen, and found it echoed in her own heart.

Aubranael's face slackened with relief, and he let out a long sigh. 'Thank you,' he said simply. 'I had nowhere else to turn.'

Sophy gave him a small smile, and turned to Lihyaen. Taking the young woman's hand, she gave her to understand that her welcome was warm indeed, and that she might stay as long as she liked. As she spoke, Lihyaen's face blossomed into a shy smile, and she gripped Sophy's hand a little too tightly.

Lihyaen was very young, Sophy realised. She and Aubranael had been of an age at one time; but the Teapot Society had, perhaps, held her in some manner of stasis for many of the intervening years. As a result, Sophy guessed that she had aged no more than seven or eight years, where Aubranael had aged more than twenty. She could well believe that the princess was in need of a stable environment: she had much growing to do, as well as healing.

'Can you sew?' she asked the princess.

Lihyaen frowned doubtfully, but she nodded. 'I learned how to do that, once,' she said, her face wistful. 'But I am not very good.'

'Never mind; you soon will be! I am in great need of an assistant, so you see, it will be of benefit to us both to remain together for a time.' This was a small untruth, for Sophy had recourse to a great deal of assistance, should she require it; Thundigle and Tut-Gut had many friends who were quick and deft with a needle, and delighted to be paid for their trouble.

But Lihyaen would benefit from an occupation; something that would keep her mind and hands busy, and afford her plenty of company. And Mary and Thundigle would teach her to cook.

Lihyaen smiled shyly and nodded, and Felebre came to rub herself past Sophy's legs in an unmistakeably affectionate gesture. Surprised, Sophy spared a moment to stroke the cat's great head. Her fur was remarkably soft, and cool under Sophy's fingers.

'Shall we get you settled in at once?' Sophy said to Lihyaen. 'I have a room which will do very nicely for you, and Mary will have it made up in a trice.'

'Thank you,' said the princess.

Sophy called for Mary, and her old friend came in immediately, followed by a flour-dusted Thundigle. They both greeted Lihyaen like an old friend, and chivvied her away upstairs to be bathed and dressed and fed and settled in her new home. Sophy watched them go, her heart glowing with affection for her two oldest friends. She could leave Lihyaen in no better hands.

But her good feelings faded away very quickly, leaving her confused, unsure and a little afraid. Would Aubranael now wish to bid her goodbye? Mr. Stanton's behaviour had latterly suggested to her that he had definite intentions in her direction; but perhaps this had been a mere product of the part he was playing, and easily shed along with the rest.

But Aubranael made no move to follow Lihyaen, or to depart. He stood rather awkwardly in the centre of the shop, his eyes downcast. He fidgeted with the buttons of his tunic, then thrust his hands into his pockets in an impatient gesture.

Sophy watched, confused. In his treatment of Lihyaen, she had seen solicitude and sincere concern for her welfare, pleasure in her company, and plentiful affection. But he did not seem mesmerised by the princess's presence; he did not hang upon her every word, nor gaze lover-like into her face. His regard for her appeared more in the character of a brother than a lover. And the fact that he had chosen to remain in the shop with Sophy, instead of following the princess into the rest of the house, appeared to her as a promising sign. But perhaps the wishes of her heart were leading her astray; she ought not to indulge such hopes.

'May I offer you some tea?' Sophy said. 'I will have to pour it myself, I am afraid, as Mary is otherwise occupied. It is likely to be dangerous.'

She had hoped to draw a laugh from him with her flippant comment, but he made no response at all—except to raise his eyes from the floor, and fix them upon her face.

'No tea, then,' Sophy observed. 'Perhaps I may offer you something edible and easily-served, instead.'

'I am not hungry!' Aubranael declared.

'Oh! Then I shall not press you,' said Sophy mildly.

Aubranael took a deep breath and said quietly: 'You will have heard by now of my—my—deception, for we must give it that name. I cannot imagine that your friends left you long without information on such a point.'

Sophy inclined her head in assent.

'You behave as though you had forgiven me, Miss Landon, but I hardly dare hope that—' He trailed off and stared at her in rather a dramatic fashion, his face stricken as if he expected to receive some great blow from her.

Sophy began to feel a mixture of amusement and impatience at this display of strange and not especially polite manners. 'I do not see any *very* convincing reason why I should not,' she said with a touch of asperity. 'I was, I admit, a little dismayed when I first heard of your charade; but it did not take me very long to see that, had I been offered the opportunity to enjoy great beauty for a few weeks, I would have accepted it without hesitation. I must be the greatest hypocrite in England, then, to treat you harshly for having done the same.' She paused. 'I only wish you had told me the truth about your identity when you arrived. I cannot help feeling that I wasted a great deal of time in learning to trust Mr. Stanton, when I had already formed a favourable impression of *you.*'

Aubranael nodded, his face an almost comical mixture of elation and crestfallen dismay. He garbled something in reply, or several somethings at once, for Sophy could distinguish nothing especially coherent from his rambling response. He stopped himself after a while, and sighed, and scrubbed at his face.

Sophy's impatience grew. Enough time had been wasted already, she felt, with his various pretences and deceptions; and while she had no desire to behave in a *bold* way, she had even less desire to continue with this detestable awkwardness. *Or* to see him leave her shop and never return.

And so, mustering her courage and drawing a deep breath, she said: 'Would you like to stay, too?'

Aubranael blinked at her.

'Well; you will not like to be very far from Lihyaen, and I would not like you to be very far from me.'

'Why, I—am not sure that—that is—' he said with admirable glibness.

'You have a great many important matters to see to, perhaps, and I should not attempt to detain you.' Sophy spoke lightly, ignoring the constriction in her throat and the unsettled, erratic thumping of her heart.

To her surprise, Aubranael laughed. 'Oh, that I do! For I am a man of considerable importance, and my time is excessively valuable.' His brown eyes shone with laughter and, at last, he smiled the wide, merry smile she had found so attractive before.

'But they may, perhaps, wait for a week or two,' she said, smiling sunnily up at him in response. 'If we did our best to be *very* entertaining.'

Aubranael nodded with mock seriousness. 'I expect to be very pleasantly detained, mind,' he said.

'I can offer you a great deal of sewing,' Sophy said promptly.

'Ah! Could anything be more enticing!'

'There is also the ironing. And if you should happen to become *very* bored, I may even have it in my power to offer you tea-pouring duties.'

Aubranael laughed, took her hand, and kissed it exuberantly. 'Then I shall consider myself the most fortunate of men,' he said. Before Sophy could object—though she was not sure she would have, given the opportunity—Aubranael gathered her up into a tight embrace and buried his face in her hair. He kissed her cheek, her forehead, her eyes, and finally her mouth; and as she returned the kiss, her eyelids fluttering shut, she reflected that she was, without doubt, the luckiest woman in Aylfenhame.

Well and well, that is the last of it! A fine ending, do not you think? There's no one so deserving as my Sophy, and I'll smitherise anyone as says otherwise.

Now, nigh on a year has passed an' all is well at Silverling. But Miss Sophy is right to wonder about Hidenory. I tend to do a bit o' wonderin' on that score meself—an' perhaps ye're inclined to as well. A woman o' that cast is no more capable o' meekness or humility or sacrifice than the most fearsome o' dragons, an' I have no doubt that there's more there than meets the eye.

An' what about that Felebre? Mysterious bein', ain't she? There's some as says Her Majesty the Queen ain't dead at all. They says she left Aylfenhame an' her husband followed; but I'm not so sure. That cat's right fond o' little miss Lihyaen, ain't she? There's sommat almost motherly about her manner. An' here's another idea: they used to say the royals had a touch o' fey magic about 'em. Could see into the past an' the future, so they said. Oh, not far; just a little way. Raises some interestin' prospects, don't it?

But thas all secret! No tellin', now! There's bad doin's afoot, an' until we can get to the bottom o' those matters, it's best not to pry.

Oh, now, on tha' topic a rumour has reached me from Aylfenhame. Shall I show what I mean? Here. See this pocket mirror? Was a gift from my old gran, an' I keep it wi' me at all times. Well and anyway, look into it closely-like. Go on; it won't bite!

Mist passes across the face of the pocket mirror, to reveal a woodland scene. A long table stands surrounded by tall, slender trees, its sides lined with high-backed chairs and its surface covered with teapots, cups and cake boxes. But nobody is sitting in any of the chairs—not even the one at the head of the table.

Interestin', no? Perhaps someone has found a way t' release Miss Hidenory, or perhaps she has released herself in some tricksy way o' hers. Either way, no one has seen or heard of her in some time...

But I've kept ye long enough, have I not? An' ye have been the best o' listeners. Now, should ye fancy another tale some way down the months an' ye happen to be in the neighbourhood, come an' see me again. Perhaps I may be able to tell the next chapter in the tale o' Sophy an' Aubranael an' Lihyaen. Perhaps I'll even be able to tell ye what became o' Hidenory.

But safe travels, now. Mind the corner into Mill Road; it's a little sharp. I'll just give yer coachman a hint.

ACKNOWLEDGEMENTS

My special thanks to my cover artist, Elsa Kroese, and illustrator, Rosie Lauren Smith, for making this book so beautiful.

Other Titles By Charlotte E. English:

Tales of Aylfenhame:
Miss Landon and Aubranael
Miss Ellerby and the Ferryman

The Draykon Series:
Draykon
Lokant
Orlind

The Lokant Libraries:
Seven Dreams

The Drifting Isle Chronicles:
Black Mercury

The Malykant Mysteries:
The Rostikov Legacy
The Ivanov Diamond
Myrrolen's Ghost Circus
Ghostspeaker

Made in the USA
Middletown, DE
09 May 2021